"I guess you don't grow up on a ranch in south Texas and not turn out a cowboy, huh?"

"Not hardly."

Amy smiled. "I always loved cowboys."

"You are making that up."

"No. I swear." She crossed her heart. "It's the character you know? The loner, the stars in the sky for a roof over your head. The one man who always tips his hat to a lady. It's a macho thing, too. The boots and vest and chaps, all that leather. All that sexy cowboy stuff."

He was laughing at her now.

"Okay, maybe it was only a romantic notion of a cowboy I loved, but when the rodeo comes to town, every girl in town wants one."

Cy gave her a long look. "You too?"

She looked back at him. Very slowly, very deliberately, she sighed. "I want this one."

Dear Reader,

Welcome to the McQuaid family—three brothers who are easy to love and hard to forget. They live their lives the way their father taught them—by The Cowboy Code.

This exciting new miniseries about danger and desire in the west kicks off with RITA Award-nominee Carly Bishop's Cy McQuaid, and continues in the next two months with his brothers Cameron, a Colorado rancher, in Laura Gordon's *A Cowboy's Honor* (February) and Matt, a Texas lawman, in *Lone Star Lawman* by Joanna Wayne (March).

Don't miss any of these sexy cowboy brothers!

Regards,

Debra Matteucci
Senior Editor & Editorial Coordinator
Harlequin Books
300 East 42nd Street
New York, NY 10017

McQuaid's Justice
Carly Bishop

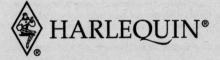

HARLEQUIN®

TORONTO • NEW YORK • LONDON
AMSTERDAM • PARIS • SYDNEY • HAMBURG
STOCKHOLM • ATHENS • TOKYO • MILAN • MADRID
PRAGUE • WARSAW • BUDAPEST • AUCKLAND

For my brother
whose contributions to my life and writing
are too many to count,

& Emily Jean, my niece and poet extraordinaire.

With a wink to Howard.

ISBN 0-373-22497-4

MCQUAID'S JUSTICE

Copyright © 1999 by Cheryl McGonigle

This edition published by arrangement with Harlequin Books S.A.

Printed in U.S.A.

THE McQUAID FAMILY TREE

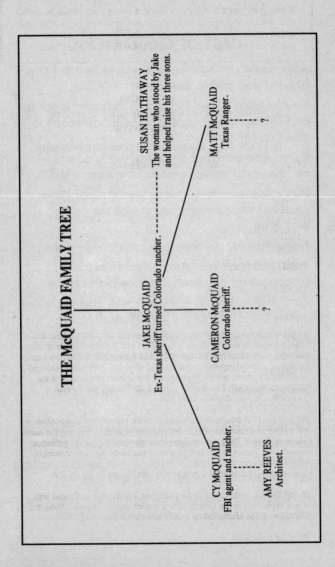

JAKE McQUAID
Ex-Texas sheriff turned Colorado rancher.

SUSAN HATHAWAY
The woman who stood by Jake and helped raise his three sons.

CY McQUAID
FBI agent and rancher.

AMY REEVES
Architect.

CAMERON McQUAID
Colorado sheriff.
?

MATT McQUAID
Texas Ranger.
?

CAST OF CHARACTERS

Amy Reeves—Only the truth would set her heart free to hear, and to love again.

Cy McQuaid—Jake McQuaid's first son, rancher and FBI agent, Cy wanted to be man enough to show up for Amy.

Byron Reeves—Had the judge made a terrible mistake, or a selfless gesture of compassion?

Perry Reeves—Amy's uncle would never have what he wanted most; power was the next best thing.

Fiona Reeves—Granny was crazy—like a fox.

Brent Reeves—Was Amy's stepbrother a scapegoat or murderer? Even he didn't know.

Zach Hollingsworth—The threat of libel had never gotten in the way of his journalistic integrity.

Jake McQuaid—Cy's father, a man of bedrock values, he never made an honest woman of Susan.

Susan Powell—Jake's woman, loyal to a fault, mother to his boys.

Cameron McQuaid—Jake's middle son, Sheriff of Chaparral County, sworn to a strict code of honor.

Matt McQuaid—Jake's youngest, a Texas lawman, like it or not, very much his father's son.

Phillip Gould—The U.S. Senator held a fearsome grudge against Amy's father and his ambitions.

Prologue

An ear can break a human heart
As quickly as a spear;
We wish the ear had not a heart
So dangerously near.

—Emily Dickinson

"Thanks. I'll pass." Zach Hollingsworth waved the senator's hovering manservant away. The refusal didn't come easily. The port wine the butler offered was exquisite. Lush. Richly scented, as full-bodied as the women Zach preferred and the news stories that had made his career.

But Zach needed to keep his wits about him. What he wanted, more than anything, was the promised tip. Phillip Gould, California's senior senator, had lured Zach to his ritzy D.C. town house with the promise of a scoop guaranteed to make his career, to forever lay waste to the lean years of scandal and allegations and he-said/she-said propositions.

What Zach really wanted was for the senator to spit it out. Either the nomination of Byron Reeves to the Supreme Court was in jeopardy, or it was not.

Phillip Gould allowed his goblet to be refilled, then directed the manservant to retrieve a portfolio that lay conspicuously on the antique sideboard. Watching below his hooded brow, the senator waited until the servant disappeared behind enormous swinging oak doors to the serving area.

He set the leather portfolio carefully to his left and gave Zach a speculative look. "Have an interest in architecture, Hollingsworth?"

"None."

"Interesting piece in the *Post* a couple of days ago." Gould pared the end off a fat Cuban cigar. "Thought you might have seen it."

"Sorry, I must have missed that one." Zach forced an easy, self-deprecating smile to mask his mounting irritation. A California golden boy in his youth, tanned, trim, blond and blue-eyed, Gould had gone to very expensive seed. Now, even the senator's sentences, lacking a subject— "*I spotted* an interesting piece," or "*I* thought you might have seen..." —were tending to annoy Zach. "What was the story?"

"An architectural design award."

"A prize." Zach leaned back, slouching a bit in his chair, letting a bit of his impatience surface. "Senator, forgive me, but is this going somewhere, or is your question—"

"An idle one?" Gould interrupted, blithely lighting his cigar. He dragged the powerful, sublimely scented smoke into his lungs and exhaled. He fixed his gaze on Zach through a blue haze curling toward the flames of seven candles mounted in an antique porcelain candelabra. His expression hardened. "I don't deal in idle questions."

"All right. Just so we understand each other. Who won the award?"

"A woman."

"Was the competition rigged?"

Gould tapped ashes into a crystal tray and blinked. "Assuredly not, or this young woman would not have won no matter how far superior her work." He shoved the portfolio toward Zach. "Tell me if you recognize her."

About as likely to identify some obscure female architect as he was to write about one, Zach cut the senator a look that said as much.

Snaring the cigar from between his teeth with a curled forefinger, Gould dropped his heavy hand on the table. "Humor me."

Zach sat forward and dragged the portfolio closer, then flipped the cover open to a black-and-white photo on newsprint, *sans* story or attribution. He had never seen the woman captured in the shot. He knew that up front. But having cultivated a near photographic memory, he searched his mind for some obscure connection to Judge Reeves and the impending confirmation hearings.

He thought the woman in the photo to be in her mid-twenties, a brunette with exceptionally fair skin, not a classic beauty, but a beauty nonetheless. "Should I recognize her?"

Gould blew more smoke, tapped more ashes, neither confirming nor denying, just…waiting.

Zach frowned at the photo again. "Reeves has a daughter who must be about her age."

The senator's fleshy lips bent themselves to the suggestion of approval. "Indeed. Her name is Amy. Interesting twist…she's deaf as a stone."

Zach skidded the photo back into the open leather portfolio. "So Reeves has a deaf daughter who won an architectural award. I'm impressed. Wonder," he cracked, his voice thick with now ill-concealed disdain, mocking the senator with his own annoying habit of speech, "what the

Judiciary Committee members will find in that to impugn Reeves's character.''

''Spare me your sarcasm, Hollingsworth.'' Gould sucked on his cigar. Smoke curled about his face, soiling his commentary. ''When a man has suffered a dry spell as long as yours since winning an award of any description, never mind the Pulitzer, perhaps one should begin to reflect upon one's own lack of imagination.''

''That's the problem for a world-class journalist these days,'' Zach snapped, reflecting instead on the approximate amount of time it might take him to cram the senator's fancy cigar down past the turkey wattle of double chins down his throat. ''So little is left to the imagination. But if it makes you happy, I'll look into it.''

''There's the spirit. An open mind is fine asset. I'm persuaded that you'll be able to set aside your preconceived notions of Byron Reeves's stellar record. Enough, perhaps, to recall where you were twenty-four years ago?''

Zach stared at the senator. ''I was at the *Trib* in Chicago on an internship—working, like everybody else, on the Jessup heiress kidnap story.''

''When the poor, innocent little heiress showed up on the security tapes in the thick of pulling off a bank heist,'' Gould prodded.

''Byron Reeves prosecuted the case. Your point would be…what, exactly?''

Gould blinked. ''Pamela Jessup was never apprehended, or charged for her crimes—despite which,'' Gould went on, honing the circle of fire on his cigar, ''the case propelled Reeves into the national spotlight. Saved him from a life of obscurity as a run-of-the-mill prosecutor and landed him a career on the federal bench.''

Zach shrugged. He was starting to believe that the senator might be about to offer him something substantial. He didn't want to risk losing it, but he wasn't going to play lapdog either. "Reeves won a conviction. They both got what they deserved."

"On the contrary. Byron Reeves," Gould snarled, "has never gotten what he deserves."

"Meaning what?"

Gould sat back, sucking smoke into his throat, then issuing smoke rings like an overfed guppy belching bubbles of air. "I believe, Hollingsworth, that if you pursue the issue with a modicum of imagination, you will find Byron Reeves at the heart and soul of a felony conspiracy."

"To do with Pamela Jessup?"

"The feds bagged David Eisman and his sidekick." Gould squashed the butt of his cigar till its stubbed sides split open. "Ever think to ask yourself how a twit debutante like Pamela Jessup slipped through his fingers?"

"I don't recall any great hue and cry going up over it. Pamela Jessup was the kidnap victim, for Chrissake. The feds would have turned her into a witness. Even if they hadn't offered immunity, her family had enough money to get her off."

"Her family," Gould reminded Zach, "refused to pay the ransom."

The subtle buzz of excitement started up in Zach's gut. He badly wanted Gould's slant to have real substance. Instinct told him to play out the line. "They would have come around. The rich do that."

"No," Gould denied categorically. "Her family knew from long experience what a conniving little liar she was." He snorted. "Trust me."

A conniving little liar? Zach thought. What half-buried hatchet was this?

"The Jessups," Gould went on, "had washed their hands of their daughter."

"And you know that because—?"

"Our families were quite close. Pamela was a wild seed from the word go. David Eisman, on the other hand, was a two-bit hood without the brains or the balls to stick up the local convenience store. Paint him in as the mastermind of a kidnap? I don't think so."

"Are you suggesting Jessup's abduction was a hoax? An extortion Pamela Jessup intended from the start to perpetrate on her own family?"

"Let me fill in the picture for you," Gould continued, with an air of forswearing subtleties in the face of Zach's tedious skepticism, "Byron Reeves was also a family friend of the Jessups—even married a poor relation."

"You're kidding."

"Not for a moment. Let me finish. It was Byron Reeves on hand for Justice the night the boys down at the local FBI nailed Eisman and his drugged-out sidekick. They both swore up and down that Pamela Jessup was locked in a warehouse closet—no way she could have gotten away without help."

"Come on! Reeves?"

Gould ignored the protest. "Byron Reeves lived and worked in the jurisdiction of the bank heist, one among a hundred or so federal prosecutors. Still it isn't outside the realm of possibility that he would be tapped to take on the case. But remember—"

"The guy was married to Pamela Jessup's shirttail relation." Zach's pulse hammered in his ears.

"And yet Byron Reeves wound up as lead prosecutor in a case from which he should clearly have recused himself. Are you beginning to get the picture?"

Zach nodded thoughtfully. Here, assuming Gould's characterization of Pamela Jessup as a wild-seed conniving little liar meant that he did in fact have some dank and unsavory agenda of his own, was a likely case of the pot calling the kettle black. But Zach's own Kansas upbringing, and years of picking his way through thickets of lies to get at the truth, left him certain of one thing.

The pot calling the kettle black didn't mean the kettle wasn't black.

Liars told the absolute truth when it suited their purposes. Whatever Gould's ulterior motive, Reeves might well have ignored a serious conflict of interest and committed a felony or two all his own. The story potential would have been explosive if Jessup were still alive and on the lam, but she wasn't.

Still.

Byron Reeves aiding and abetting the escape of a fugitive, failing even to indict Pamela Jessup for her crimes, was the big time.

Zach had to ask the obvious question. He didn't bother to cloak the query in watered-down euphemisms. "Senator, if you knew Reeves was covering up a conflict of interest, why in hell didn't you go screaming bloody murder twenty-five years ago?"

"I did." Gould sat back comfortably, unintimidated. "The Jessups were personal friends. But unlike Reeves I put my civic obligation, however painful, ahead of the loyalty I had to her family. I informed the Justice Department."

"You're telling me the Attorney General of the United States blew you off?"

Gould sneered. "Let's just say Reeves has friends in high places."

Which, Zach thought, only made it all the more heinous. A man who aspired to sit on the bench of the highest court in the land in judgment of his fellow citizens sure as *hell* should never have thumbed his nose at the law, even if the extent of his complicity was in poor judgment.

"About Reeves's daughter…"

"Amy?" Heaving himself from his chair, clearly signaling the end of the interview, Gould smiled. "More than meets the eye there."

Chapter One

"'Wishing a thing,' my grandfather used to say, 'don't make a thing so.' But there was one thing he taught us a man could depend on—besides," Cy McQuaid joked to the friends and neighbors gathered to mourn his namesake's loss, "the love of a good woman."

Bittersweet smiles, a few heartfelt chuckles came. "I believe it too," Cy went on. "He believed that working the land, carving out a living from a couple thousand acres of godforsaken earth, a man could trust that everything is exactly what it seems. Nothing more, nothing less, nothing hidden, nothing secret. Little else in life happens that way."

Done with what he had to say, Cy stepped back on the craggy, windswept hill next to his youngest brother, Matt, and let the Reverend Bleigh take over.

He heard the ritual words, the return of His faithful servant Cyrus McQuaid, dust unto dust, unto his Lord and Creator. But in his mind's eye, Cy imagined his granddad's spirit, free at last to appreciate the rugged, good-for-nothing landscape, so barren only the hardiest scrub oak survived.

Cyrus McQuaid had spent the whole of his life cooped up in an accounting office, shaping perfect numbers in

rigid columns in search of a buffalo-head nickel's worth
of profit. If he'd ever found it two years running, he'd have
bought the Circle Q himself. Instead, he spent his twilight
years railing at his son, Jake, Cy's father, for sinking his
money into the place.

Even so, Gramps had known in his heart of hearts ranch-
ing wasn't about profit, it was about a way of life. You
had to love the land for its own sake. You had to take your
pleasures where you found them, as damn few and far
between as they came. You had to believe your seed would
sprout and produce enough grain to keep your livestock
alive—or money enough in the bank to make up the difference.

And when the calving started in the middle of the night
and an ice storm hit with the first steaming calf to drop,
you put everything else aside. Which was exactly what
happened the night Cyrus's daughter-in-law, Cy and Cameron's mother, died.

Jake McQuaid, Cyrus's son, hadn't made it back from
calving till her body had gone stone-cold.

After that, Jake boarded up the house, sold off the ranch
in East Texas, and went back to sheriffing in the next
county over. Then he'd gone through another wife he
didn't have the heart to love, and had another son, Cy's
youngest brother Matt.

Jake kept a few horses and taught his boys to ride. They
learned to lasso, practicing at first with an old sawhorse.
They tore up their hands learning to repair barbed-wire
fences, which was just the beginning of how tough they
grew up to be.

Jake had spared them none of the harsh realities. Cy
could still remember the day, the hour, the way the air was
choked with dust baked dry in the heat of the Texas sun,
when Jake was obliged to fetch the rifle he carried in a

gun rack mounted against the back window of his '76 pickup and put a snake-bitten dog named Millie out of her misery.

The mangy sheepdog who had saved all their skins more than once, had put herself between Matt and the rattler he tripped over.

Even a number-crunching old fart like his grandfather knew all this. A man did what a man had to do, at the business end of a pencil, astride his horse, on his ranch, or behind the badge he wore.

Especially behind the badge.

A man did what was right and honorable and just, and mercy didn't have hell of a lot to do with it.

Cy stood in the biting wind beneath the cloudless blue Colorado sky, hat in hand for a few moments after the rest, his father, Susan and his brothers had all turned away. His right hip and leg ached like all billy-hell. Always would. A small fortune in titanium had reconstructed bone enough for him to function, even to ride. But he wasn't willing to swallow ibuprofen to the tune of a couple thousand milligrams every four hours for the rest of his life, so he had learned to live with the pain.

He lingered because he wasn't ready to face Susan, but when he turned, certain that she would have gotten into the old tank of a Buick with his father, she stood waiting for him. Her hands were shoved deep in the pockets of her black coat, her graying blond hair framing her face under a black lace mantilla. He had no idea how the thing stayed put on her head.

"I asked Cameron and Matt to ride back with your dad." The crow's-feet about her hazel-green eyes deepened with her bittersweet smile. Even as grown men, the McQuaid boys had mostly done what Susan asked them to do, even when it was pretty much the last goddamned thing they wanted to do. She linked an arm through his and they began walking back to his car. "Thanks for coming, Cy. It means a lot to your father."

"I'd have come regardless, Susan. You know that."

"Still and all."

"How did you get Matty here?" he asked, falling easily into Susan's diminutive for his youngest brother, the only one of the three of them who'd left Colorado in his rearview mirror, with no intention of ever returning. Matt was a Texas Ranger now.

"Why did you come?" she countered.

"He's my grandfather, Susan. It's family. Matt cut himself loose a long time ago."

"Matty feels the same, Cy," she chided. "I think he feels it more because he's cut himself off." She shivered. "Texas can be a very lonely place."

He helped Susan into his pickup. They drove back to the ranch house in a silence more uneasy than he was accustomed to feeling with Susan. She had something to say to him, doubtless to do with his father, but she had tried too many times to make a case that wouldn't be made in his father's behalf. Not where Cy was concerned, or either of his brothers, for that matter.

He pulled up in front of the wide veranda and shoved the stick into neutral, leaving the engine on for some heat inside the cab. He sat a few moments waiting for her to get up her nerve to say what she had to say.

She straightened, huddling inside her coat. "Your father's birthday is coming up in a couple of months. His seventieth. I'm planning a spring barbecue and I want you to be here. I want you to come for a celebration."

He knew about Susan and birthdays. "I'll try to make it."

"I know you will. You're the oldest, Cy. I'm hoping if you come, Cam and Matty will see their way clear, too."

Cy felt his jaw stiffen. His leg was giving him fits. All she had to do was say, *Do it for me, Cy,* and he would come. She knew that. Cameron too, though Matt was another story. But it would be meaningless then, because she would know he had come for her sake, and what she wanted was for him to come to honor his father.

What she wanted was for all Jake's sons to forgive him, and that was as unlikely as hoarfrost in July. In the words of all too many hackneyed country-and-western songs, Jake had done Susan wrong. He had lived with Susan Powell, taking her to his bed, letting her raise his sons and cook his meals and keep his house and wash his shorts, all without marrying her. And he'd been doing it since the night that Cy and his brothers had carried Susan limp and unconscious, bedraggled and near-dead, home to their father.

But Susan had never given up trying to reconcile the boys, now long since men, to what they considered their father's utter lack of honor where she was concerned. *Do as I say, not as I do,* was the long and short of it where Jake was concerned.

Cy didn't want to fight with her. "I'll talk to Cameron, but that's all I can promise."

"Now?" she pressed him. "Today, while you're all here?"

He nodded.

She flashed him a smile, and reached to pat his cheek. "You're a good man, Cy. A good, decent, wonderful man."

He wondered if she would think so when he asked her about the woman in the photo on his dash. He debated doing it now while he had her to himself, but his father, lean, lanky and stooping in the shoulders a little bit, was pacing the veranda waiting for her to come in. Cy wanted to talk to Cam about it first anyway.

He got out and went around to help Susan out. Jake bowlegged his way down the stairs and took her back up again and inside. Cy followed and started looking for Cameron among all the locals, ranchers and their wives and kids milling around with paper plates piled up with food. He got waylaid by the preacher and his daughter.

"Good to see you, Cy," the Reverend Bleigh said, offering his hand to shake.

"You too, Reverend."

"Sorry about the circumstances."

"Yeah."

"You remember my daughter Marcee?"

"You remember, Cy." She laughed. Plain as a mud fence by her own account, she considered herself the poster girl for spinsters. "Marcee, marriageable Marcee?" She gave her dad a long-suffering look. The reverend flushed and moved on.

Cy grinned and gave Marcee a peck on the cheek. They'd known each other since ninth grade. Even gone to a couple of Sadie Hawkins dances together because Cy didn't know how to say no to a girl.

He had Susan to blame for that. Certainly, by his example, his father had nothing to do with it.

"How are you, Marcee? Still busting your butt down in the trenches? Last I heard, you were running an outpatient clinic for…what? Substance abuse babies?"

"Yeah. My funding dried up though. But I lucked into a five-year grant to evaluate hypnotherapy with cancer kids—you know, getting them to imagine their cells as hordes of little guerrillas attacking their tumors from all sides."

Cy grinned. Marcee as director of guerrilla warfare wasn't a big stretch of the imagination when it came to cancer. She hated anything that hurt kids.

"What about you?" she asked. "Still counting coup in the Bureau? I heard from your dad that you got promoted to head of the terrorist squad."

"Lucky me." Cy grinned. "They had to give me a desk job, Marcee. The switchboard position was filled."

His joke didn't take her smile very far. "Dear Lord, what am I thinking? Cy, I'm sorry. I'd forgotten all about your leg. Your rehab obviously did wonders."

"Yeah." He gave a weary grin and shook hands with a couple of his dad's friends making their way out. "Twenty-seven months later," he went on. "But then, having had it nearly blown off, I'm lucky I came out with my leg at all."

She shook her head. "Two years, Cy? That's awful. I should have thought to visit you. Did it drive you crazy too, being laid up like that?"

He shrugged. "I had a roommate. This deaf kid I fell for like a ton of bricks. I learned to sign. He quit smoking like a chimney."

"Show me," Marcee demanded. "Show me what 'smoking like a chimney' looks like in sign language."

He showed her. "My version, anyway."

Her face lit up. "Look at you! Do you even know what a soft touch you are?" she demanded. "How wonderful. There you are in a hospital bed not knowing if you'll ever walk again—"

"Yeah." He cut her short to stifle the praise. "I'm wonderful." Just not enough. The job aside, he supposed it was a testament to time passing that he could even talk about Seth without choking up.

"You are, you bum. Listen, Cy, I've really got to run.

I want to get back over Vail Pass before dark. Call me sometime, if you ever need an old friend to talk to, will you do that?''

"I will, Marcee. Thanks. Shall I walk you out?"

"Don't even think of it. You have a houseful of people to see."

But he watched her go, nevertheless, watched until her car disappeared up over the dirt road. He hadn't thought about Seth in weeks. Now, twice in a week's time he'd been slapped with the memory. Slapped hard. Now the dam was well and truly broken, he knew what energy he'd been putting into not thinking about the kid.

He went looking for Cam, shaking hands on the way, making all the right noises for the folks who had come to break bread together in the wake of his grandfather's funeral. He spotted Matt sitting on the hearth in front of the massive stone fireplace. The three of them looked enough alike, a head taller than Jake's five-eight frame, all within an inch or two of each other, dark-haired with steeply slanted eyebrows, that most people didn't know Matt had a different mother. Or that Susan wasn't their mother, for that matter.

Matt was the real loner. Susan was the only mother he remembered at all. Cy piled his plate with fried chicken and went and sat with him a while. They exchanged maybe fifty words between them, but a lot got said between the lines. And a lot went understood.

He polished off the last of the chicken, bounced a fist off Matty's knee and said they'd talk more later. He found a toothpick, then his middle brother, Cameron, gnawing on a sparerib in the midst of a bevy of admiring women. "Need a rescue?"

"Do I look like I need a rescue?" The women all laughed, an old girl named Lettie who used to pass out

suckers and doggie bones at the bank the loudest. Cam
dropped down to his haunches and asked his littlest ad-
mirer if she would do him a personal favor and take his
plate to the garbage pail. Thrilled even to be noticed, she
took the paper plate and darted away, pigtails bouncing
behind her. "Begging your pardon, ladies?"

Cam led the way out the door into the kitchen. The
linoleum was worn through after thirty years from the
scraping of work boots. The cabinets were freshly painted
a cheerful yellow, though, and Cy saw the old man had
finally sprung for a new dishwasher. He backed up to lean
against the countertop opposite the sink while Cameron
washed his hands.

"What's on your mind?"

"A couple of things." He worked the toothpick to the
corner of his mouth. "Susan hit me up on the way back
from the service."

Drying his hands on a tea towel, Cam turned around.
He wore a crisp white shirt and bolo tie, dark trousers and
snakeskin boots their father would mock for "duded up."

"I wondered what that was all about. What was she hitting
you up for?"

"The old man's birthday. She wants to have a party to
celebrate."

"And she wants us to come."

"Yeah."

Cam clamped his mouth shut hard, which meant what
he had to say wasn't suitable for uttering in Susan's
kitchen. If he knew how much he looked like Jake when
he did it, he'd have cut his tongue out before it happened
again.

And if the good folks of Chaparral County knew what
a grudge their sheriff carried in his heart against his own
father, they might have quietly taken him down from the

pedestal they'd put him on. Folks here didn't hold with grudges, but that's how good Cam was.

No one knew.

Cam would manage to be occupied with pressing county business for Susan's party. Everyone would say what a shame it was that he couldn't make it, and Cam would go right along with it.

"What did you tell her?"

"That I'd talk to you."

"Fine. You've talked to me. What else is on your mind?"

"Maybe Susan's right, Cam. Maybe we ought to let it go."

"You know, I might just be willing to do that if the old bastard were to marry her. Even now. But he won't."

"Come on, Cam. They've been living together so long they're common-law anyway—"

"Yeah, and the whole thing is getting long in the tooth too. Isn't that the point? Since when are you inclined to forget it?" But Cameron's lips clapped shut. "It's the kid again, isn't it? Seth?"

Cy exhaled sharply. "Partly." He had come as close as a man gets without having his own babies to knowing what it felt like to be a father. To love a kid so much that his pain was worse than your own.

But Seth was a hard sell. He hadn't believed for one second that when Cy got out of the hospital he'd ever be back, so Cy got rejected, spit on, sworn at and ignored out of existence so damn many times he'd almost given up and proved the kid right.

"If the old man feels half what I felt when Seth…" He couldn't go there after all. Anyway, Cameron knew it already. "Yeah, okay, so I know how the old man has to feel. Leave it at that."

Cam took a deep breath. One of the neighbor women came through the swinging kitchen door. The voices from the dining room spilled through the open door. Seeing them, she turned and scuttled back out. Cameron turned back to Cy.

"There's a difference, Cy. You did everything humanly possible to set things right for Seth."

He didn't want to go into what he had and hadn't done for Seth. Whatever it was, it wasn't enough. He stuck to his point. "Jake did all right by us."

Cam knew that. Nobody could fault the upbringing Jake had given his sons, but on the other hand, the passing of years couldn't heal what hurt most. All three of them had a festering burr under the saddle when it came to Jake making an honest woman out of the only mother they had ever really known. "All he ever had to do to make things right was to marry Susan."

Cy plucked the toothpick from his mouth and flicked it into the trash like a cigarette butt. "I want to show you something. You need a coat?"

"Will we be long?"

"Maybe."

Cameron headed for the door out through the mudroom and garage to the outdoors, snagging one of Gramps's coats from a nail. It took a couple of minutes to get back around the house. Cam stuffed his hands in his pockets. The wind plastered his pitch-black hair to his head. Along the way he asked, "You gonna help me fill in Gramps's hole?"

"If my leg holds out."

"Wuss," Cam jeered.

"Up yours," Cy returned affably. He opened the door of his pickup and reached up on the dash for the envelope. He didn't want the wind to rip the photo out of his hands and blow it to Kansas, so he kept the cab door open for a windbreak and pulled the dossier photo up most of the way.

Far enough, anyway, if the five-by-seven was going to strike Cam at all.

His brother frowned; sharply slanted-down eyebrows like Cy's own pulled together. "Quite a looker."

Cy rolled his eyes. "When I need your help figuring out if a woman is good-looking, I'll let you know."

"Well, she is."

Cy gritted his teeth. "Are you going to be serious?"

"Are you saying you aren't?" Like, if Cy didn't have the hots for her, there was some screw or other loose.

"If I did you'd be about last damned one to know." He didn't really care what his brother knew about who he was seeing. They didn't see each other often enough anymore for Cam to make a federal case of it. All the same, he wasn't carrying Amy Reeves's picture around to brag or check out whether Cam approved.

"All right, all right. Don't get your shorts in a twist." He studied the photo again, squinting. The wind had his hair standing on end now. He shook his head. "I don't recognize her."

"You sure?"

Cam nodded. "Why? Should I?"

Cy shrugged. "When I first saw it, I thought if Susan ever had a kid, this would be her."

"Sorry. I don't see it. Where'd you dig it up?"

"The picture? I didn't dig it up. It belongs to a case file I was handed a couple of days ago."

"Holy hell…you mean, I mean, was Susan…"

"No." He saw where Cam was headed. Susan wasn't the target of any FBI investigation. "But something about her, the shape of her nose and mouth, the widow's peak, made me think of Susan. I wanted to check it out with you.'' He took the picture out of the envelope and put it in the breast pocket of his suit jacket. "God knows why."

"Because I'm smarter than you," Cam jibed.

"In your dreams."

"What else?"

Cy let the wind slam the cab door shut and began walking back around the house. "You've been around Susan long enough to see a resemblance if there was one."

Cam shook his head. "Since when have you needed me to back up your instincts?" He wasn't buying. Cam was smart, that was the trouble. He didn't need writing on the wall to know any resemblance to Susan wasn't the whole issue. "You gonna tell me what's going on with you?"

Cy grimaced, pulling up short at the door into the garage. "Nothing."

"As in, nothing yet?"

"I haven't even met her, Cam," he snapped, which was pretty stupid, giving himself away.

His brother cut him a look. "So what. Are we going to stand out here in the freezing damn wind till you get up the *cojones* to spit it out?"

"This woman—she's a possible witness to the alleged murder of her mother."

"Okay. So?"

There were other salient details, like the fact that she was only five at the time of her mother's death, so his piece of the investigation was likely to take more than a couple or three interviews with her. Or that her father was not only accused of the murder, now, twenty-some-odd years later, but was a federal appellate court judge on the short list for nomination to the Supreme Court. What Cy told Cam was a matter of his own discretion. But of all that what he said was, "She's deaf."

Cam's head jerked up. "She's yours?"

"Mine to handle. Yeah."

"What genius decided that?"

"Mike Brimmer. Special Agent in Charge." Cam knew who Cy's boss was. Every lawman in Colorado and Wyoming knew the head of the FBI division. The point was, the assignment came from the top and wasn't open to debate.

"Tell him to find someone else."

"Yeah. That'll go over real well."

"Tell him you forgot everything you ever knew about signing. Tell him you're too rusty." But he could see Cy wasn't going to do that. By the time the McQuaid boys hit puberty, even the hankering to fabricate a load of b.s. had been knocked out of them. "Tell Brimmer the truth, then."

"What? That I got my heart busted by a deaf kid and I don't want to go there again?"

"Just say you have a conflict of interest and leave it at that." He looked gently at Cy. "It's the truth, isn't it?"

"And the next time it comes up?"

"What? Another deaf witness? How likely is that, Cy?"

He shook his head. "It doesn't matter, Cam. The thing is, I don't want to deal with it, and we both know life just keeps handing you the same old crap till you do."

Cam cussed, short and sweet, but the wind blew it away. Walking away from your heartaches wasn't one of those things that had survived their breeding, either. A man played the hand he was dealt and he didn't cry about it or jaw it to death, and damn straight he didn't flinch. It was some sort of natural wonder the two of them could even discuss this.

"Maybe it won't be a big deal to talk to her," Cam offered. "Slam, bam, thank you, ma'am. Ask your questions. You're in, you're out, you've done what you had to do."

Nodding, Cy straightened and pulled open the door. He would do what the job required. Behind the badge, a man just did.

Inside, Cam raked a hand through his hair. "So. You gonna show the picture to Susan?"

"I haven't made up my mind." Cam had to have an inkling what purpose it would serve to confront their stepmother with the photo, or he wouldn't have asked. Amy Reeves was not Susan's kid, but the likeness of a woman the age to be Susan's daughter had set him to thinking.

"The thing is," he lowered his voice now that they were out of the wind, "what if Susan did have a kid? What if she already had a husband? What if the old man not marrying her was over some obstacle like that?"

"A kid. Susan with a kid."

"Yeah."

"You're kidding. Tell me you're kidding, because if you're not kidding you need to get your head examined. Tell Brimmer—that'll get you off."

Cy's jaw cocked hard to the right. "That's always been your problem, Cam. You just never know when to let up."

Cam swore again, shorter, uglier, but this time there was no wind to carry it off and it hung between them. "Cy, I'm sorry. I didn't mean…"

But it was out. He'd get over it. They both would. "Forget it."

Cam nodded. Swallowed hard and let it go too. "Cy, we're talking Susan, here. Do you really think she would cut out on a husband and kid? I don't buy it. Not even if the sorry son of a bitch beat her black and blue every Saturday night. Not Susan."

"All I'm saying is that ever since we were kids she's

defended the old man. You can't believe her in one instance, like you trust she wouldn't have run out on a family, and then turn around and ignore her defending Dad.''

"The hell I can't,'' Cam argued. He took off Gramps's sheepskin coat and tossed it at the nail where it caught, then lodged a boot on the fender of the old blue Buick. A line of glass bricks just below the eaves around the top of the garage let in daylight enough to see by, though not much more.

"Come on, Cam. We're not kids anymore. We both know nothing is ever so cut-and-dried that—''

"I thought I might find you two out here.'' Susan stood in the doorway, framed by the light behind her since the garage was half-dark. Slipping into a sweater, she closed the door tight behind her. "What's not all that cut-and-dried?''

"Go on back inside, Susan. Cam and I are just hashing a few things out.''

She shook her head. The boards were tight enough no draft got through, but the wind still whistled through the rafters. "Neither one of you sounds too happy with the other, right now. I don't want you to come to blows over this. I'm right, aren't I, assuming you were talking about coming to your dad's birthday celebration?''

"Not exactly.''

"What then?''

"It's back to the same old same old, Susan,'' Cam answered respectfully. "Why you tolerate the old man.''

"Tolerate? Cameron, you listen to me, and you too, Cy. Try to finally get this through those hard heads of yours. Your dad treats me fine, and you can believe he 'tolerates' me every bit as much as I do him. What is it with you men?'' she chided, her voice going lower as she got more passionate, where most women would get shrill.

She squared off with Cy. "How is it that you can stand up there on that hillside recalling your grandpa's words about a man being able to depend on the love of a good woman, and then deny your father has any right to it? And you," she turned to Cameron. "What can you be thinking?"

"Susan—" Cam began, but she cut him off. She knew exactly what their beef was. What it had always been. She understood it well enough back in Texas, when they were kids and how the ugly names the other kids called her for living with Jake landed them in fistfights all the time.

"Cy? Are you going to tell me what's going on now?"

The two looked at each other over the top of her head. She looked to Cy, as she had always looked to him, being the oldest, to explain. He took the photo of Byron Reeves's daughter out of his coat pocket and handed it to her without a word.

She took the picture and studied it for a long, long time, but she didn't betray the slightest emotion. Somehow, Cy had thought she would.

"I'd ask what you were thinking, but I guess I already know." She looked up from the photo. "She's a beautiful young woman, just the age to be a daughter of mine. Is that what you want to know, Cy?"

He shook his head. "I know she's not yours, Susan. She's the daughter of a federal appellate court judge."

Dragging in a ragged, halting breath, she shivered so hard that the picture fell from her fingers and fluttered to the floor.

"Susan?"

As if she hadn't heard Cy, she jerked forward to reach for the photo. Cam held out a hand to stop her and sank to his haunches to retrieve the picture and exchange a what-the-hell-is-this-about glance with Cy.

"Susan, are you okay?"

"I'm fine." She shivered again, crossing her arms and digging her fingers into the sleeves of her sweater. "It's just...I wish she were mine, Cy. Not having my own child was..." She broke off. Tears welled up in her eyes. Finding only more to hold against Jake, Cameron swore. Cy waited for her to finish. "It's about my only regret."

Cameron's look wanted to know if Cy was satisfied yet. "It didn't have to be that way, Sus."

Susan bucked up, just as she always did, defending their old man more fiercely than ever, more disappointed in the two of them than she had ever let show. "Your father has always done what he had to do and so have I. We don't get everything we want in life. You don't have to understand the choices your father made...or I made. You don't get to judge them either. You want him to do the honorable thing by me. I'm telling you, he has."

Turning away, she went for the door. "I'd appreciate it if you'd find Matty and the three of you go bury your grandfather now, before it gets dark out, or snows."

Chapter Two

The old Chamberlain mansion unnerved Amy Reeves. It always had.

Midway to the top of the hill overlooking Table Mountain Mesa, the mansion sat among a stand of enormous Colorado blue spruce, protected on all sides by an intricately designed twenty-foot wrought iron fence.

The edifice was constructed of native moss rock. Classic cornices stood out above artfully carved friezes. Huge stone griffins, fabulous marble renditions of the mythical half-eagle, half-lion beasts, decorated the capstones at the gates and the pinnacles of arches on the front door and each window.

Amy was an architect, and could appreciate the balance of materials with the artistry of design, but on her its charm was lost, for the wrought iron spikes on each upper window of both wings were far more functional than decorative.

Chamberlain House was where her grandma Fiona had lived ever since they put her away, years ago. As a child she had never arrived to visit without wondering if they put children away too.

The wind whipped around the estate in fierce arctic

gusts, and even her classic black wool business suit wasn't enough to prevent the January cold slicing through her.

She lowered the trunk door of her Lexus and eyed the edge to make sure it had locked shut. Then, altering her grip on her oversized blueprints portfolio, she turned and made her way through the parking lot to the entry of the upscale sanitarium. Granny Fee wanted to see the designs for which Amy had won the prestigious Bechtel Award in architectural design.

The doorman, a veteran of Chamberlain himself, smiled at her and mouthed a good afternoon. Amy nodded, smiled back and went past the portly old gent. Though outside light slanted through massive windows at the central landing of wide twin staircases, the interior felt dark, cavernous and deserted.

She left her blueprint case at the bottom of the stairs, then turned and walked back across the lobby area to sign in, feeling the heels of her pumps ricocheting against the marble flooring.

She signed her name in what was euphemistically called the guest register beneath a couple of names she didn't recognize, which didn't often happen. The middle-aged receptionist, whom Amy had sometimes caught snoozing, carefully ignored her. This was nothing unusual, for the woman had never believed that Amy could possibly read her lips.

Still, the tension radiating from the woman disturbed Amy. Something was terribly wrong. Was it Fiona? Amy whirled away, snatched up her case and flew up the stairs.

She turned into the west wing. Her grandmother's room was at the far end. A flurry of activity near Fiona's door urged Amy to hurry down the long carpeted hallway. Orderlies milled uncertainly nearby. Other patients stood peeking fearfully out of their doors.

Then Amy saw the head nurse, Faith Dunston, dart out of Fiona's door, headed for the room where the narcotics were locked up.

Alarmed, Amy pushed past the attendants and entered her grandmother's room. A well-remembered, if heart-breaking, scene met her eye. Fiona had dozens of music boxes lining the shelves of her room, and the frail woman was going from one to the next winding each, turning them all on.

Amy heard none of them, not one. Nor could she hear the two strangers, men standing near the far wall in business suits, exchanging glances and speaking to each other. But though she couldn't hear them, their expressions betrayed their complicity in pushing Grandma Fee into this bizarre behavior.

For one desperate moment Amy relived the chaos, a sliver of time years and years ago when she could still hear, and Grandma Fee had been reduced to this same sad activity. The "Blue Danube Waltz" clashing with "Lara's Theme" clashing with Joplin and Bach and Sondheim till Fiona couldn't hear herself think, let alone the voices that plagued her.

The clamor, the sheer din of a hundred music boxes playing at once had spelled the end of Grandma Fiona living at home.

Fending off the powerlessness of her child-self to do anything about it, and the sensation of vertigo the memories thrust upon her, Amy cast the two men a withering glance. She dropped her blueprint case and shoulder bag on the floor and crossed the small room to Fiona's side. Angling her body between Fiona and the shelves of music boxes, she caught her grandmother's hands.

Garbed only in her soft lavender dressing gown, Fiona was regally tall, matching Amy's height, but her body had wasted away, gone painfully thin. For a moment Fiona's rheumy violet eyes met Amy's without a hint of recognition and dismay shuddered through her rigid body. In the next instant, Fiona threw her arms around Amy.

Sobbing, she crooned words Amy couldn't hear. Still, Amy clung to her grandmother, absorbing the shudders, the vibrations of sound, stroking Fiona's shriveled, bony back. The two men stood by looking too large, too ridiculously masculine in Fiona's small, indelibly feminine Victorian room. One of the two, the shorter, stockier, balding and vastly more uncomfortable one, stared uneasily out the window, clearly unwilling to encounter the wrath in Amy's expression.

The other met the angry reproach in her eyes over Fiona's shoulder with studied disregard. He was well over six feet tall, and dark-haired, with steady, unnerving chinablue eyes. Broad in the shoulders, slim in the hips, he had an air of unequivocal control.

As brazenly masculine as he was indifferent to the turmoil he had caused, he reached with his left hand into his pocket and came out with a leather case that fell open to a badge and federal credentials. With his right hand, he spelled, then signed to her as he spoke.

"My name is Cy McQuaid, FBI, Denver. This is Special Agent Ted Povich. We have the permission of your father to interview his mother."

Deeply shocked at his ability to sign, Amy blanched, dismissing him, signing, "My father did not intend this result when—if—he gave his permission." She turned away, asserting her own power. McQuaid could not make his explanation if she refused to look at him, to read his lips or watch his hands.

She wanted him and his embarrassed sidekick out of

here, away from her. Away from her beloved, distraught Granny Fee. Surely he would leave.

Faith, Fee's nurse, returned with a syringe in hand. Amy stepped away from Fiona to block her administering the hypodermic, gesturing *no*.

No.

The nurse came at her head-on. Unlike the receptionist, Faith Dunston had never had any difficulty believing that Amy understood her perfectly. "Get out of the way, Amy. Your grandmother—"

No, Amy repeated. Her cheeks flamed. She had rarely felt more vulnerable. She managed in the hearing world every day of her life. Managed brilliantly. But she felt undone by the indignity of this perfect man with his undoubtedly perfect hearing who had caused this disaster, watching her mutely confronting her grandmother's nurse, and she resented him all the more for it.

Faith Dunston ignored everything but Amy and Fiona, who had begun again to wind her music boxes, one after another. "Must I call the orderlies, Amy?"

Yes, Amy signed. *To get them out of here.* She knew that Faith would not understand her ASL, but McQuaid might. And Faith would get her meaning. The intruding men had caused her grandmother's hysteria. They should be made to leave.

Faith shook her head. "Amy, I would respect your wishes under ordinary circumstances. Fee would calm down herself alone with you. I know that. But it is important that these men speak with her. You must either leave or stand out of the way. Now."

Amy drew a deep, shaky breath. She had no authority to refuse the medication, even on her grandmother's behalf, only Faith's regard for her. There was nothing she could do to prevent the nurse from administering the sedative.

Amy winced. She had no intention of abandoning her grandmother to these self-important, uncaring men, but she couldn't bear to watch the drug-induced, unguarded euphoria descend on Fiona's dear old face.

She veered away, acutely aware of the taller of the two men. Of the power of his body as he brushed by her. Of his intention to silence the melee of music boxes.

She stepped in his path. If the only thing she could prevent was his touching Granny Fee's most cherished possessions, it would have to be enough.

CY BACKED OFF, let Amy Reeves take over. He wanted a cigarette. Badly. It had been a long time since he'd been party to an interview that had deteriorated as quickly as this one had. His beat was terrorists and felons. He was about as far out of his element as he could be dealing with a woman like Fiona Reeves.

Or her granddaughter.

He could bum a smoke from Povich. What he couldn't do was take it outside, which was what he would have to do if he wanted to smoke. He couldn't leave. Or more to the point, take his eyes off Amy Reeves in the flesh.

She was all in black, from her leather pumps to the designer suit, the slim skirt split to mid-thigh, the shoulders lightly padded. Black silk stockings molded to her shapely, athletic calves. Her hair, spilling like a cut of raw silk over her shoulders, was a very deep red, nearly brunette. She wore unusual cuff earrings, white gold or platinum, that wrapped around the outer curve of her ears. He searched for references in his mind to adequately describe the color and texture of her skin, and found none.

Alabaster.

Maybe.

But now her cheeks and neck were mottled, stained by her outrage at the turmoil he had caused.

To stand his ground he focused on the expected resemblance to his stepmother. Like Susan's, Amy Reeves' mouth was too wide, her lips too full. There were other superficial similarities, but if Cy had met her before he ever saw a photograph, he'd have been hard-pressed to draw the comparison.

Susan was strong.

Amy Reeves had a certain unyielding, willful femininity that defied so simple a characterization.

Susan inspired comfort.

Amy Reeves sparked tension. And if he were to be truthful about it, he'd have to label it sexual—and admit to himself that his response to her, his attraction to her was one-sided and none of her doing. The last thing this woman meant to convey was a come-on.

As her grandmother flinched with the needle stick, now crying out with no more energy than a mewling kitten, Cy could feel the force of Amy Reeves's will as she touched, then silenced, in turn, each music box that gave itself away to her by the tiny vibrations on her fingers.

He watched her long, slender hands flit over the music boxes, her fingernails coated in a striking iridescent mauve like sparkling amethysts at the center of a Colorado geode.

Because of Seth, Cy had reason to suspect the extreme sensitivity of her hands. But the stray and licentious notion that popped into his head about her hands shook him to his righteous, straight-arrow, lawman core. He cleared his throat, thrust his own hands into his pants pockets and turned to Povich.

"Not playing out as a run-of-the-mill investigation, is it?" Povich muttered.

Cy exhaled sharply and shook his head. "Give me the hard-asses from hell any day." It should have been a cakewalk. "Fiona Reeves doesn't have it in her to swat a fly."

"Still, she's no lightweight."

Cy agreed. Despite having lived for so many years in what, despite its gracious appointments, amounted to an insane asylum, he couldn't fault Fiona Reeves's memory. Names, dates, places, events—Fiona Reeves could not be tripped up.

But the *summa cum laude* Radcliffe graduate, class of '30, was also known to suffer acute recurrent auditory delusions, a classic symptom of paranoid schizophrenia.

About to make some other idle remark, Cy stopped short. Povich was nodding almost fearfully at Amy.

Cy turned. She stood with the now silent music boxes at her back.

Her eyebrows were shiny and dark, perfectly shaped over her deep, angry hunter-green eyes. Signing, she demanded, "What is this about? What gives you the right to upset my grandmother so badly?"

He looked directly at her, chilled by her expressive eyes and the body language meant to establish herself, and though he knew she could lip-read him, he signed to establish with her his competence in her language. Against her strength, what he knew she must have been through in her life, he felt like a wad of putty.

"I have a job to do whether you like it or not, whether you approve or not. You are welcome to stay if you will not interrupt."

Her chin went up. "Do all FBI agents sign?" she asked.

Her hands were exquisitely inventive, conveying much more than the letter of the words. He gave a half-amused smile though he nearly choked. "I've never seen sarcasm—" he spelled the word, then brushed the backs of his fingers off his chin in an internationally recognized gesture of rudeness "—quite so cleverly done."

Amy stared at him. If she'd assumed he'd learned to sign for reasons as simple as a job requirement, she must know now his reasons were personal, even...painful. But she obviously resented his intrusion, the disruption, that because of him Granny Fee sat glassy-eyed, rocking her chair back and forth, and her cold eyes told him she rejected out of hand any need to know the smallest detail of Cy McQuaid's pain.

"What did you say to my grandmother," she signed, "to upset her?"

"Enough that she would turn on all the music boxes at once?" he responded, speaking now. "Why don't you tell me about the last time she pulled this?" Instinct led him to the question. He had no idea whether Fiona Reeves had ever used her music boxes to drown out voices—or anything else for that matter—before this day.

He had only the smallest of cues to go on, her swallow, the slide of her throat, the barest flicker of pain in her eyes, but adding them all, he had his answer. It had happened before, and Amy Reeves remembered it. Was it the night, he had to wonder, that her mother died?

She recouped with uncanny speed. "You're outside your milieu, Mr. McQuaid—"

"My what?"

"Milieu." She spelled the word at a pace a kindergartner could follow. "My mother's death can have nothing to do with a background check meant to clear the way to my father's nomination."

"The background check is over. That's not our purpose here."

"Then," she signed dismissively, "you have no busi-

ness here at all. Get out. Get out,'' she gestured power-
fully, *''now.''*

"I'm afraid I can't do that. A week ago, noon Friday,
your father turned over to the FBI an extortion attempt
alleging that your mother's death was not an accident."

Amy shivered involuntarily. "That is absurd."

"Nevertheless, the allegations are there," he countered.
"As you must know, even the appearance of impropriety
must be dealt with."

"What impropriety? My mother's death was an accident."

"Was it?"

"Yes. My mommy…my mother fell and hit her head.
It was as simple as that."

Her use of "mommy" didn't escape him. "Did you see
her fall?"

"No. It…it happened to her outside, very late at night."

"Were you up late at night, or in bed?"

"I don't…I don't remember."

"Did you see your mother after she died?"

"No."

"Do you know what led up to her fall?"

She crossed her arms, her meaning clear enough. *I can't
help you.* Her hands flew again. "This is all ludicrous."
She spelled the word so he would not mistake her opinion,
but he had to guess anyway because her fingers flew and
he didn't catch anything after l-u-d-i. "My mother," she
went on, "died in a fall outside the house. No one saw
her fall."

"That wasn't my question." He felt outwitted only because he fell behind her signing so fast that he had to fill
in the blanks himself, and his delay in responding gave
her a certain advantage. "My question was, what led up
to her fall?" She shrugged, implying, he thought, that it

didn't matter. "Amy, I need to know what you remember, what your grandmother remembers of the night your mother died."

"I would love to help you." Everything about her body language contradicted her silently effusive remark. "But I can't. My grandmother can't help you, either. I'm deaf. She's crazy."

Wildly out of context she elaborated on "crazy," forming then holding the signs for "brick" with her right hand and "bat" with her left so he could read them left to right and make no rookie mistake about it.

Crazy as a brick bat.

Even Povich got the essence of the brutal characterizations Amy made of herself and her grandmother.

Cy yanked on the knot in his tie, loosening his collar. He'd known Amy Reeves less than an hour but already she had the knack for jerking his chain. He didn't like it. The conversational landscape felt strewn with explosives she scattered, clearly intending to maim him long before he got across. If she wanted to get down and dirty so soon, he'd accommodate her.

But if she thought he would buy into her calculated invitation to dismiss her in some asinine belief that being deaf somehow equaled being stupid, she had another think coming.

Slowly he shook his head. "Sorry, Amy, but as my Arkansas grandfather would have said, that dog won't hunt."

Again the faint slide of her throat, her hands flying to distract him. "I don't know what you're talking about."

"You're a liar. Worse, a bad one." He reverted to signing again to keep it between them. "The allegations made against your father are serious, so don't waste my time. And don't insult my intelligence again."

She would not flinch. He'd seen the same deathly still

control in Seth. Her careless shrug denied even the remote possibility that she had underestimated him. He watched as she shoved the weight of her hair over her shoulder.

The movement, natural and wholly unconscious, gave him the barest glimpse of the lace and silk of a mauve-colored camisole beneath the black lapels of her suit coat. His eyes lingered an instant too long, and when he met her gaze, he found her regarding him steadily.

"Do you like it?" she signed, letting her fingers hover near the delicate lace of the camisole, her small wrist cradled between her breasts.

His lungs ceased, the breath in him froze. Had his pupils flared? He imagined they must have. He'd forgotten what terrible intimacy was required to speak to the deaf. Like Seth, Amy missed nothing, gauged every nuance of expression, caught every telltale sign. He understood perfectly that she wasn't coming on to him with her gesture or her question.

Quite the opposite.

She had not intended to set him up, but she moved with a blinding speed to press any advantage. To make him pay. To embarrass him by drawing attention to a ridiculously small indiscretion.

To make him back off.

He got it. Daring and brazen and tough as a winter-starved she-wolf, Amy Reeves would strike at any vulnerability he was dense enough to show her. *But if she truly believed her mother had died as the result of an accident, what was there to defend so fiercely?*

Despite her clear advantage in the pace of the interview, she hadn't met her match. Yet. And Cy had a job to do.

Her gaze was still locked on his. Povich cleared his throat nervously, excluded by the silence from this subtle clash of wills. Maybe Povich would have backed off.

Cy refused to give in. As with a wild horse, if he cut her so much as an arm's length of slack, he'd lose. Period.

Her hand had fallen away from her breast, but he let his gaze drift down again and signed, "I like it. Yeah." He let his hand suggest the shape of a caress, let even his gaze linger before finding its way back to hers.

Her throat clutched. He saw it. She hated him for the havoc he had caused but she could so nearly feel the caress his hand intended from five feet away that her heart sped as if she had never been touched there before.

For one wild and improbably long moment, before God and Granny Fee and Agent Povich, she wanted the caress of his hand more than she wanted him to leave and take the havoc with him.

And Cy saw it.

He had only meant to fight her fire with his. To play her game and beat her at it. To let the weighty pause suggest, with sarcasm as deep as her own, that he would in fact prefer the camisole off her altogether. Instead, the unguarded look in her eyes stormed the root of him.

He put his hand away, first into his pocket and then in a single word. "Truce?"

Amy broke off, staring instead at her own hands. Instinctively, he knew what she was thinking. She *had* underestimated Cy McQuaid. A hearing man who read her innuendoes so unerringly, who met her every deadly thrust with an equal or superior parry, deeply unnerved her.

She would not make the mistake again.

On the other hand, he had been sent on a fool's errand. The sooner he understood that, the better. "Maybe you should just leave and take your investigation where it needs to be. Out doing whatever it is you do to put an end to lies and vicious rumors."

Her hands flew so quickly that he only caught "rumors,'' but it was enough. "If this were a matter of squelching rumors, Amy, I wouldn't be here. The President himself wants an answer. The charges are not without foundation, and they bear investigation whether the subject is painful to you or not.''

"The President should have the courage of his convictions. And *you* don't have the least idea what is painful to me.''

Cy shoved his hands into his pockets again. For a moment, the ache in his chest to do with Seth reared its ugly head again. For the first time in what seemed hours, he took his eyes off Amy, looking instead at Fiona Reeves sitting patiently in her rocker, a sweet smile on her face, as placid as if she were the deaf one.

He had only caught "you" and "least" and "painful,'' but she was wrong. He had more reason than a deaf kid who broke his heart to know exactly what hurt Amy. He was more or less a motherless child himself. He let it go and turned his attention to Amy.

"I don't understand your opposition. I would think, Amy, that you would want to help me lay the allegations to rest. Your grandmother is very pleased…'' *thrilled,* he signed, "that your father may well be the next man seated on the bench of the Supreme Court.''

"I am thrilled for him as well. I would help you if I could. My father is a great man, a wonderful judge. He deserves the nomination,'' Amy signed, and for once he felt marginally sure that he had followed her signing accurately. The feeling didn't last. "My point is not that I don't want to help you, or that I don't want my grandmother to help you, but that there is nothing to be helped. Nothing. People make mountains of molehills.''

Seeing that she had lost him, she backed up, slowed down, elaborately spelled out "molehills.'' "You asked me to tell you about the last time my grandmother began to turn on all the music boxes, as if that had some deep, dark significance.''

"Can you be so sure it doesn't, Amy?"

"Yes. It's simple. My grandmother is old, was old, even then. She is also schizophrenic.'' Her hands mimed her grandmother's brain splitting in two, each half falling away from the other. He doubted the sign would be found in any ASL text, but it made her bitterly eloquent point. "She hears things," Amy went on, "voices, God knows what. I was five then, and I had accidentally fallen into a mine shaft—''

"You *what?*" Cy interrupted.

"I fell down a mine shaft. A—'' her brows drew together, then she corrected herself, spelling the word ''—a ventilation shaft to an old silver mine. That's when I went deaf.'' She shrugged as if it were nothing. "You didn't know?"

Cy exchanged sharp looks with Povich. "No. We didn't know. Go on."

She drew a deep breath as if to go on.

Cy swore under his breath.

"What is it?" she signed. "What?"

"Nothing.'' He shook his head. "I just should have known."

Her hands hung at her sides, waiting.

She wouldn't go on until he'd explained. He still had a lot to learn about the willfulness of Byron Reeves's daughter. "It's your breathing, Amy."

"What of it?"

"No one who has been deaf from birth takes a deep breath before they begin to speak. They don't need to. You still do it. I, uh…'' He frowned. "I should have known. I'm sorry."

Her hands hung more limply than before. She had nothing to say. She turned away, went to the small fireplace in the corner. She sank to the tiled hearth, and turned on the gas log fire.

She stared into the flames, deeply confused by a man who would purposely shove her grandmother to the very brink of hysteria, dare to take her on over his own faux pas, admitting that he liked what he saw, and then...then what? There were no words to describe the quality of Cy McQuaid's attention to her. It was simply, far and away, light-years, quantum leaps beyond her experience of a hearing man in all her life.

And yet he'd apologized for having failed to notice when and how and why she took a breath.

At last she turned back, aware herself now, of the breath she took, forcing herself beyond wonder to chalking it all up not to the quality of the man but the practice of his profession. She went on signing, picking up where she had left off. McQuaid was waiting patiently.

"I had fallen into the mine shaft earlier that day. My brother Brent was out of control, blaming himself. My mother was angry that it had taken my father so many hours to get up to Steamboat from Denver. My uncle had spent the day working with a mountain rescue team to get me out. And then my mother tripped in the dark and hit her head and died. Is it any wonder," she demanded, pausing for emphasis, "that my grandmother just went over the edge? Is there some evil slant that could be put on any of this?"

Cy sank down onto a small, delicate bench at Fiona's vanity. She had been crystal clear, waiting after each statement to be certain he understood, clarifying when he did not. He answered her question with one of his own. "Two deadly accidents in one day, Amy? It kicks the hell out of any theory of a random universe.''

She swallowed. "How is it possible," she signed, "for you to notice every breath I take and still so completely miss the point?"

He shook his head. "Your point isn't lost on me at all. And I don't think mine is lost on you."

She sighed deeply. "I don't know what you want from me. I've told you everything I know."

"How old was your brother?"

"Twelve."

"Did your father blame your fall on your mother?"

"My mother wasn't there when it happened. Why would he—"

"Isn't that the point? Why wasn't she there? What kind of mother expects a twelve-year-old kid to keep his little sister safe from harm?"

"Most mothers," Amy signed, her hands conveying clearly how badly he needed a reality check if he believed otherwise. "I had been out with Brent dozens of times. Nothing bad had ever happened to me."

"Until that day."

She stared at him. "This is the case you want to build against my father? That in his anger at my mother over what had happened to me in my brother's care, my father flew into some homicidal rage?"

She had made no effort to make her syntax easy to follow, or tone down the complexity of her protest, and he understood that was also a measure of her anger. Her nuance suggested his thinking, his "case" against her father, was on the same scarcely competent level as his ability to follow her meaning.

And by extension that he was hardly man enough to deal with her.

She expected him to turn tail and run. She didn't have his measure yet. It shouldn't have mattered to him, but it did. He let his silence, his unbroken gaze, grow uncomfortably long.

"I'm not interested in making a case against your father, Amy. The country loses out if your father isn't vindicated. But if you think things can't go so bad between a man and his wife when something like this happens—so bad that one of them winds up dead—you're wrong."

Heat and anger flared in her cheeks, but she was too focused, too keenly observant because she depended on visual cues, to miss either his refusal to back off—or the faint tremor at the cleft in his chin. She guessed his experience of things going so wrong between a man and his wife was deep. Personal. Nearly buried, but not quite.

She looked away. She didn't want to know anything about him. Not about the strength she kept testing, not the pain. Instead she stared out at the bleak winter landscape beyond the window with the iron bars that tried so earnestly to seem decorative but were intended to keep the residents of Chamberlain House from throwing themselves out of the windows to their deaths.

At last she faced Cy again. "Do you have any more questions for my grandmother?" she signed. "This was supposed to be a small celebration. It's my birthday and I would like to spend some time alone with her."

He gave her a look that might have hinted at small regrets. "Happy birthday, Amy."

"Thank you."

"I'm sorry, but we do have a few more questions for Mrs. Reeves."

She gestured that he should get it over with. He stood, and winced as he rose, stretched, then lifted the vanity bench in one hand and placed it in front of Fiona. Amy stood and went to sit on her grandmother's bed, near enough to hold Granny Fee's hand, and at an angle to lip-read Cy's questions. Povich moved into place as well.

"Mrs. Reeves." Cy smiled. "I understand you're about to have a small celebration here."

"Yes." Granny Fee squeezed Amy's hand and smiled at her fondly. "My granddaughter is famous now."

Cy signed Fiona's response for Amy's benefit, then, "Is that right? Why?"

"She's won a design award." She turned to Amy. "Show him your blueprints, sweetling?"

Amy gestured "later."

"I understand," Cy went on, eyeing her blueprint case, "this is also Amy's birthday."

"Oh, my dear, yes! Her twenty-eighth."

She knew exactly how petty it was, but Amy resented the small kindness he offered in interpreting for her, almost as much as she resented the reality check Cy imposed on Fiona's mental status—and that Granny Fee had failed. "Twenty-nine," she signed.

"Twenty-ninth, isn't it, Mrs. Reeves? Amy's twenty-ninth birthday?" he said, then signed, "Off by a year? Not an issue, Amy. She knew it was your birthday." He turned back to Fiona. "Twenty-eight, twenty-nine. What difference does it make?" He smiled with Fiona, signing as he spoke to her, signing her responses. "She's still a baby, isn't she?"

"Not exactly," Fee demurred softly. "But I remember quite clearly when she was."

"What kind of mother was your daughter-in-law?"

"Julia?" Fee gave the question several long moments' thought. Cy's hands went still, waiting on her. "Irresponsible," she said at last. "Resentful."

He lowered his eyes, deciding in the split second to spare Amy her grandmother's answer. "How did you—"

"Wait!" Amy interrupted him, leaning toward him, refusing to be spared anything. "What did she say?"

He wanted to make something up. He couldn't. If he once began to lie to her, he would lose forever whatever ground he had gained with Amy Reeves. He spelled the words to eliminate any small matter of interpretation. "Irresponsible. Resentful."

"What does that mean? Ask her," Amy signed, "what does that mean?"

Fiona suddenly understood through the gentle haze of the hypodermic drugs what effect her unguarded answer had had on Amy. She closed both her gnarled hands around Amy's. "Sweetling, do you remember that you could once hear?"

But Amy had never been able to read Fiona's old lips well, and she turned to Cy, who repeated Fiona's bizarre question.

"Granny Fee," she signed, "what does that have to do with the kind of mother Julia was to me?"

Fee's eyes swam in sudden tears. "You heard everything, sweetling. You were a difficult child to love. You heard everything."

Cy cleared his throat. "Mrs. Reeves, do you know, did someone in the house cause Julia's death?"

"Amy knows," she uttered softly, so unguardedly Cy knew it could only be because she had been medicated beyond any discretion. He signed her response to Amy.

She stopped breathing. Her hands trembled. "How would I know that, Granny Fee?"

"You knew, sweetling," Fiona insisted. "You...you heard," she cried, a drop of spittle leaking from the corner of her withered old lips, "what terrible trouble there was in that house."

Chapter Three

Amy stood, bow and arrow in hand, in Hank Takamura's barn, which had been converted to a practice hall. At the far wall was a bank of sand, and mounted in it, the circular target batt. She had been trained to become as one with the target. To disregard herself, her wishes, even her intent to hit the bull's-eye.

Her breathing slowed; she felt herself struggling to keep other thoughts at bay, other feelings that had no place here. Hank Takamura bowed toward her, then attached a target face to the tied-grass batt.

Backing away, he more closely resembled an ascetic Zen monk than a wealthy business magnate. The nearest neighbor to her father's property, Hank presided over the largest privately held electronics company in the world.

Hank was a nisei, born in America of Japanese immigrants. He had returned to Japan for his education, and become a master in the art of *kyudo* archery. He considered himself an American though, and when he uttered some unanswerable Zen koan, it was with tongue in cheek.

More grandfather than neighbor to Amy, he had troubled himself far more than her uncle or brother to learn ASL, and far surpassed even her father's ability to appreciate nuance and complexity. In short, he had learned to understand her.

An hour ago, seated near the waterfall in Takamura's rock garden, she had relayed to him the gist of her encounter with Cy McQuaid and Fiona's drug-induced revelations. Takamura watched her closely, so closely that she was reminded constantly of McQuaid, but it was clear to her that her beloved aging mentor did not approve of the emotional turmoil she was experiencing.

"What is it that you want, Amy?" he had asked. "To find the kernel of truth, or to undo what has happened?"

She had felt chided as she hadn't in many years. Scolded like a stubborn child. Nothing could be undone or unsaid. The question was not meant to remind her of so simple a truth, but to demand she reach deeper. Even if she could stop McQuaid's probe, would she do it?

"If he continues—"

Takamura had cut her off with a slicing motion of his arm in the air. "Can you stop him?"

She swallowed. Shook her head. "No."

"Then to rail against what will be is a self-indulgence unworthy of you."

Watching the koi swimming about in the deep heated pond at the base of the waterfall, she felt so shaky that she was unable to think even what it was she feared from Cy McQuaid or his investigation. It was true that she had discounted all her life what had happened that day, made light of it, made the accident seem less than it was even if ever after she could hear nothing.

It happened.

She had lost her hearing. So what?

The truth was that she had never really looked the enormity of her loss in the face. She had lost her mother as well, but it had taken Cy McQuaid, almost twenty-five years later, refusing to let her belittle her losses, to shake her up.

And then Granny Fee had driven home the point. *You knew...you heard what terrible trouble there was in that house.*

Takamura, flat-footed but crouched deeply beside her, his arms about his knees, had touched her arm to regain her attention, his expression softer, gentler. "Are you fearful that your father will be proven to have murdered your mother?"

"No. He is a good and honorable man. He couldn't have had anything to do with her death. I believe that with all my heart."

"It is a dangerous thing," he warned carefully, "to believe with your whole heart in another human being. You must be prepared to deal with the truth as it is, Amy, and not as you wish it to be."

She rose then, and led the way onto the path away from the garden through the winter-bare aspen trees and enormous Scotch pine to the barn. At the door, held shut by a couple of bolts, Takamura stopped her. He had waited until he had her full attention again. She wouldn't set foot inside quite yet.

"If not for your father, then what it is you fear?"

"Only this," she signed. "If McQuaid continues, if it matters somehow whether I knew what was going on in the house in Steamboat, then...I don't know what will happen to me."

"Then you have nothing to fear. The worst has already happened."

"What do you mean?"

Takamura said nothing. His face remained impassive. He believed she did know.

"It's not a matter of whether my mother found me a

difficult child to love. I don't even really remember her. But for Fiona to suggest I knew what terrible things were going on in that house—''

"Consider, please," he interrupted, brooking no protest, idle or otherwise, "the possibility that you did know. And then, please, consider what must occur. When a child hears what no child is meant to hear, when she knows what she knows yet is told she knows nothing of the sort, what do you think becomes of such a child?"

She goes deaf....

Her throat locked. She felt unable to breathe or think or examine the metaphor, if it was one at all, but he gave her no time even to think. He had opened the barn door, in a clear signal to her that the discussion was over. The issue was not to be brought into his practice hall. She must put it all aside now, and become one with the instruments of her art, for to do so was a true test of her resolve and her art.

She stood poised to shoot, distanced from the target by twenty yards. She adjusted her leather arm guard, then drew a breath deep into her lungs. The question Takamura had raised went to the core of her being; she feared Cy McQuaid for what he was prepared to do to her life on behalf of her father's nomination. But Takamura would end her practice before she began if he thought her mentally unfit.

One after another, she plucked arrows from the quiver, and shot. After every sixth time she collected her arrows while Takamura replaced the target on the tied-grass batt. At her sixtieth arrow, she sensed, by some altered quality of light, that the door of the practice hall had opened. That someone had entered and now stood, unmoving.

No one who knew Takamura would have dared enter uninvited. He ignored the intrusion; he expected the same of her. She emptied her quiver again. Collecting her arrows, she returned to her mark, battling the temptation to turn and peer into the darkness, to confirm what her own wary instincts told her, that the intruder was McQuaid, half hidden in the deep shadows behind her.

She knew by his careless, arrogant trespassing, and by her intuition. Her heart beat hard. The air around her seemed fraught with tension and despite her effort, her composure fled. Takamura ignored all that. Taking the arrows from her hand, he set each with infinite respect into the ground quiver, and by his care, she knew he had found nothing to praise in her shots. Though each arrow found its mark within the bull's-eye, the faulty angles reflected the tension riding every nerve in her body.

"You are distracted, Amy." This was not an accusation, but an observation. "Accept a thing as it is," he commanded, "and you will recover."

She straightened. Such a remark was a gauntlet from Hank Takamura. His advice went far beyond her next shot to whether she would finally turn and face her past. To confront the emotional danger Cy McQuaid represented to her. She had no choice. She would not hide. She nodded.

Takamura inclined his head toward her in an abbreviated, Americanized gesture of great honor and respect; Amy mirrored his motion. Then he took a taper from a box, lit the wick and placed it in a pottery candle holder on the floor so that the circle of its glow fell well short of the target.

Takamura backed away from the target. When he doused the lights, he would expect her to draw the bow spiritually, effortlessly, then let loose her arrow into the dark, like an infant letting go of a finger, trusting. Trusting. Without effort or conscious thought, her shot must show Cy McQuaid what Byron Reeves's daughter was made of.

LEANING AGAINST the back wall of the remodeled barn, Cy crossed his arms over his chest. An outbuilding on the forested ten-acre property—by covenant the smallest parcel of land in this ritzy Evergreen development, the barn had been built for very expensive, very pampered horses, and it was large enough to serve as a small indoor arena. The roof had to be thirty feet above the wooden flooring.

The loft was truly impressive. A rich man's indulgence. At one end deep enough to serve the usual purposes, the loft continued around all sides of the barn in what he imagined must have served the owner as an observation deck.

Cy's foray into Amy Reeves's territory had upset her. He could feel her anxiety. He suspected she knew he stood behind her. Knowing nothing of archery, watching her shoot, he took her disciplined refusal to acknowledge his presence as a bid for dominance in a struggle neither of them had quite yet defined.

She discarded a windbreaker. He knew from her dossier that she always wore black. Always, as if in perpetual mourning, just as she devoted every Saturday morning to her archery practice with Henry Takamura.

This morning she wore a black tank top and sweatpants that more molded to her long, lean haunches than masked them. He could see the tension in her slender, powerful shoulders and in the sleek muscles of her back. Despite her awareness of him, or perhaps because of it, shot after shot flew absolutely true to his untrained eye, cleanly piercing the bull's-eye.

Then Takamura spoke almost soundlessly to her, so that she could read his lips but Cy could not hear him. Cy had no basis for understanding the old man's gestures of displeasure with her. The near-silence unnerved Cy as well, and he was not a man to tolerate such weakness in himself. For years, with Seth, he had seen firsthand the paranoia of not hearing. Now, for the first time, because of Amy Reeves, he began to feel it.

He fought the awareness of his attraction to her. She was a beautiful woman. Sleek, controlled, dangerous, and for all that, still vulnerable. He knew the force of personality, the strength of character it took to thrive, deaf, in a hearing world.

He couldn't afford to be drawn to her, to admire her, to understand her, to cut her any more slack than he would an unbroken filly.

He suspected the investigation would cost her dearly.

He couldn't afford to care that Amy was the sacrificial lamb on the altar of an answer the President himself wanted—yesterday.

But Cy was already in deep trouble with this investigation. He hadn't slept last night. That was a first. He could always sleep, even when he had lain half paralyzed for months on end in rehab. He had schooled himself in the ability.

He straightened his slumped shoulders. He hadn't expected to be as disarmed by Amy Reeves as he'd been by Seth, but the stricken look in her eyes when her grandmother alluded to trouble in her childhood, when Fiona had said what a difficult child she was to love, when she maintained Amy knew what had happened the night Julia Reeves died, was enough to make him sick.

And leave him sleepless.

He was no rookie in the dirty-tricks department. He had a job to do and he did it. His conscience never bothered him. But Amy Reeves was tailor-made to make him despise the callous disregard of it all.

Under the influence of the hypodermic drugs, calmed out of her usual wariness, Fiona Reeves had spilled her guts where her daughter-in-law was concerned. Amy had been blindsided, and Cy couldn't even comfort himself that he had had no reason to know it would happen.

That kind of thing happened all the time.

So his conscience hacked away at him now, even as he understood that he couldn't endure the slightest emotional investment in another deaf human being.

Despite all this, his sex, not his heart, had hardened. And that hadn't happened in all the months—forty-six of them—since his right leg had been nearly blown from his body...

It was a brass-jacket hollowpoint, Cy, ripping through your groin. You're lucky to be alive. You're damned lucky to be walking. Give it some time.

He gritted his teeth, clenched his fists. Relief swamped his soul.

He watched Takamura nod to her, and Amy acknowledging with a nod of her own. Takamura backed away, lighted a long, thin candle and placed it ten feet to the side and fore of the target.

Cy's gaze caught on Amy. She stood stock-still, her shiny black bow raised, her arrow nocked, her stance open and to the side.

He held his breath. He felt something extraordinary happening. The silence was complete now; Takamura approached Cy soundlessly. His obsidian eyes glancing neither left nor right, he passed by as though Cy existed in some other reality. The old man stood by a bank of light switches, crossed his arms and closed his eyes.

Amy breathed. Cy watched the torturously slow rise and fall of her rib cage as his own stiffening eased. He thought her respirations were easily under five per minute, signaling exceptional focus. As if at some indiscernible signal, Takamura reached for the light switches and flicked them all off, plunging the practice hall into darkness pierced only by the light of one thin candle.

Cy heard the sharp *whap* of the bowstring slapping the leather arm guard Amy wore, the arrow sundering the air, the deadly thud of the arrow piercing the target.

Seconds passed. Minutes, he'd have sworn, if he hadn't his own heartbeat to gauge the time. He heard her draw another arrow from the quiver. He imagined her nocking the arrow. He couldn't see her.

Irrationally, he felt...fear. He imagined that she was his judge and jury, that she had found him accountable, that she had turned toward him to exact her revenge.

That her next arrow would penetrate his heart.

That he would die in this dark, too-silent hell.

His fists balled up again and his heart hammered. Not now, he thought. Not now. He wanted to live long enough to make love to a woman again.

Too late to move he heard the *whap,* the air sundered, the lethal thud.

She had struck the target again.

Relief poured through him. He'd been in bad situations where he thought he'd surely be dead in the next second. He'd been scared before—but never with such fleeting reason.

Takamura turned on all the lights. If the arrows piercing the target had been welded together, they could not have been more closely aligned. Amy turned away and unstrung her bow. Staring hard at Cy, she signed an apology to the old man.

"Next time, Amy," he assured her. "When it matters."

Next time. It was all Cy could do to stir from the back wall of Takamura's practice hall and follow her out the door.

CLAD AGAIN IN her waxed cotton windbreaker, Amy walked briskly down the paved, spruce-lined lane toward her father's property. The sun shone brilliantly in the foothills to the Rockies, but a biting wind had come up.

She made it nearly impossible to walk and carry on a conversation. McQuaid didn't try. She credited him for his patience, but she sensed an edge about him that she hadn't seen before. A sudden spike in whatever respect he had for her? Maybe.

She lived in the small guest house now, to the rear of her father's mansion. McQuaid probably knew that, so she took him to the front door of the main house and rang the bell. Pixielike and Irish, the live-in housekeeper answered the door and gestured them inside the foyer.

Amy turned momentarily to Cy and signed, "This is Moira Kilbride. Please tell her hello for me and introduce yourself."

Cy turned to Moira and translated for Amy, then reached for his badge and credentials and introduced himself. Moira paled and darted a glance toward Amy.

Amy touched the housekeeper's thin shoulder reassuringly, then turned to Cy again. "I'm sorry. I forgot Moira is having troubles, at her staggering income level, with the IRS. Can you reassure her you are not here to take her away or to threaten her?"

Cy quickly eased the woman's fears, then waited until she had disappeared down what must be a service hallway in the enormous Tudor-style house. He turned to Amy. "Why are we here, Amy?"

"As opposed to…where?"

"The guest house," he answered. "Your home."

She stared for a moment at his lips, which already she knew too well, then shrugged out of her windbreaker and hung it on the brass coatrack. She led him to her father's study. She would not take him where she lived, where she must later tolerate remembering Cy McQuaid's presence.

She sat in the oxblood leather-upholstered wing chair, and drew her long legs up beneath her. He took the near end of the matching sofa. At last she answered his question. "I thought you might like to see where my father spends his time. The study of a brilliant and dedicated jurist."

He didn't follow the descriptives, only guessed at the hyperbole by her effusive signing. "Trappings don't make the man, Amy."

"Nor does a badge. Do you think you could even pretend to a shred of honor?"

Sticks and stones and arrows, he thought. Her aim with words was as just as deadly. She was calling him on his tactics. "Amy, I didn't intend to upset your grandmother—"

"Yes, and dragons don't breathe fire."

He missed the subject of her reply entirely. "Again?" he asked, repeating the sign he didn't know.

"Dragon," she answered, spelling the word, repeating the fire-breathing creature with her hands. "You intended no harm—dragons don't breathe fire."

He didn't have to think much about what forces had gone into making her so flinty, or her language so damned impenetrable. She was deaf and in her silent version of a very noisy hearing world, she had to fight every moment for her place in it.

Still, she refused to dumb down her meaning.

He looked straight at her, taking her on, maybe harsher than he meant to be because of her physical effect on him. "What is it, Amy? What do you want?"

"The truth, McQuaid. The truth about what you're doing, why you're doing it. Why you're here."

He grimaced. "You're not alone."

"What does that mean?"

"It means I don't know." He hadn't been made privy to the full extent of the charges against her father. He didn't have any real understanding of the quality of the evidence either way, and that fact pissed him off no end. He told her as much. "For whatever reason, I was—I *am* being deliberately kept in the dark."

She didn't believe him. Not fully. "What about my grandmother's music boxes?"

"What about them?"

"You knew when you asked me that she had turned them all on before. That she had done it the night my mother died."

"I didn't know, Amy. It was a just a lucky guess."

Her chin notched up. "And do you have a lucky guess as to why you would be kept in the dark?"

He nodded. "Yeah." He looked at her. "When your father reported the extortion attempt, it wasn't only the manner of your mother's death came into question." What he suspected, he told her, was that he believed he had been set up to unwittingly exploit the deadly intersection of a possible homicide, a child going suddenly stone-deaf and an old woman swallowed alive in an insane asylum, all in a matter of twenty-four hours, twenty-four years ago.

Fending off a shudder, maybe just unable to take any more, Amy got up and crossed her father's study to the French doors. She stood with her back to him, her arms crossed, her head and shoulder resting against the highly lacquered white door frame.

He gave her a few minutes, then joined her there, wondering idly how she could bear the weight of her hair caught up in long tortoiseshell pins. He wanted to let it down for her.

He leaned against the door opposite her, facing her, watching her watching a pair of Siamese cats perched on a low stone fence, taking turns bathing each other with their tongues.

He waited until she turned to face him again, then went on. "I'm guessing that whoever was looking into the case had a hunch that you might have seen or heard something the night your mother died that would prove crucial to resolving the case against your father."

"Clearing the way," she signed, "for his confirmation hearings—or sparing the President the embarrassment of nominating a murderer to the Supreme Court."

"Exactly."

Her throat constricted. He could see her battling back tears. "So what you needed was to orchestrate my grandmother assuring me that I knew what happened that night?"

"There's no way I knew that would happen. No way anyone knew."

"Are you saying you weren't informed that I would be there?"

"Yes. That's what I'm saying." And it was the truth, so far as it went. Professionally, he couldn't fault the approach. What setting Amy up against her grandmother lacked in sensitivity it more than made up in usefulness. Bottom line, it had knocked Amy off her position before she could even stake it, forcing her to reexamine her certainties about what had happened in that period of twenty-four hours, and what had not.

He might have agreed to the scheme even if he'd known how it would work out. Probably would have. Pitting one story against another was a time-honored tradition in the annals of Getting at the Truth. But the image of himself as the blind leading the deaf to her emotional slaughter gnawed at his innards like a hungry rodent.

"Amy, look. God's own truth. We don't go looking for the most Byzantine route to the truth of what happened. If the charges against your father could be tossed out on the basis of the facts on record or the autopsy, he would have been exonerated and it would have been unnecessary to speak to you or your grandmother. That didn't happen, and since it didn't, I have to assume that even the taint of the charges will stick."

"Unless I can remember what really happened that night?"

"Yeah." It would at least give the investigation another angle of approach if what they had was as badly stalled as he suspected. "Anything, Amy. Any leverage into this is better than nothing."

Clutching both her elbows with her hands, she sighed deeply. Outside, the cats continued washing each other's faces and she stood still watching them, her attention splintered, Cy thought, between her conflict with him and the peaceful, utterly sensual behavior of the cats.

Chapter Four

"Can you guess," Amy signed, turning away from the outdoors, her signing less eloquent, more jittery now, "what was the purpose of my last arrow?"

"No." He straightened against the doorjamb. Became conscious of the pain in his leg and hip that was never very far from the surface. He had no idea where she was going, what she was asking. "What?"

"To split the shaft of the one before it."

He stared at her, knowing he had understood her meaning perfectly, doubting it all the same. "You're kidding."

"I'm not."

"Is it possible?"

"I grew up watching Takamura do it."

"Have you ever—"

"No. That's the point, Cy."

He cupped her cheek with his hand, couldn't get the images of the cats' stroking out of his own mind now. "Amy, I'm not asking anything like that—" He was interrupted by the abrupt appearance of a man at the door of the study. Stepping back, lowering his hand, Cy recognized Perry Reeves, Amy's uncle, Judge Reeves's older brother.

He had a full head of silver hair, very dark, flashing

eyes, a nose and ears too large for his head. No taller than Amy, he wasn't handsome. Still, Reeves radiated charisma—and the air of a man to be reckoned with.

Surprise flitted across his plain features. "Amy. What a pleasure it is to see you." Cy's first instinct was that her uncle was not as pleased as he claimed to be.

Amy signed a hello and blew her uncle a kiss. He tossed a thick file of papers onto the desk. "And who have we here? A suitor, I presume?"

She shook her head in answer to her uncle's question, then looked at Cy. "I'll be right back. Introduce yourself." She turned and unlocked the French doors, then went outside.

Reeves introduced himself and offered a handshake.

"Cy McQuaid, sir." He took out his credentials with his left hand, shook with his right. "FBI."

"Not a suitor then?" His complexion darkened visibly. "My mistake." He went around behind the glossy mahogany desk and planted his fingers. "I suppose you're here about this ridiculous extortion attempt on Judge Reeves."

Ignoring the "suitor" remark, Cy confirmed, "Judge Reeves turned the threat over to us, yes. As he is obliged to do, given his position."

"Of course. I fully understand my brother's responsibilities under the law. What galls me is the thought of lending these ludicrous charges any credibility at all."

"I'm sure most of the country would agree with you, sir." Cy moved on quickly from the acknowledgment. "I understood you were in Washington, D.C. Our intention was to get in touch with you there."

"Must have missed connections, hard as it is to believe in this day and age, with cell phones and all. I'm here now, but I'm off again in a few hours. A number of fronts need to be covered in Judge Reeves's business interests. Still, I suppose I can spare you a few minutes."

Cy didn't much care for Reeves invoking the judge's name or interests. It smacked of privilege, the kind of consideration which a federal appellate court judge might be accorded—but which in no way extended to his brother.

"How can I help you?" Reeves prodded. "Assuming," he paused, letting his gaze find Amy out on the terrace, "assuming, of course, that you haven't already gotten what you need from my niece?"

"Mr. Reeves." The man's carefully deadpan tone nevertheless insinuated that Cy had already gotten a good deal more from Amy than the necessary answers in an ordinary investigation. Amy was coming back inside now, one cat in her arms, the other darting through the door she opened. "Let me warn you that it is not in your best interests to piss me off."

Reeves blinked. "I wouldn't dream of it." Taking the judge's chair behind the mahogany desk, he settled himself. "Please. Sit down and let's get on with it."

Amy curled up into the chair with one of the cats. Cy sat again on the end of the leather sofa. "I'll be signing to make the interview accessible to Amy." Her uncle gestured impatiently, as if such a consideration was a given, when in Cy's estimation he had already discounted her presence. "You have no objection to your niece being present?"

"Of course not. Why would I?"

Amy signed, "Delicate family issues, Uncle Perry. Fiona has already weighed in."

Obviously unable to understand her, Reeves waited for Cy to translate, then scowled. "What a waste of time." He looked sharply at Cy. "I assume you know my mother is a paranoid schizophrenic, not to mention senile."

Translating for Amy, since her uncle seemed oblivious to the need to speak so that she could see his lips, Cy nodded. Senile was carrying it too far. He was liking this man less every time he opened his mouth. "The Bureau fully appreciates the nature of your mother's condition."

"That surprises me, Mr. McQuaid, because if you truly understood her 'condition,' as you call it, you would know anything she has to say to you is both unreliable and inadmissible in a court of law."

"I had no expectation of learning anything from your mother that might later be ruled admissible or not."

"Then—"

Curious to see what Amy would reveal to her uncle, Cy watched her interruption.

"Granny Fee only offered her opinion that Julia was a resentful mother." Cy spoke her words aloud.

"Well, that much is true." Reeves looked at Amy, finally. "I'm sorry you had to hear that, sweetheart. It's irrelevant in any case." He faced Cy again, repeating for emphasis, "Meaningless to your investigation. My brother has often wondered in private just what jackshit they teach you boys at Quantico these days. I have to say—" He broke off, suffering Amy's animated interruption as she confirmed with Cy her uncle's meaning, down to spelling out the insult.

"That's *not* true, Uncle Perry."

He turned a sympathetic, almost pitying look on her. "How would you know, sweetheart?"

Himself stunned by the callousness of her uncle's remark, Cy watched Amy absorbing the shock.

Reeves backed off, bowing his head for an instant, then apologized. "I certainly didn't mean that the way it came out."

"I think you did," Amy signed.

A silent clash of wills, of strength, a meltdown, something between them which Cy had no way of understanding, ensued. Was it the echo of some distant battle between them? Or only the emotional fallout of what Amy saw as a very deliberate and considered insult?

Cy watched her throat grip, her rib cage freeze, her beautiful green eyes dart away, and all he could think was of panic winning out under the force of her uncle's scorn. He thought of Seth, of the countless slights, both intended and innocent, that he had endured. What stamina and strength of character it took to stand up to them.

He didn't want Amy to lose this one. It shouldn't have mattered to him one way or the other.

When she looked up, he could find no hint of the raw emotion that had threatened her, only the woman he had first encountered, the one who knew how to protect herself, when to launch an offensive and where to strike to get it done.

"If I asked my father to his face," she signed, "if he had ever wondered in private what 'jackshit' they teach at Quantico these days, what do you think he would say to me?"

Reeves was just as gifted as his niece in controlling his demeanor. Her uncle never looked away from her face while Cy gave voice to her words, nor did he wince or hesitate.

"He would lie to your face to protect you, Amy, from the harsh realities of life, just as he has always done. And given what you've been through, I won't fault him for it."

"Would he also lie to me about what happened to my mother?"

"Don't be absurd," Reeves snapped after Cy had verbalized her question. "We were speaking of a philosophical attitude your father has most assuredly had occasion to raise. And questioning a certifiably insane old woman in regard to Julia's accidental death is a clear example."

She would not be bullied or distracted. "Fiona believes I know what was going on the night my mother died."

"Fiona believes— Well. There you have it, the gospel truth. I have only one question. Where has such knowledge been locked away all these years? Are we to rely upon the memories of delusional paranoid schizophrenic in her eighties and a five-year-old child? The fate of your father's career, his reputation, his *life* now depend on what you knew as a preschooler? Amy?"

"Of course not!" she signed. She started to go on but Cy cut her off.

"Mr. Reeves." He'd had enough of the man's emotional badgering. More than enough. "Judge Reeves's *fate,* as you put it, rests on the facts of the case, nothing more. Just give me the facts as you know them."

"Fine." Reeves sat back in his brother's chair and let his arms stretch out the length of the armrests. "Where would you like me to begin?"

"Wherever you'd like."

"All right. Early in the day of my sister-in-law's death, I was in the middle of very delicate, very time-consuming real estate negotiations at the First National Bank in Steamboat. Fiona called me there, interrupting my meeting. She was already hysterical. It took me several minutes to get out of her that Amy had fallen down the ventilation shaft of an old silver mine located on the property adjacent to ours."

Looking confused, Amy shook her head. "That isn't what I—"

"Recall?" Perry interrupted Cy's translation. "Why doesn't that surprise me?" he asked, making an example of Amy's clear inability, as a child, to understand what she thought she knew.

Amy's expression remained neutral, but a flush stained her cheeks. Her uncle folded his hands over his abdomen and looked down as if hurting her hurt him worse.

"In any case." He sighed. "I called 911, which Fiona hadn't had the presence of mind to do. I left instructions with my secretary to get word to Byron, and then I left.

"The mountain rescue team showed up along with a couple dozen locals. They had to dig and reinforce every few feet. The threat of a collapse was there every minute. Amy would have been buried alive.

"My brother," he went on, "didn't get there till hours after the sun went down. Minutes before we finally pulled Amy out. Julia was panicked. Hysterical. Hyperventilating all day long. She was asthmatic. Hell, if there hadn't been oxygen tanks right there with the rescue equipment, I'm not sure she would have made it through the day."

"Was she on medication?"

"Yes. The oxygen merely made her more comfortable."

"All right. So now, who takes Amy," Cy asked, "when she's pulled out of the hole?"

"Julia tried. Byron shoved her out of the way. Amy reached for him, clinging to him and her stuffed rabbit like she would never let go. It was eerie as hell." He looked at Amy, his eyes seeming to tear up. "Not a peep, not a whimper out of you. Your little legs and arms and hands were scraped up pretty bad. Your face was all dirty, and we saw tearstains, but you just put your head down on your daddy's shoulder and tuned out.

"Christ." He rubbed his eyes.

His recital was emotional. Other than his instinctive dislike for the man, Cy had no reason to doubt its veracity. "So Judge Reeves carried Amy back to the house?"

"Yes."

"How far?"

"A good half hour in the dark."

"The kids got that far away." Cy shook his head. He posed the question. "Was Julia that neglectful?"

Perry shrugged. "Apparently, since it happened that way."

Amy interrupted. "She was packing to leave when she sent us out to play."

"Do you know where your sister-in-law intended to go?" Cy asked, following up on Amy's beliefs.

"My understanding was that she had intended to join my brother in Denver for the weekend."

Amy shivered, her signing pensive, her motions crabbed and clumsy. "I thought she was running away." She rose swiftly out of her chair. "I'm going to go get my jacket."

She departed, leaving the door open. Dropping his hands, relieved to be spared signing for her, Cy watched her uncle watching her leave.

He knew all about mothers dying, mothers leaving. Susan was the only exception in his life. "*Was* she running away, Mr. Reeves?"

Startled, Perry jerked his attention back to Cy. "Julia, you mean. Running...I thought you meant Amy for a second." He paused. "I can't answer that. Julia was...erratic at the best of times."

Amy returned clad in her jacket and sank back into the leather wing chair. Cy asked how long it had taken anyone to worry about her loss of hearing.

Reeves answered. "Amy was in shock, McQuaid, as you might imagine. We didn't have any idea for a couple of days, maybe as long as a week. When it became evident that she wasn't hearing us, we took her to every specialist this side of the Atlantic. No one could find a physiological reason that Amy couldn't hear, but she tested profoundly deaf over and over again."

Cy dropped his head into his hands. The tragedies that night had just kept raining down till hell wouldn't have it. He scrubbed his face with his hands, then looked up at Amy. "It's traumatic then, your deafness."

"'Strangulated affect,' they call it," she replied, spelling the words, miming "strangled." "Or just 'hysterical.'"

Watching her delicate, amethyst-tipped fingers going through the drill of repeating the diagnosis, Cy felt as if one of her arrows had found its mark in his guts. Shadows haunted her eyes, leaving him no stomach for the task at hand.

He turned to her uncle, because if he didn't move past the visceral revulsion over what had happened to Amy Reeves, he'd lose it. "Judge Reeves was upstairs alone with Amy. What happened then?"

"An argument broke out, downstairs in the parlor. Julia was furious that Byron had sent her away, and she took it out on Mother."

"On Fiona?" Cy clarified.

Perry nodded. "Fiona retaliated. Lit into Julia like a cyclone for having let anything happen to Amy. Brent became defensive, but Julia already had it in her head that Brent had stuffed Amy down the ventilation shaft on purpose."

Cy cut him off, told him to wait. "Amy." The color had drained from her face. "Is it true? Did Brent push you down that shaft?"

She shook her head. "Cy, I don't remember. Everything happened so fast, and then nothing happened for hours and hours. But no. I don't think he did. He was so angry with

me that for the most part I couldn't even keep up with
him.''

"Why angry?" he signed *anger,* for emphasis. "I didn't
get that yesterday.''

Amy shrugged, confused. "She had sent us out. And it
is true that nothing bad had ever happened to me with
Brent. He did like to taunt me, blame me when he got into
trouble, but no more than any older brother might. He
could also be wonderful, though, Cy. He made up all these
magical voices for my stuffed animals.''

"Like the rabbit you were holding when they pulled you
up?''

"Yes," she signed, smiling. "My March Hare.''

"Do you remember why he was mad at you that day?''

"He was just scared, Cy. She was packing, and he didn't
want her to go. He never wanted her to go, even for a
weekend.''

Cy knew well enough about anger and resentment and
being scared in a twelve-year-old kid. If he hadn't dis-
played enough of it in his own misbegotten adolescence,
he'd gotten it again with Seth, in spades.

Amy might not believe the kid could have meant to stuff
her anywhere she would be out of his face. Cy knew better.

He turned back to her uncle who had sat silently by,
listening to Cy interpreting Amy. "What happened when
Julia accused Brent of pushing Amy down?''

"She slapped the kid." He straightened, then leaned
back. "Brent knocked her down. Maybe she fell. I don't
know. I don't remember now, but she—''

"That's a rather important detail to be missing from
your otherwise remarkable recall, don't you think?'' Cy
interrupted.

Reeves glared, his eyes narrowed. "She was still alert,
although she started the wheezing and gasping again. Brent

threw her inhalant atomizer at her and ran out. By the time Byron came down—Amy, you must have been asleep or he wouldn't have left you—but by then Julia was terrified that something would happen to Brent outside in the dark, alone. Byron threw on a coat and went out to look for the kid.''

"Julia didn't go with him?"

"She must have slipped out a few minutes later...when I had to put Amy back to bed.''

"I thought Amy was already asleep upstairs.''

Reeves frowned. "So had I. But I thought I heard her talking to herself outside the parlor.''

Repeating for her in sign, Cy looked from Amy back to her uncle. "Was that unusual for Amy, to get up like that?''

"No.'' Perry exhaled sharply through his nose. "She was up at all hours. I found her huddled in her little nightgown on the landing of the stairs.''

Amy nodded. "I remember that.'' She swallowed. "There was this flocked wallpaper along the wall by the stairs.''

Her hands flattened, the fingers of one searching, seeking, stroking the palm of the other in describing the way she touched the velvety wall while she sat trying desperately to hear what was happening. "I must have been—'' She hesitated, searching for a word. "Sleepwalking.''

Her hands went still, her body tense, her gaze soft and unfocused, or focused inward. Cy edged forward on the sofa. Her uncle demanded to know what was going on. Cy ignored him.

He was willing to wait for her to find her way through whatever dark maze she had come upon in her mind. Wait till hell itself froze over if that's what it took.

His mind seized on the image of a tiny little girl, bruised

and exhausted, huddled in her nightgown, listening too hard for what she shouldn't hear. Comforting herself against perils she didn't understand by the touch of her hands to the downy soft textures she found against the wall.

Chapter Five

He sat through the long silent moments, his body language alone warning her uncle not to interfere.

What Amy Reeves had seen or heard, somehow witnessed in her sleepwalking that night, was key. He knew it, trusted the instinct as he trusted the sun was going to come up tomorrow.

But when she looked up again, he saw that she'd lost it.

She shook her head. "I'm sorry. Something...I don't know what. Something happened before Perry saw me, before he took me back up to bed."

"It's all right, Amy. It'll come back."

"I was afraid." She couldn't let it go. "I was so scared. I didn't know what was happening." She looked up at him for the first time since the fragment of memory had taken hold of her. "Cy, I'm not sure, not at all, that it will come back. Or if it does, that I'll know what it means."

Her uncle interrupted, agitated by his exclusion. Cy took the time, first, to reassure her. "If it matters, Amy, you'll remember it." He sat back and spoke aloud. "She remembers sleepwalking, being scared, not knowing what was happening. Go ahead. You took Amy back to bed, and Julia left?"

"Yes."

"And you went after her?"

He nodded, his handsome face clouded. "I was ready to kill her myself. She was in no condition, emotionally or physically, to be chasing after that kid. That's why Byron went out in the first place."

He gave a small shake of his head and went on. "I found her lying on the ground. She hadn't gotten more than fifty yards from the house. She had tripped or stumbled, twisting her ankle so that she fell backward and hit her head on an outcropping of granite. As I understand it, the impact would have paralyzed her autonomic functions, killing her almost instantaneously."

Stumbling over the technical language, Cy resorted to spelling out "autonomic." Amy nodded that she understood, giving him a thumbs-up for making the attempt.

He stood to stretch his leg, pace off the numbness, shake out the tension in his hands from the near ceaseless signing he had done. Reeves's account of the events leading to Julia's death painted a plausible scenario. He made no attempt to hide or even minimize the tension riddling the family—or to spare himself.

Cy hadn't seen firsthand either the original autopsy report or whatever evidence of foul play the extortion attempt purported to have. Julia Reeves might have been dead or already dying before her head struck the protruding rock. Her fall could well have been as a result of a physical altercation.

Cy checked in with Amy. "How are you holding up?"

"I'm fine, McQuaid. You're looking a little the worse for wear."

He knew she understood exactly how challenging, how draining it was to do the work of talking for all parties in a complex language that wasn't his own and never would be.

"You're doing fine," she told him. "You give a damn. I appreciate it. Are you nearly done?"

He nodded, considering his next question.

Nothing in Reeves's polished, emotional recitation of the events had yet ruled out the possibility that Judge Reeves, one way or another, was there when his wife died. Cy just didn't see it happening. It wasn't impossible to imagine a man of Byron Reeves's caliber lying in wait to kill his wife, or even argue with her in the frozen night out of earshot of his family. It was simply unlikely.

Cy respected the odds. He just didn't trust them.

"Mr. Reeves, I understand the events around your sister-in-law's death came at the end of a long, trying day. But sir, the question remains. How can you be certain Judge Reeves—or her son Brent, for that matter—had nothing to do with her fall?"

Reeves sighed impatiently. "I know because I called the police immediately. The state patrol was already headed up to the house with both of them in the vehicle. It would have been physically impossible to lie in wait for her, shove her to her death, and then get five or six miles down the road and into the police cruiser headed back to the house before I could even report the accident."

"Not even if you didn't make the call for, say, fifteen or twenty minutes after you found her?"

"You could make that case," Reeves returned, his flinty look at odds with the complete absence of any sarcasm in his tone of voice.

At some deep, inexplicable level Cy felt toyed with. "If there is another case to be made, sir, I suggest you spit it out."

"All right," Reeves snapped. "Here it is. The unvarnished truth.'' He directed his words to Amy. "Many years ago, after my own brilliant law school career, a stint on the *Harvard Law Review,* a clerkship with the federal district court judge in northern California—in short, with a rather rosy future secured, I was disbarred for life. An unfortunate drug bust. Possession, intent to sell.''

Amy stared at him. Cy could feel her disbelief in the way her hands clasped together. Her uncle having done something so stupid, so self-destructive, when he had so much going for him clearly stunned her.

She might have felt sorry for him, Cy thought, except that what he had done he'd brought on himself.

She signed to him, depending on Cy to translate. "It must have been hard, all these years, to watch my father getting everything you dreamed of for yourself.''

He nodded, musing. "As it turned out, I have lived my life vicariously. I stood by your father in all things, all ways. At every turn I was there making sure he didn't stumble because if I couldn't have it all—the judgeships, the respect and admiration of my peers on the bench, the appointments, then, I swore by all that's holy, by *God,* my brother would have it.''

"Uncle Perry,'' Amy signed, "this is unnecessary.''

He fell silent. "Long story short, then, sweetheart. I have done whatever was necessary to guide and protect your father's career. I am a realist. I am practical. I do what is expedient because I don't care where the chips fall, so long as they do not litter your father's path or mar the reflected glory I enjoy.

"But it would have been quite pointless to postpone making that call to the police. Julia was dead. There would have been nothing I could do to salvage the situation, however inclined I might have been. We may all have it in us, somewhere, to take another life. But for your father to then lie to protect himself? No.

"Had he tried, he would have gone as crazy as your grandmother. Crazier."

ZACH HOLLINGSWORTH jackknifed the pencil in his hand over the stacks of documents littering his desk, and jerked his aged Underwood nearer the edge of his desk. Cramming a piece of fresh white paper into the roller, he cut loose both his forefingers to hammer away at the keys.

No matter which way he came at the decades-old case, he couldn't ditch the slant. Byron Reeves should have taken himself off the investigation before the dragnet of Pamela Jessup's accomplices ever went down.

So how did a man like Reeves justify hanging in? Zach wanted to know. That was the question, the sticking point, since all he could come up with in his research was that Reeves held himself to such an unbelievably high set of standards that he'd drop the dime on his dear, crazy old mother if she got herself crosswise of the law.

Gould claimed to have informed the Justice Department. Zach now doubted that the slimeball senator had done or said anything to the attorney general. Too many people had too much to lose if Gould had ever leaked so much as one word of Reeves's family connections to the press.

What turned Zach's crank was the murky possibility of a nastier, deeper sensibility about Byron Reeves. If he had never intended to prosecute Pamela Jessup, or the kidnappers, then in his own mind at least, he could assure himself there was no impropriety in his role. But if you had to walk a mile to turn that crank, Zach thought, you might as well have walked the mile in the first place.

He sat back thinking about getting his protégée, Frani Landon, in on this story too. He didn't believe Reeves capable of such tortured logic, but he'd have liked to run it by her. Frani had a mind on her that wouldn't quit, and the talent to take her smarts and her instincts right up there with the best of them, and he didn't only mean the females in international news, either.

He would call her, he decided. He didn't need Frani's take on the possibility that Reeves let Pamela Jessup escape the feds' dragnet though. Unlike Gould, the photographs in the case files could not shade the truth under an umbrella of innuendo. At least, there was no possibility of digitally altered photographs twenty-five years ago. The photos were gruesome, sickening. Pamela Jessup had clawed her fingers to the bloody bone trying to escape the closet where David Eisman kept her locked up.

The cops and forensics boys had concurred and still did. At some point, several hours at least ahead of the operation that had netted Eisman, Jessup had finally managed to kick a hole through drywall, and crawled from there, her hands bleeding and raw, through several hundred feet of dead space to daylight she could only have dreamt she'd ever see again.

Reeves probably did have something to do with the decision not to indict Jessup. He had sources lined up to work over that angle, but it hardly seemed worth his time. The poor little rich girl who gave her family the metaphorical finger was dead anyway. Within a year and a half of her escape, she'd drowned in the pool of some seedy backwoods motel. Drunk, destitute and very much alone. A worse fate by far than what befell her so-called kidnappers.

Zach knew now where the story *wasn't* leading. Gould had fed him a line the senator had to know wouldn't hold, which left only one possibility—he believed Zach would sort through the dross until he hit pay dirt.

Although no evidence ever surfaced, he typed, *that*

Reeves actively aided and abetted the flight of the Jessup heiress, we are left to wonder why an up-and-coming young prosecutor would fail to reveal his ties to the family—unless the stakes were personal...or higher than we knew.

The impropriety of Reeves prosecuting Jessup's kidnappers was one meager little snowball. But with any luck, set rolling down the mountain, Zach's snowball would trigger an avalanche.

"YOU INTERVIEWED Perry Reeves?"

Mike Brimmer wasn't known for asking questions to which he already had the answer, but sitting in his house on a snowy, lazy Saturday afternoon, off duty, and deeply into the AFC playoff game at home, Cy's boss had been ambushed. More or less, considering the presidential pressure and attendant urgency of resolving the "situation."

"The guy walked in," Cy answered. "It seemed like the thing to do at the time."

"Wait a minute." Brimmer waited till the Broncos scored another big one, then muted the TV entirely. "Walked in where?"

"Byron Reeves's study." Cy sucked the foam off his glass of beer. "I went to see his daughter again this morning."

"Why?"

"Did Povich turn in a report of our interview with Fiona Reeves?"

Brimmer nodded.

"Then I don't have to tell you it didn't go well. The old lady had to be drugged to calm her down. The judge's daughter wasn't much better off." He looked straight at Brimmer. "I don't know whose bright idea it was to hold out on me, but I don't like it, Mike. I don't like it at all."

"Noted. Fair enough."

Cy nodded. An acknowledgment of his anger was all he was going to get out of Brimmer, which told him the decision had been made at higher levels.

"So you went back to see the judge's daughter again."

"I had a few more questions."

"And Perry Reeves walked in on that?"

"Yeah. She'd taken me to her father's study. Her uncle showed up there. I introduced myself. Right off the bat he said he'd missed our calls in D.C."

Brimmer scowled. "You think he was ducking us?"

"No. He's too smart for that—but I don't think he's too eager to talk to us, either."

Shaking his head, Brimmer flicked a crumb off the arm of his chair. "I don't get it. You'd think he'd roll out the welcome mat. He's been Byron Reeves's spinmeister for thirty years."

"Maybe not talking *is* his spin on the situation, Mike. Anything else looks defensive."

"Except that it's likely to backfire. Forensics won't get off the fence." Brimmer gnawed on the inside of his lip. "Can't really blame them. Julia Reeves's body was cremated. All they've got to go on is the official autopsy—which the coroner—a pathologist, by the way, recanted."

Cy nodded. This was what had triggered the investigation in the first place. "Recanted when?"

Brimmer's brows lifted. "Almost immediately, is what I understand."

"And that's the basis of the extortion attempt?"

"Yeah."

"What did the doctor say in the letter was the cause of death?" Cy dragged a hand over his head. "I mean, either she died of the head injury—"

"Two things," Brimmer interrupted. "One is that other

bruises on her body indicate she may have been pushed, and so fell and struck her head, which takes it out of the realm of capital murder. The other is that she was already dead when her head hit the rock. There were strong indicators of oxygen starvation. She might have been smothered first, which indicates intent, and takes it beyond manslaughter.''

"Why hasn't this come up before now?''

"Because Courson, the coroner, put his change of heart in a notarized letter which somehow failed to surface until a couple of weeks ago.''

"Now I don't get it.''

"Me either,'' Brimmer admitted. "The crime lab has authenticated the letter. The paper, the typewriter ink, the notary seal—all of it is at least twenty years old. The type matches an old electric typewriter found in Courson's home office, and the signature on the letter matches up stroke for stroke with Courson's signature on a couple of hundred other autopsies.''

"I suppose Courson is dead?''

"Yeah. He died three weeks ago of complications he developed after some heart-valve-replacement surgery.''

"Which is when the letter showed up,'' Cy guessed. "So who's responsible for the extortion?''

"Courson's son. Apparently the widow came across the letter, but she's seventy-some years old.''

Cy returned a surreptitious wave from Brimmer's three-year-old son, the youngest of a couple of kids in a second family. The little kid scampered off, snickering at having gotten a wave to Cy by his dad when he was supposed to be playing in the yard outside.

"Go ahead. Laugh, McQuaid. One of these days I'm going to make a point of coming around to watch you change some loaded diapers.''

"Don't hold your breath, old man." Cy got up with the same old aches. "What am I missing? Why would Courson bother recanting his ruling of an accidental death if he wasn't extorting the Reeves family in the first place?"

"Maybe he decided his judgment call was right in the first place and he just stuck the letter in some file and forgot about it. That's the problem in a nutshell. He's dead. We can't ask him. The problem is that Byron Reeves cannot be exonerated by official records." Brimmer scowled again, this time provoked by an empty bowl of chips.

"So…what? Reeves's nomination goes down the tubes on nothing more substantial than a letter Courson himself never made public?"

Brimmer heaved a sigh. "I wouldn't count Byron Reeves out yet. Did his brother the spinmeister give up anything useful?"

"Just a recital of the events." Cy summarized Perry Reeves's account, leaving nothing out—not even Reeves's crudely veiled implication that Cy had gotten something more than answers from the judge's daughter. "What about the extortion attempt? Was he handling that for Judge Reeves too?"

"In a manner of speaking. He's the one who brought the letter to us last Friday. A million bucks or the letter would go straight to the press. Judge Reeves himself was in court. His docket is a nightmare. There was no way he could have—"

"C'mon, Mike. Are you telling me if a federal appellate court judge summoned you to his home in the middle of the night, you wouldn't be on his doorstep inside of an hour?"

Brimmer smirked. "Not me. I'd send *you*."

"You know what I mean."

"Granted. But by the same token, if a federal appellate court judge chooses to have a letter of extortion delivered by carrier pigeon, I'm not gonna argue with him. Would you?"

Cy polished off his bottle of beer. "I might."

"Always the cowboy," Brimmer razzed.

Cy shrugged. The shoe fit. He didn't give a damn what anyone thought, and he sure as shooting wasn't going to start toadying to the powers that be at this point in his life. "My point is, Perry Reeves had it in his power to head off the investigation when the extortion could still be dismissed as a fruitcake threat—unless ducking us for a couple of days gave him time to fit the story to the coroner's recanted version."

"Christ." Brimmer lowered his head and kneaded the muscles on the back of his neck. "I can hardly wait till the jackals in the press get hold of this." He looked up at Cy. "You know what you're saying? If Perry would do anything to protect his brother, to head this thing off…"

"Yeah." Cy nodded grim-faced. "Then why the hell didn't he do it?"

Chapter Six

Sunday morning, as Cy was in the middle of pushing himself through a grueling five-kilometer course, his pager vibrated at the waistband of his shorts. He snatched the thing up, looking for a reason to cut his run short. What he found wasn't quite excuse enough. The coded entry wasn't a phone number but a message that he had E-mail, which hadn't even gone through the Bureau switchboard.

The sun shone so brilliantly that if you weren't outside, you wouldn't suspect the temperature was near freezing. Still, sweat poured off Cy's face and soaked his shirt. If he hadn't lifted weights first, his leg might not be giving him such fits, but the therapists and trainers, he supposed, knew what they were doing when they set the order of his torture.

He'd have given his soul, just then, to have back the body he had before the Sig Sauer .45, loaded for bear in the hands of a freaking madman, had taken him down.

A few days ago he'd have traded his soul for evidence that he might have sex again some day. He figured his soul was safer now than it had been with that particular bargain.

He ground out the remaining couple of kilometers. The return leg of his course was more downhill than up. He ran alongside the frozen streambed that meandered across his fifty acres of prime mountain pasture. A small herd of Angus lowed as he went by. His horses, five of them, were corralled, lazily rolling in the dirt, gnawing on salt licks, breaking out in a frisky fight now and again.

If what had happened to him had happened to one of his horses, they'd have had to put a bullet through his head.

He made it back to the ranch house, shaving a couple of seconds off what any reasonably fit woman could have done, and paced off the acid buildup in his muscles outside, then entered the foyer, closed the door and sank down on the cold flagstone floor.

He rested there a couple of minutes, then forced himself to go turn on the computer in his den and access his E-mail. What he found was a short message from Amy Reeves.

Working, it said, *at a renovation site at 6th and Holly. Need to see you. Urgent. Pack a sledgehammer & lunch is on me. Amy.*

He wondered what she would consider urgent. When he left her yesterday, he thought he might not see her again at all.

She had promised to contact him if she remembered what she might have witnessed the night of her mother's death. Even if she had, he couldn't help wondering if her recall, along with the truth, wasn't going to prove a moot point.

It hacked him off, but in the long run, it probably wouldn't matter. Brimmer was right. The press would savage Fiona Reeves's assertion that Amy knew what had gone down the night her mother died. The woman was a diagnosed paranoid schizophrenic. Her usefulness would be turned into a bad joke, and at best, for all her trouble, Amy would be labeled unreliable.

What really got Cy's goat was the certainty that Perry Reeves was playing chicken with them all. He was going to hang for it, and hang high if Cy had anything to do with it.

First he had to get Amy clear of the hell that might just bust loose.

He stood under the hot shower for less time than he'd planned, skipped the shave and dressed in Levi's and a long-sleeved turtleneck. He threw on his sheepskin coat, then his tan Stetson and went outside, cutting across the front yard toward the barn for a sledgehammer.

The scent inside the barn, the hay, the horsehide, the leather, filled his nostrils, slowing him down long enough to wonder what in the Sam Hill he was doing.

Amy Reeves was not only the daughter of a federal judge involved in a pending investigation, she was deaf, which for him made any further involvement with her an emotional disaster looking for a place to happen. But here he was, whistling a happy tune, and it scared the hell out of him because he wasn't kidder enough to kid himself.

He wanted to see her, which meant he must have lost his ever-loving mind.

His horse, a seventeen-hand white Arabian stallion, officially "Knight to Kings X," unofficially Charlie, sneaked up on him from the corral side of the barn and gave him a mighty nudge in the butt, just when what he needed was a swift kick.

"Funny." He turned around and clouted the beast on his hard head. He'd swear Charlie was grinning, pointed ear to pointed ear. "Real funny, you clown."

He reached for treats out of an old coffee can, and scratched the whorl of hair on Charlie's face while the horse went through the handful.

He wondered who usually interpreted for Amy Reeves.

He wondered why he didn't just tell the Bureau to find
some ASL-competent female agent, assign her to Amy
Reeves and let him off the hook. If she never heard from
him again, chances were she'd get off unscathed by the
events her father's nomination had triggered anyway.

The last thing on God's green earth Cy McQuaid needed
was to drive on down to Denver and remind himself why
he wasn't going to do that.

He was going anyway.

He shoved hard on Charlie's chest to back the animal
out of his path, and on his way out picked up a sledgehammer, grabbing up a pickax for the hell of it. He slung
the tools in the toolbox mounted behind the cab window,
then got in and pointed his pickup down the frozen ruts
of County Road 45 and out of the foothills west of Denver.

AMY TOOK A BREAK at ten o'clock, grabbed up a couple
of sodas and gave one of them to the neighborhood boy
who was helping her load the brick and debris from the
renovation onto the flatbed trailer.

She went back inside and examined the painted brick
façade serving on either side as room dividers between the
octagonal living room and the dining room. They were not
load-bearing, merely decorative, if you could stand the
designation, which she really couldn't.

The previous owners of the smallish Victorian mansion
had bricked in fifteen-foot pocket doors. The construction
laborers were scheduled to remove the phony brick façade
tomorrow, but Amy didn't want to wait.

She needed something to do, something physical, to dis-
pel her tension, to take her mind off the nightmares. A
little masonry demolition, something inherently destruc-
tive, suited her mood.

She wished now that she hadn't E-mailed McQuaid. She

needed to think things through. But maybe he wouldn't come.

She climbed the scaffolding, took a bandanna out of the pocket of the blue-jean overalls she wore over a sleeveless black T-shirt, tied it over her nose and mouth for protection against the cement dust and began chipping at masonry with a two-pound sledgehammer.

She'd worked her way down nearly four feet from the ceiling, ridding the wall of the brick façade on both ends of the scaffolding when she saw Cy letting himself in the front door. She gave one last swing of her sledgehammer to dislodge a brick hanging dangerously loose, then climbed down off the scaffold and pulled the bandanna down about her neck. He took off his hat and coat, and hung them both on the newel post.

"Hi." She felt…awkward. Jumpy. Her leather gloves got in the way of saying anything else. He was so big. He hadn't shaved and didn't smile. Why had she invited him here?

He cast a critical eye on what she'd accomplished. "This a hobby of yours?"

She nodded, though her renovation investments in historic properties paid her very well. Better, often enough, than her day job as an architect for the design firm of Sykes & Bladestone, where a commission basis meant occasionally lean times.

"Looks like I'm just in time to help lower the scaffolding."

She turned on the heel of her construction boots and moved to the far end of the scaffolding. They worked together lowering the ten-by-twelve pieces of lumber from eight to four feet above the floor. She stripped off her gloves and pounded the dust out of them against her leg, then stuffed them in her back pockets and faced him. He was watching her.

"Thanks."

"You're welcome."

A few clouds broke loose outside. Sunlight streamed through the plain clerestory windows she would replace with leaded, stained-glass windows, as close to the originals as she could find. "Do you ever smile, McQuaid?"

"How do you know I'm not grinning my fool head off inside?"

"At seeing me?" she joked.

"Sure."

"Are you?"

He delayed. "Yes."

She wanted to turn away. Somehow she sensed, now, that he had come as much to see her as to learn what was on her mind. She wasn't averse to flirting, but this didn't feel as harmless as flirting normally did.

She felt reckless because she knew that the pull between them wasn't going the way of any idle flirtation in spite of her intentions or his investigation or the emotional turmoil it had already caused her.

Being deaf ruled out such social luxuries as turning aside with some flippant remark, not if she wanted to see his face or know what he said in answer. The intimacy of this, which she should have been used to, was somehow almost unbearable with Cy.

"I shouldn't have asked you here."

He tilted his head. Swallowed. He was as answerable for coming as she was for asking. He had the luxury of looking away till he was ready. "We're grown-ups, Amy. We can deal with it."

"I did have a good reason."

"I guess you needed one." He looked around, gauging

what was left to be done. "So. Do you want to finish this up now, or talk first?"

"Finish."

He nodded, turned around for his tools, then hoisted himself onto the lowered scaffolding with her.

Eyeing him, she pulled off one glove. "What's wrong with your leg?"

"An ugly encounter with a weapon of mass destruction. Nasty illegal ammo, anyway." He scowled. "I was hoping it wasn't so noticeable anymore."

"It's not."

"Should I be flattered?"

"Why?"

"Because I've been killing myself just trying to get back to some semblance of normal. So if you noticed what isn't so noticeable it must mean something, huh?"

"Yeah, it means something, McQuaid." He really needed to shave. She noticed that, again, too. "It means you're full of yourself."

"Or maybe it means you're doing a lot of looking."

"What I'm looking for is a set of beautiful old bi-parting doors behind all this brick."

"Don't you usually hire muscle for this kind of thing?"

"Yes."

"Why not this time?"

"Today," she signed, "I felt like bashing brick myself."

His slanted brows drew together. He didn't have to ask why. She eyed his monster sledgehammer. "Take it easy with that thing."

He gave her a snappy salute, then turned and set to work on the middle third of the brick façade at his end. In an hour they had knocked off all the old brick, save across the top, and she could see the full fifteen-foot height of the still-glossy finish on the ends of both pocket doors.

She wiped down each one so far as she could reach with her gloves. He watched her stroking the finish, watched pleasure and satisfaction wash over her at uncovering the doors, and he felt a kick of pleasure for her.

But he thought she was reminded, when she looked at him to share her delight, of what it was she'd been avoiding while she uncovered her antique doors.

Her smile faded. Tossing her gloves aside, she shrugged. "It was almost enough."

"It is enough, Amy. All the rest is just, just…what do they say? Sound and fury—"

"Signifying nothing," she signed, her long slender fingers fading to "nothing." He thought for a minute that she might go along with it, but she didn't. She tossed her gloves aside and went to the sideboard in the dining room. She held up the front page of the Sunday *Post*. "Did you see this?"

He could see from where he stood the file photo of her father below the fold, and headlines that read simply, Justice Reeves?

He strode toward her and took the copy. The byline was Zach Hollingsworth, no lightweight. He read quickly through the copy and looked at Amy. "Did you know about any of this before you read it here?"

She shook her head. "All I've ever known, Cy, is that my mother's mother was named Jessup—and that her family were very wealthy California vintners. I wouldn't know it now but Jessie—a friend, also the interpreter I employ in my own work, called early this morning to warn me."

Cy nodded. "Is your father upset about this?"

"Apparently not. I haven't heard from him." She took

the paper from him and put it aside. "But what I want to know is whether or not you believed my uncle."

He met her eyes. "Why don't you let this be, Amy? Let yourself enjoy—"

"Will you answer my question?"

"I had a few doubts, but—"

"Can you tell me why?"

"I'm not sure that would be helpful—or that it even matters."

"Well, I think we were being spoon-fed, Cy. I'm not good at ferreting out hidden agendas—"

"Just doors, huh?" He touched her hair and gave a bit of a smile. "Trust me, Amy. On the whole this has to be a lot more gratifying."

She fumed a little. "I don't want to make a career of it, McQuaid. I just want to know what your doubts were."

Right now his doubts were running high that after rattling all the family skeletons, it wasn't going to matter. She had too easily dismissed the Hollingsworth piece, but maybe that was simple healthy skepticism.

"All right," she signed, taking his silence for a refusal to share his doubts. "I'll tell you mine." She turned and walked through to the dining room and took a picnic basket off the built-in sideboard. Spreading a checkered cloth on the floor, she indicated he should get drinks from the cooler. "Wine for me." He twisted the top off a bottle of beer and pulled the pewter-topped cork on her bottle of Chardonnay, pouring a large plastic cup half full for her.

"There's egg salad, or tuna." She produced a tray of relishes—hearts of palm, pickled okra, olives, a couple of banana peppers.

"Egg." He bit into a pepper. "I love eggs. Love them." He took a pull of the bottled beer, then wiped the back of his hand over his lips. "Amy, what is this about?"

She finished doling egg salad onto thick slices of bread, then put them on two plates and passed him one. She left hers sitting there untouched. "I don't trust that what my uncle told us is the whole truth."

Cy cocked a brow up. "You were only five. How would you know what the truth is?"

He was mocking her uncle's comment. "I grew up with the man, Cy. He's patted me on the head like that most of my life. It bothers me, but it wasn't all that surprising."

"Come on, Amy. I was there—"

"No. I was hurt and I looked away, it's true. I didn't want to see that condescending attitude in him. But then he was looking at me, staring hard, you know? Like you do when you're warning someone to shut up or quit arguing or to stop doing what they're doing."

She paused, checking to see if he had followed her meaning. When he nodded, she went on. "He did the same thing to me the morning after my mother died."

Cy frowned. Trouble was, he believed her because he had one fairly uncivilized attitude toward her uncle already. "Did you know what had happened to your mother then?"

She shook her head. "I only knew she wasn't there."

"Did you look for her?"

"Everywhere, yes. But I knew I wouldn't find her. I don't know what I thought. Maybe that she had run away after all."

"They must have taken her body away the night before."

"Yes. When I couldn't find her I went outside. My father was out there. I was hiding in the shadows on the porch when the men in white coats—honest to God, that's how I thought of them at the time—took my grandmother away."

Cy swore under his breath. She wasn't telling him anything he didn't know, except the details, but it was through the finer points that he was finally beginning to understand.

She nodded. "It was horrible. They carried Fee out on a stretcher, and there was this posey thing—"

He interrupted her. "What kind of thing?"

"A posey. It's made of cloth, sort of like a straitjacket with wrist restraints, but it's intended to keep a patient tied to the bed—sort of like a doll, you know? How dolls come in boxes tied to the cardboard?"

"I don't have a lot of experience with dolls."

"But you know what I mean?"

He nodded. The image made him sick. "Where the hell was your father all this time?"

"In the car with my grandmother."

"He went with her?"

"Yes." Her chin quivered once, and if that wasn't enough, tears pricked at her eyelids. "After they drove off, Uncle Perry turned around and saw me standing there on the porch. He started coming toward me."

"Tell me, Amy. Tell me what happened."

Her gaze fell away. She spoke with her hands, describing what she saw in her mind's eye. "Our house was…is secluded. It's tucked away up on a silent mountain surrounded by pine. No one was ever around who hadn't come there on purpose. No neighbors." The sky she described was gray, overcast, dropping fat snowflakes. "I was so scared."

"Of your uncle," he signed, because she wasn't looking at his lips.

"Yes. His eyes…"

He had to ask, had to be clear. There was too much at stake to make a mistake. He drew her attention to his face. "Are you sure, Amy?"

"Sure that he was threatening me?"

"Are you certain that what you were seeing wasn't just how appalled or upset your uncle was that no one was there to make sure you didn't—"

"I *am* sure." A tear spilled. She backhanded it. "My uncle is not a stupid man, Cy. He knew there was no one left to watch over me."

Chapter Seven

She had no one.

It was as simple as that. No one but her uncle. Her mother had disappeared, her grandmother had been carted off and her father had gone, too, accompanying his mother on her short trip to the ritzy asylum.

Cy had never known what it was like to be as alone as Amy must have been. He'd lost his mother and had fallen out with his father, but he'd at least had his brothers, Cameron, and later Matt. And Susan.

Even Brent couldn't be counted an ally for Amy, whether he had ever intended to hurt her or not.

"So what you saw when your uncle turned around and found you standing there was…what? A threat?"

She nodded. "He had that little-pitchers-have-big-ears look that meant all this—everything that had happened—was my fault."

Fault was about all he understood in everything she had signed. "Your fault?"

She nodded again.

"I don't get it." Frustration began to gnaw at him. Time and again he'd been in the same position with Seth, and the memories choked him. "Amy, I'm lost. I don't know

what you're telling me, beginning with 'little pitchers.'"
He repeated her signing. "Is that what you meant?"

"Yes." She slowed down. "Fiona used to say it. 'Little
pitchers have big ears.' It was a nonsense thing she meant
as a veiled warning to the others to be careful of what they
were saying around me."

He caught it this time. "Because you might overhear
something you shouldn't?"

"Exactly." Her head dipped low, then she looked at him
again. "That's what Granny Fee meant, I think, when she
said I was a difficult child to love." Again she waited to
be sure he was following. He was. "They could never be
sure what I saw, Cy, or what I heard. I wouldn't stay in
bed. I wanted to know what was going on."

He picked up his egg salad sandwich, but it never got
close to his mouth. He had no appetite, just an ugly opinion.

"I'm not a little pitcher anymore, Cy. Don't treat me
like one."

She meant that he shouldn't edit what he was thinking,
shouldn't not say what was on his mind. Maybe she
needed to know to be sure she wasn't making these things
up.

"It makes me believe Fiona was right, Amy. It makes
me want to know what was going on inside that house that
made it necessary for a five-year-old child to turn herself
into such a vigilant little pair of ears."

Her eyes lingered on his lips, it seemed to him forever
long, until she signed, "Me too."

She had intended no intimacy with her prolonged gaze.
Still, an awareness spiked like a fever between them. He
dropped his gaze, studied the beads of cold sweat on his
beer bottle.

"I have to find out, Cy. I need your help."

He felt his Adam's apple plunge. She drew him like a moth to a flame. She refused to be quelled, silent, too nice, not herself, or to stay put at all. She sat here baring her soul, asking for help, willing to expose the lies in what she had always believed. He didn't know another woman as honest as Amy, or as daring.

The others, the women he'd known, were no more substantial in his memory now than paper dolls.

Against all odds, Amy was the woman that had made him feel like a man again. He had to weigh all that against the fact that she was deaf, that he didn't know if he could cope with it.

He had every intention of exposing whatever game it was her uncle was playing, but he meant to do it himself and he meant to spare her. She might be accustomed to being dismissed by her uncle but he was only the tip of the iceberg. It took no imagination to see the press painting the FBI just bent enough on clearing Byron Reeves that it would court the "recovered memories" of a woman gone deaf by the trauma of her fall. Let alone the murder of her mother by her own father...

Most of all, he didn't know how he could help her without getting in deeper, without caring too much what became of her. Without putting his heart into bridging the chasm between hearing and not, and having her later hack the bridge to pieces when she discovered he didn't have it in him to go the distance with her.

Then some jokester part of him laughed inside his head. He already cared too much.

Still he struggled to keep a distance. "Amy, there is no way that you were responsible for what happened."

"Is that a 'no,' McQuaid?"

In English the question was plain enough. In her hands, "no" took on shades of hedging, the aspect of running

scared, allusions that captured his feelings so well that another image, of Amy as the starving she-wolf, paralyzing
her prey with her eyes alone, invaded his head.

He felt ridiculous. She was asking for help, not the right
to mother his children. It was his own fault to imagine the
distance between one thing and the next wasn't so great.

His answer was no answer at all, only another question.
"What I don't get, Amy, is what your uncle thought he
would accomplish by scaring the hell out of you. Or by
what stretch of the imagination he blamed you for everything that had happened."

She left her focus on his hands only so long as was
absolutely necessary. "That's the whole point, isn't it?"

"You weren't responsible for what happened."

"Maybe not directly."

"Not even indirectly," he argued. "Think about it,
Amy. You were a *child*."

"But if my grandmother is right, I *knew* things, even if
I didn't have the least idea what it was that I knew, even
if there was nothing I could do about it."

"For example?"

"As far as my uncle was concerned, my mother was
getting ready to leave for a weekend in Denver with my
father. That's not true. She was packing to leave us."

"Maybe both things are true, Amy. Maybe she intended
to go to Denver to break off with your father."

"The end result is the same. She was leaving us, and I
knew it."

He shook his head. "Amy, don't take this the wrong
way, but you were only five, and it's been a very long
time. The only way you could possibly have known that
your mother was running away was if she told you—"

"No," she interrupted, signing, "I knew it when she
sent Brent away and told him to take me with him." When

he said nothing, only waited, she went on. "I know this isn't what I said before, but—"

She broke off so abruptly that he knew she was having a hard time accounting to herself for glossing over the gritty details two days before when she had always known better. "The truth is, I was expected not to make a scene, to pretend and go out to play as if everything was all right. As if she wasn't planning to ditch me...us."

Her hands clasped tightly together. Sometimes her brilliantly expressive signing betrayed her. He knew what she was thinking: *If only I hadn't been a such a difficult child to love, my mother might never have conspired to ditch me.* Her slender knuckles whitened. The last time he'd noticed such a thing, his own mother was clutching her bible while the life remaining in her body bled itself out.

Amy's spine curled inward. Her shoulders sank low in a weary, bone-tired sort of posture. She nibbled the spoonful of egg salad off the bread, washed it down with half the wine he had poured her, then straightened.

He could barely swallow, hardly speak, but he mouthed the words and it was good enough. "Spell it out for me, Amy."

"There was something terribly wrong in my house long before my mother died. Something that had to do with me."

He turned and wedged the cooler between the side wall of the dining room and his back so that he could lean against something and stretch out his leg. "My mother died when I was a kid, too."

Stricken, she waited for him to go on, every aspect of her attention pinned on emotion she couldn't even hear in his voice. He didn't know why he'd started this. He didn't want to notice how he needed to tell her.

"She miscarried. We lived twenty miles out of the nearest town. An ice storm had come up out of nowhere, but the calving started that afternoon and my old man had taken the pickup out to try to save what few he could. The phone lines were down. I couldn't have gotten her any help if I tried.''

Cy couldn't even put into words how devastated he'd been because his dad had left him in charge, and his mother died on his watch. ''I prayed really hard instead, right up until I fell asleep.'' He broke off.

He cleared his throat. ''I always believed she wouldn't have died it I hadn't fallen asleep. Kids are like that. They always blame themselves.''

''I'm sorry about your mother.''

He shrugged, still trying to ignore her eyes welling up on his account. It was just like her. ''I was making a point. I don't remember my mother very much anymore.''

''That doesn't make the loss any less painful.''

He swallowed. ''No. It doesn't.''

Her tears subsided and she went on, letting him off the hook. ''Cy, I wish I could believe that blaming myself as any child would do is all there is to this. I could even accept that I imagined the threat to me in my uncle Perry's eyes after they took Fiona away. But I wasn't imagining the same look yesterday when I contradicted him over my father's opinions. You saw it. Tell me. Am I wrong?''

''No.'' Cy shook his head. ''You're not wrong, Amy.'' Perry Reeves had intended to embellish the doubt and uncertainty, to make mercilessly clear that nothing she remembered could be taken seriously.

Being deaf, she couldn't possibly know or have heard her father's opinions on any number of subjects.

What could she know for sure, at all?

What could she have heard?

And finally, what did she really want—her father's career to be destroyed based on what a crazy old woman believed a five-year-old had known?

He stared at the piles of brick and rubble, and knew exactly why she'd taken on the job of destroying the brick wall facings herself.

Tears glittered in her eyes, but suddenly she smiled through them. It pierced him to the heart. He found himself trying to memorize what amusement looked like in her eyes, on her lips. Despite her teasing over his never smiling, he hadn't seen much merriment from her either. "Tell me."

"I was just picturing myself in that big old Gothic house, a forlorn little urchin with this huge pair of ears." She paused, still smiling. "They couldn't lock me in my room. At least, no one ever did. And I didn't mind very well—obviously."

For a man who needed a tight rein on his attention, he wasn't managing well. Still, he thought maybe now she could be dissuaded or distracted from needing to find out for herself what had been so wrong in her house. A slow grin took over his lips.

"What?" she signed.

"I'm betting not a lot has changed. That's all."

She sat very still. "That depends upon who wants what from me."

His breathing grew suddenly shallow. He could no longer be certain at all of her meaning, but suddenly what he wanted from her became the issue.

What he was doing here.

Why he had come.

What else besides his investigation he had on his mind. The attraction he'd believed they could contain. From the moment he had touched her cheek in her father's study, they'd been at this risk.

He remembered the first instant when he knew he would lose her if he once lied to her. He'd thought then that losing her only meant sacrificing her cooperation with the investigation, but even then he'd been kidding himself.

"Are you asking, Amy?" He knew better than this, too. Like he knew the hills and creeks and valleys and draws on his land, he knew that even coming here he had violated half a dozen rules writ large in the book of ethical conduct about a witness in an open investigation. And that if he kept going, he'd violate half a dozen more. "Are you asking what I want?"

Her eyes lingered on his hands after the necessity of that was past. If he thought speaking with his hands would alleviate the tension, he was wrong.

"Yes." Her pulse throbbed at her throat. She looked up, met his eyes. "I'm asking what you want."

He cleared away his bottle of beer, her wine, the bowl of egg salad, the baguette of bread, their plates. All the clutter that lay between them.

She had plenty of time to retreat if retreat was what she wanted.

He had the time as well but not the inclination to stop himself. He straightened and sat back on his heels, took her hand and pulled her between his splayed thighs. She came easily enough. Almost eagerly.

Kneeling so close to his body, she was still as a church mouse. He was going to kiss her, maybe touch her. He thought she knew it. He didn't think she could still be a virgin, not at twenty-nine, but he had the notion that she was not practiced, not an old hand at seductions, but at dodging them instead, only she wasn't dodging him.

Still he was leery. The physical attraction between them had already flared up more than once. He wasn't convinced this time that it didn't have as much to do with his willingness to try to understand her as it did with her wanting him.

But then her eyes went to his lips and she touched her fingers to his whiskered jaw and his need of right reasons slipped away.

"Amy."

Her fingers darted to his lower lip like a blind child exploring, or a deaf one learning the shape of spoken words. He spoke her name again, then again, because the sensation of her fingertips on his lips was as close a thing to heaven just then as he'd ever known.

The heat of her body, the scent of her, cement dust and egg and chardonnay and some musky, deeply feminine scent all mixed together. Made his belly damn near cramp with wanting her. She leaned closer, drew her fingers lower to scrape her nails over the whiskers in the cleft of his chin. Her eyes followed the course of her fingers till they fell closed when he couldn't stand it anymore and covered her parted lips with his own.

Maybe it was the months, the years of abstinence forced on him by his injuries, but he lost himself so fast in Amy's sweet silent lips, so hard deep inside himself, that he forgot what restraint was.

What taking it slow meant or how scared he'd been that he'd never suffer such pleasure again.

He pulled the long decorative pins from her hair, let them fall clattering to the floor, and thrust his hand in the spill of her hair, tangling his fingers, cradling her head.

She was under his skin; he wanted to be under hers.

Sunlight poured through the clerestory windows, warming Amy's back, and shimmering above her shoulders. Cy's hand held her head, pulled her hair, cradled her neck to deepen his kiss. The tenderness shook her more deeply than the touch of his lips or the heat and damp of his tongue, which—as it was—moved her to a place of sensations and heavy, indelible pleasure she didn't remember ever feeling before.

The pleasure had more to do with her heart and her mind, her soul, than even the sum of all that. McQuaid believed her, more than she believed in herself. Beneath her hands, splayed on his chest, she felt the pounding of his heart, the subtle tactile vibration of a groan, the beading of his nipples, the hardness of his pecs.

The evidence of his desire for her laid waste all her jaded expectations and she wanted more than anything to feel her body tight up against his.

She arched nearer. His arm closed around her waist, drawing her deeper into him, closer. He felt her heat now, more than smelled it.

A small whimper of pleasure came from her then, the only sound he had heard her make, and he knew it was one that he would remember as long as he lived, for her small cry pulled him out of his trance and pointed out to him how weak and shallow he felt.

What he craved was the sound of her voice, his name on her lips, and it loomed like some terrible fault in the landscape of his selfish and narrow little mind that he would never have it no matter what countless other ways she fit him.

He had all the proof he needed that the icy sensation in his gut when she'd asked for his help was real. Amy was deaf, and he wasn't man enough to cope with it.

He tried to chalk the fault up to something more symbolic, less damning of his character, than that he would never hear her voice. Like a righteous, realistic, honest fear of never truly knowing her.

It wasn't that far-fetched.

He'd thought he knew everything there was to know

about Seth. What the kid needed, what he wanted, what he dreamed of what, what he was made of, even when Seth didn't know himself. But he'd only been guessing, and his guessing was lousy. He knew if he hung around with Amy long enough to make what they had too important to back away from, sooner or later he'd start resorting to his faulty guessing again.

And so would she. Start thinking she knew what was in his heart, filling in the blanks of their flawed and imperfect communication for herself, finally imagining the worst because she was only human and that's what humans did best.

He had only his experience with Seth being deaf to go on, but he also knew promises were hard enough between a man and a woman when they spoke the same language. When they didn't, when one of them hobbled along and the other had to spell it out all the damned time, pretty soon the effort would begin to feel less like a payoff and more of a burden.

Something always got lost in the translation.

He knew what to do, how to kiss, where to put his hands, apply his lips, touch his tongue to hers. What he didn't know was how to end it, not because he wanted to end the kiss or because it had run its course, but because it hadn't.

He pulled away, put his hand on her hips and gently pushed her down. Their foreheads came together. His heart clopped like a lame horse. His breathing felt as ragged as hers.

Between them she signed with one hand. "That was lovely, McQuaid, but…surely it's a little early for r-e-g-r-e-t."

He couldn't misunderstand that. She must have tasted the emotion in him. He didn't know how to answer. He let his ragged breathing excuse his silence. He stretched out his leg and sat and faced her, not knowing what would happen. Whether the hard and certain reality of falling head over heels in love with her would add up to anything lasting, even if he could get over her unending silence.

He just couldn't throw in the towel on himself—or her—yet. If nothing ever came of it, if whatever there was between them wasn't meant to last, he wanted to know it wasn't because he hadn't given them an even chance. He wanted to show up, be man enough to love her if she wanted him, to be more than he thought he was right now—more than he'd been for a deaf kid.

He wanted it more than he needed his honor. He chose his words carefully, leading her to believe it was the job, which while true, wasn't the truth.

"It shouldn't have happened, Amy."

"Ever?"

He looked at her, leading her further. "Ever is a long time."

She nodded, believing him, accepting at face value that he both wanted to kiss her and would again, eventually, maybe when his investigation was done.

She got up and brought him another beer, poured herself another half-glass of wine, then looked steadily at him, measuring, he thought. Gauging anew whether he could be trusted or whether he would lie to her.

He twisted off the cap and took a swig. His heart was still clopping stupidly along. He dragged his sleeve over his mouth. "Where were we?"

She sipped at her wine, putting herself back to the point she'd intended to make before they kissed. "You were agreeing that I hadn't imagined my uncle's threats yesterday."

Cy nodded. "They were real enough, Amy, but I'm not convinced—"

"Of what?" she demanded. "That he meant them? That he intended to scare me off? You're not convinced of that? Because, Cy, if my uncle really has nothing to fear from me then what's the point? If nothing I may have seen or heard that night matters, if there really is nothing more to my mother's death than exactly what he told you, then why the intimidation tactics? He isn't usually like that. He doesn't bully people—"

"He bullies you, Amy, and if what you're telling me is accurate, he always has."

"But why? The only thing that makes any sense of his treating me that way is that I'm a threat to him. A threat he has to…somehow…contain."

Now was the time to edge her out, to do what he could to keep her safe from the fallout. "Amy, did you see your mother fall outside or not?"

"No."

"Then whatever else you saw or heard or knew or even what your uncle suspects you knew is meaningless."

"I don't understand."

"Nothing short of an eyewitness to your mother's accident is going to be enough to prove or disprove the truth of half-assed allegations made against your father."

"That isn't what you said yesterday," she signed.

"I know, but—"

"Yesterday you said that what I knew was the only thing that was going to save my father's nomination from the taint of the accusations." Her eyes fixed on his. "Something has changed since then. What is it, Cy?"

He drew a deep breath. He'd long since given up trying to distract Amy or dissuade her. He hoped she might still listen to reason, still take the way out he wanted her to take. He wasn't optimistic, but he owed her the explanation of his own change of heart.

"I'm convinced, Amy, that your uncle knew enough—before he ever turned over the extortion material to us—to discount any possibility that we would take it seriously."

"Please. Say that again," she signed.

He complied, nodding to indicate he understood her confusion, that he'd been confused himself. He went on to explain the discrepancies between the official autopsy and the letter recanting the ruling of an accidental death.

"The ruling turns on whether the bruises indicate your mother was shoved, fell down and hit her head, or whether she was already dead when her head hit. Her tissues indicated a severe lack of oxygen."

"Which could be the real cause of her death?"

"Yeah. One interpretation of that is that she had been smothered to death before her head ever hit the rock."

Distractedly, Amy covered the egg salad and got up to put the bowl in the cooler, then turned back to him and stood leaning against the built-in sideboard. "Isn't there any way to tell?"

He began to get up as well. "I'm only guessing, Amy. I haven't seen—" The stiffness made his leg buckle and his knee cracked hard against the hardwood floor. Amy reached to steady him but he held up a hand to fend off her help. Grimacing, he stood up and leaned with her against the sideboard.

"Cy, your face is white as a ghost!"

"I'll be all right." He breathed deep a couple of times to disperse the pain, then went on, signing because he was gritting his teeth and she wouldn't be able to read his lips very well. "I haven't seen either document, but I'm assuming the amount of bleeding was the issue. If the heart isn't pumping, then the amount of bleeding is minimal.''

Her ill-concealed concern for him led her question. ''What does that mean?''

''All I know for sure, Amy, is that the cause of death isn't clear, and it's never going to be. What I'm getting at is that your uncle's version of what went on in the minutes leading up to your mother's death accounted for both the bruises and the indications of oxygen starvation.''

''Case closed?'' she signed.

''More or less.''

''Except that Perry let your investigation get under way before he bothered explaining what had happened.''

''That's my take on it.''

She shook her head in disbelief. ''Why? If he knew what it would take to clear up whatever questions were being raised in the extortion attempt, then why wouldn't he just do it?''

''It's possible that it took him a while to come up with his explanations for the hypoxia angle.''

''It's also possible he's deliberately sabotaging my father's shot at the Supreme Court, isn't it?''

''The thought occurred to me too,'' Cy admitted. ''Can you think of sweeter revenge, Amy, for all the indignities he suffered? He spent his whole life watching your father get what he believes he was entitled to himself—and now it's in his power to take it all away.''

She shook her head, wadding napkins and throwing them into the paper sack. ''He can't be that despicable.'' She spelled the word for the sake of accuracy.

''Can't he?'' Cy argued, knowing he was largely arguing her case against her uncle. ''It won't even reflect poorly on him. He may have allowed the investigation to get far enough that one way or the other, it costs your father what he's worked a lifetime to achieve. But now, stepping in with the crucial information, Perry gets to be the hero of the story again. It's his explanation of what went down that makes the autopsy results spin one way or the other. In effect, he's the one standing between your father and a felony murder charge.''

"It's not that I would put it past Perry, Cy, but I don't buy it. He's too vain, too good to at what he does to let my father go down the tubes. To let anyone beat him. He intends to pull this off.''

Cy straightened. "Pull what off?''

She swallowed. "I think my mother was murdered. I think he knows she was because he's the one who killed her.''

Chapter Eight

"I think he just decided my mother was too much of a liability to endure—"

"Amy, slow down. Too much of a what? To do what?"

"A liability," she spelled.

"So when the opportunity arose to dispense with her, he grabbed it?"

She nodded, convinced of it, still slowing herself. "Don't you see? It really doesn't matter whether she was dead before her head hit that rock or not. One way or the other, he got to her. All he had to do was make it look like an accident—for my father's benefit if nothing else. And now he's playing us all for fools. There's nothing more he has to do now to get away with it."

Cy swore under his breath. The logic of the scenario Amy drew with her hands stunned him. "It plays, Amy." Not least because it also explained why Perry Reeves would risk letting the investigation get under way. "Once he accounted for the discrepancies that made the coroner change his mind, the case file on your mother's death would be closed forever. After an official FBI inquiry, the likelihood is zip of anyone raising the possibility of foul play in your mother's death again."

"And all the while," Amy signed, "the possibility of

his guilt never even comes up.'' She stopped. Her hands fell to her sides. Her fingers gripped the top of the sideboard behind her for the few moments before she resumed signing. ''Will he get away with it, Cy?''

He wanted to give her his macho cowboy lawman assurances, to promise her that if Cyrus V. McQuaid had anything to do with it, the murder of her mother would not go unavenged or unpunished. His record spoke for itself, and for him. He intended to dog the hell out of the case while he could. But he wouldn't lie to her.

Her scenario was too compelling by half to discount. And if it was true, then Cy would bet the farm her uncle had been right there, taking charge, doing for Judge Reeves what he did best. In that case, Perry Reeves had served his own interests as well, making damned sure Julia Reeves's final resting place would be some fancy urn for her ashes, so there would be no body to exhume and later make a liar of him.

''Based on what we know right now, Amy, assuming he did the deed, he's *already* gotten away with it. And all this is just another opportunity for your uncle to pull your father's fat out of the fire.''

''And thumb his nose at you.''

His jaw tightened. She'd managed to reduce to a single visceral image exactly what he'd been thinking. He didn't know if by ''you'' she had meant him or the whole system of justice Perry Reeves's brother was destined to preside over, but Cy was taking it personally.

''What will you do?'' she asked, her hands hovering in the air, posing the question.

''I don't know, Amy. Anything I do now to keep the investigation open is likely to compromise your father's nomination process. Especially if the press gets wind of it.'' He turned his head toward the front of the house. "Someone's knocking at the door. Do you want to get it?"

"It's probably Paulo. I forgot all about him." She went to let the boy in, and gestured for him toward the piles of brick that needed to be removed. The boy grinned, ran out to fetch a wheelbarrow and began loading up the rubble.

Cy began picking up after their meal, polishing off the remainder of his sandwich. Amy knelt to take up the cloth she'd spread out on the floor, then sank down on her heels. "Your time is very short, isn't it?"

"To make the case against your uncle?" he asked to clarify. When she nodded, he answered, "I'm not sure the window of opportunity hasn't already slammed shut, Amy."

"Then I'll have to do it. I want to go to Steamboat to see my brother first, but it's now or never, Cy. Perry will keep stonewalling until it all goes away," she signed, holding up one hand like a cop stopping traffic, the other slithering off. "That's the only thing he has to do now. If he has a problem, I'm it. I'm the wild card he can't control. You know that."

Cy folded his arms. He knew she was right. He also knew she could have no concept of what it was like to play hardball with a man like her uncle.

If they were right, Perry Reeves had murdered once, clearly demonstrating he would stop at nothing to ensure he got what he wanted since what he had *really* wanted had been out of his reach since the hour he'd taken possession of street drugs he'd intended to hawk.

Cy scowled, congratulating himself on having achieved the exact opposite of his intentions in coming here at all. Amy was unlikely to back off now. "Do you want to know what will happen if you pursue this?"

"It doesn't matter."

"That's easy to say, Amy, but you have to think through the consequences. How will you answer when your father asks you what you're trying to prove? If we nail Perry, do you think he won't take your father down with him? All he would have to do is say that your father knew exactly what had happened. Do you think he wouldn't at least make that threat? Or that your father's career would survive the accusation even on the federal bench?"

"My father would be the first to throw your argument out the window."

"We're not talking abstract principle here, Amy—"

"No. We're not. I intend to ask him. I think he would survive it—but that isn't even the point, Cy. If it came to that, my father would resign from the bench first."

She waited for him to say something. When he only looked at her, she looked at Paulo scurrying around loading bricks into the wheelbarrow. Cy could see the struggle going on inside her. If she couldn't persuade him that her uncle had committed murder, then maybe she was wrong to think she could take it on.

"You think I'm being naive, don't you?" Her hands spoke of a babe in the woods.

He had the feeling there was more going on inside her heart than he knew. That she felt herself a babe in dangerous woods her uncle lorded over, and equally, unwilling to be bullied anymore.

"The thing is," he answered, "your father won't ever get to make that call because the buck stops with you. You're the one who has to decide. Now we know that's what was going on yesterday. Your uncle was putting it right there on the line, Amy. He was saying, *Cross me and see what happens to your father's career—not to mention his life.*"

"Yesterday," she went on stubbornly, "I was afraid of what would become of me if you kept going."

"You weren't wrong, Amy. You're not wrong now. If you could make the case for your father, if you went to him and just laid out what you believe right now, how do you think he would decide what the truth is?"

Her eyes filled with tears but she began to laugh. "He would probably call the men in white coats to come take me away."

Cy's heart thumped hard because her laughter wasn't anything like the unpleasant noise Seth had made when he was amused because he couldn't hear and didn't know better, but a beautiful, bittersweet laugh a hearing woman would envy.

Her smile faded. "This isn't about him anymore, Cy. It's about me." She looked at him, in his eyes. "Do you want to know how I know that?"

Choked with an emotion he didn't even begin to understand—hope, maybe—he asked. "How?"

"Because in my dreams last night—a nightmare, really, I knew I could still hear, if only I weren't so afraid."

ON THE WAY TO Steamboat Springs early Monday morning, they stopped in the blink-and-you've-missed-it town of Kremmling and had lunch. An hour later, Cy shifted into four-wheel drive to accommodate the deeply rutted, snowy mountain road. Headed up an incline of twenty, maybe twenty-five degrees in places, the road led to the secluded Victorian mansion where Amy had spent her first five years.

This was where it had all begun, and ended, and the place Amy chose to start. To cross the line her uncle had drawn in the sand.

The sky was overcast, it was snowing fiercely, and the

wind didn't blow so much as suck massive clouds of the white stuff down the naked swath cut through the ever-greens. The weather was fit for nothing.

Cy let the pickup come to its own stop in the drifts. Amy raised her hood and got out by herself, trudging through the snow to the front porch. The place filled her with foreboding. She hadn't been inside it, save in her nightmares, since her father bought the house in Denver next to Hank Takamura.

Brent lived in the old mansion now. Freeloading, according to Perry. Brent pretty much did exactly what he wanted to do and little else, tending bar or filling in on ski patrol when he needed cash, skiing otherwise, or chasing women.

Enormously popular, he had a reputation around the ski town for hard drinking, doing the hot-dog jobs—volunteering on the fire, rescue and avalanche control teams—and a flair for uproarious impromptu standup given a mike in the bars.

Amy hadn't seen him in over three years.

Cy waited behind her while she rang the doorbell several times. When she got no answer, she knelt next to the wooden bench and retrieved a key cleverly hidden in a small crevasse-like compartment of one of the wooden slats.

She handed the key to Cy.

"Are you sure we should just let ourselves in?"

She nodded. "He knows I'm coming. He rents out rooms, too, so yes."

Cy opened the lock, then shoved the door open. The darkness inside made Amy think of a yawning abyss. She shook off her mood and crossed the threshold, turning on entryway lights in hanging fixtures so old they had had to be converted to electricity.

She pulled off her other glove, then shed her coat. The temperature, at least, was welcoming. Scraping snow from his boots outside, Cy took off his Stetson, went in and closed the door behind him.

"This is it," she signed. "There are the famous stairs, the library," she pointed to one side of the stairs, then the other, "the parlor."

Looking around, he hung his hat up. "Is it pretty much like you remember it?"

"It's exactly the same, Cy." Nothing had been done to update or redecorate the house in all the years that passed. It was clean enough, but not even the position of the furniture had been changed. It was still sitting in all the familiar places. She glanced into the parlor, to the magnificent old bric-à-brac shelves cluttered now with ski trophies and the like. "Everything but that. There, on those shelves, is where Fiona's music box collection was when I was little."

Cy crossed the age-darkened hardwood foyer to the extraordinarily wide staircase. A worn runner, itself three feet wide and tacked at the top of each riser, ran up as far as the eye could see.

He took the first seven steps two at a time to the landing where the staircase changed direction and sat there, looking for something.

She drew nearer to the wall directly beneath him and looked up. "What?"

He looked down at her from between a pair of balusters. "This is where you sat listening to them all when you came down at night?"

"Yes."

He nodded.

From her vantage point, she knew he could no longer see anywhere in the house but straight ahead and down into the foyer. Nor, she thought, could anyone have readily seen her sitting there. "What are you doing?"

He shrugged. "I was looking to see if I could tell where you used to touch the wallpaper."

Confused, she signed, "Did you find it?"

"No."

She went up the stairs, passed him, and sat on the step above the landing. "Here. Where it's gone all shiny. See? Should I turn the light on?"

He shook his head. Now that she'd pointed out the worn place on the wallpaper, he wasn't looking at it.

"Why?"

"Why...what?"

"Why were you looking for this?"

"No reason, Amy."

"No?"

"It's just been on my mind, is all."

"Me touching the wall has been on your mind?"

He gave her a long look. She could tell he wanted to shrug it off. He wanted her to leave it be. She didn't know how to leave it alone if the fact of her touching that hideous old wall was occupying his thoughts.

"Cy—"

"Amy. Look. It's not some weird pervert thing about you touching things."

She swallowed. She began to feel her heartbeat. "I didn't think it was."

"The image just stuck in my mind, okay? It just...stuck in my mind."

But she guessed, then. It made her stop breathing. Made her stop forming witless, awkward questions in her own mind. There was a tender and deeply human emotion inside him for what she had gone through, crouched here in this exact spot trying to hear things in the dark to reassure herself, trying desperately to feel safe by the touch of the velvety wallpaper.

"Cy." She touched his cheek, stroking opposite the direction his whiskers grew with her thumb. Feeling maudlin, she dived overboard the other way. "You are an idiot."

He cracked a smile. The feel of it beneath her hand, reaching his cheek, filled her up with emotion.

"I'm flattered."

She shook her head, signing with her other hand that no, she was the one who was flattered.

He turned his head ever so slightly, till his parted lips reached the mound of her flesh below her thumb. Her pulse began to speed, to hammer. A tremor of desire rose inside her. His breath warmed her skin. She watched his lips part further and close over her skin, pressing kisses to the wildly sensitive inside of her wrist. And she watched the tip of his tongue slowly, slowly trace the creases and hillocks of her palm and then she couldn't watch anymore because the sheer rocketing pleasure of it became too fierce and the sensual aches inside her scattered so near and so far, so hard and deep that her neck arched. Her head fell back, exposing her throat, inviting his lips, his kiss, his tongue nearer her heart, nearer her tightening breasts.

But his lips never reached her throat. Instead he pulled back, lowered her hand, his jaw clamped tight, his frustration thick.

Afraid to know why, she forced herself to meet his eyes.

"Your brother is coming."

She jerked her hand away from him. He laughed because the alternative would have been to cut her brother off at the knees when he walked through the front door. Standing, he pulled her to her feet, then loped casually back down the stairs with her at his back.

Brent Reeves came barreling through the door. When he saw her behind Cy, he jerked the shotgun he was holding up and away.

"Jesus, Amy! I could have blown you to kingdom come." He glared at Cy. "What are you doing here?"

"Why don't you put that thing away so we can tell you," Cy snapped.

"Yeah? And who the hell are you?"

Cy pulled out his credentials. "Cy McQuaid. FBI. Put that thing down *now*."

Brent turned around and set the shotgun down in the corner of the foyer nearest the door. "There. You happy?"

Cy blew off the surge of adrenaline. "Happier." No one mistook him for mollified.

"Brent," Amy signed. "We didn't mean to alarm you."

"I can't understand you, Amy. What is—" he repeated what he could remember of her signing.

Cy translated for her. "She said we didn't mean to alarm you."

"Yeah, well." He rubbed his forehead. "You did. And I already talked to you guys. This guy Chuck Something-or-other."

"Jones."

"Yeah. Him." He dumped a pile of mail on the small telephone table and shrugged out of his coat, turning to Amy. "I got your E-mail, but I thought you were coming alone. I thought it'd be just the two of us."

"When has it been just the two of us since I went deaf, Brent?"

He looked at her, trying to act like he got it, but he didn't have a clue.

Cy repeated aloud what she'd signed.

Brent flushed. "Well, it's all kind of useless anyway,

isn't it?'' he demanded. "I mean, I already told them everything I know. What can I tell you?''

"There are things only you and I know about growing up in this house, Brent. I'm hoping you can help me remember some of it.''

"Why? What good'll it do now?''

"To see if anything I remember is accurate for one thing." She signed to Cy, "Tell him we just want to sit down and talk, okay?''

He nodded. "Look. Brent. Your sister just wants to talk, and I didn't come here to go over the same ground you already covered with Jones. Do you mind if we sit down?''

"Would it matter if I did?''

Cy shrugged. "Your call.''

He looked at Amy again and heaved a sigh. "Might as well take your coats off. I don't care. If she wants to talk it's no skin off my nose. Come on back to the kitchen.''

He led the way through the parlor and dining room to the kitchen beyond a heavy old varnished oak swinging door. Amy dumped the teapot sitting on one of the burners, refilled it with water and turned on the gas. Brent opened the back door to the closed-in back stoop and let in an aging golden retriever whose tail thumped wildly when she spotted Amy.

He sat in the yellowed vinyl chair at the far end of the table, took off his boots and angled his feet over the corner of the table.

Sitting opposite him, cradling the retriever's head in her lap, Amy smiled. "Granny Fee would have a heart attack.''

"Nah," Brent returned amiably after Cy had translated what Amy signed. "Nothing's going to kill that old lady. You seen her lately?''

Amy nodded. "A couple of days ago. She really is getting fragile. You should go see her. She'd like that."

"You're kidding yourself, Ames. She didn't have any use for me or Mom either."

He was wrong. Fee had asked about him many times, but Amy knew how he might feel as he did. Her grandmother wasn't always easy to be with, and she loved Amy more than any of them.

"It's something Fee said to me that I wanted to ask you about."

"How is it," her brother asked, giving Cy a sideways look, "that you can sit talking to Granny? She can't understand you either, can she?"

Amy smiled. "No. But she's patient enough to sit writing notes back and forth."

"Well, hell. She's got a lot of time on her hands, I guess." He laughed at himself. "Like I don't. Geez, Ames. Sorry I was such an asshole."

"Don't worry about it," she signed. She looked to Cy. "I can't tell if he means it or not, Cy." She got up to take the whistling teapot off the burner. "Where are the tea bags?"

Brent frowned. "How'd you do that? How'd you know?"

"To get the teapot?" She smiled. "Your faces."

"I'm impressed." He got up and got a handful of mugs and a box of mixed teas. Cy just grabbed one. Amy chose a mint flavor. "So what did Fee say to you?"

She dunked her tea bag, then let it steep for a moment. Cy was translating as fast as she could sign. He half-knew what she was going to say anyway. "She said Amy was a difficult child to love."

Brent choked on his sip of tea. "Geez, she just cut right to the chase, didn't she?"

"Come on. I couldn't have been that bad."

He'd grown more comfortable, watching Amy, listening to Cy. "Are you kidding me? You were a holy terror."

"How?" Cy asked, not waiting for her.

"Hell. She was...you were like this little phantom shadow. Nobody could turn around without falling over you. No conversation was safe. You weren't a tattletale, exactly, but I was in trouble *all* the time because of you."

"How, if I didn't tell on you?"

"How? You really don't remember? You went around parroting everything you heard, so any smartass remark I made got right back to Mom. It was just you jabbering to your dolls or your stuffed animals—no. Mostly it was Beeka. If it wasn't your rabbit it was Beeka."

"Oh, wow!" Tears sprang to her eyes. Cy didn't get it. "Beeka," she signed, "was my imaginary friend. I'd forgotten all about her. There was HooDoo too. And Pilly."

Cy grinned. "HooDoo?"

She gave him an arch look. "I still have my Pilly. She's this really ratty old pillow. I'm allowed to say that, by the way. You're not. Say what you want about HooDoo, but do not disparage Pilly."

Straight-faced, Cy held up his hands in a *Who, me?* gesture, then just mentioned the other names of her imaginary friends for Brent.

"Yeah. She had a regular menagerie."

Cy sucked up half his tea. "Sounds more like fun than trouble to me."

"The judge thought so." He shrugged. He'd rarely referred to Amy's father as anything but "the judge." "But when HooDoo spoke—trust me, Amy was putting on a goddamned one-woman, three-character act *all* the time, I was in deep shit."

Cy poured himself more hot water, dunked his tea bag again, then helped himself to milk from the refrigerator.

"Me too," Amy signed. "To the top."

He filled her mug. "So how did your mother know Amy wasn't just playing, making things up as she went along?"

"Half the time Amy was repeating things Mom said. You know. Not just the general drift. I mean verbatim. Words she probably didn't even know the meaning of. It wasn't hard to figure out." He looked at Amy. "You couldn't have had any idea the things you were saying. Fee thought you were a clairvoyant, only with hearing things." He frowned, thinking. "Clairaudient she called it."

"That was your fault," she accused. "You were the one—"

"What?" Surprise, angry surprise flitted over Brent's expression. "What's that supposed to mean?"

She'd meant her accusation in fun, but something had been lost in the translation.

Incredulous, Cy didn't take the time to straighten it out. "Wait a minute. You mean like hearing voices?" he asked incredulously. "Joan of Arc stuff?"

"Yeah." Brent looked hard at her, then shrugged it off. Whatever it was. "Fee thought so. Pissed ol' Unca Perry off—big time." He turned around in his chair and grabbed a half-empty bag of Oreos out of a drawer. "He was convinced the old lady'd singlehandedly turn Amy into a schizo like her. What a farce."

Amy stared at the stale bag of cookies, trying to see the humor in it. The most irrational fear of her life was of being locked away like Granny Fee for hearing voices that weren't there.

"Look, Ames. We had fun, too. It wasn't all that bad."

She mistrusted his sudden attempt at reassurance. She

couldn't have pointed to any change in his demeanor or give a reason, but it seemed phony to her. Was he trying to see if she remembered the good times, or only the bad?

"I remember you making voices for my stuffed animals." She shook her head. "It's hard to remember hearing. Could you make your voice come from somewhere else?" If Fee thought she could hear voices, part of it at least, had to do with Brent's vocal tricks.

"Like where?"

"Like, across the room."

"Who told you that? The old lady?"

"No one. I was just trying to remember—"

"You were a kid. God knows you had an imagination that wouldn't quit. So. What else?"

"About the day I fell."

"And Mom croaked. What about it?"

She exchanged looks with Cy. It wasn't her imagination. In the past few minutes, Brent had grown a lot less willing to talk. Defensive, maybe. "Something must have set her off that day, Brent. She was…livid. Isn't that so?"

"She was screaming mad, all right."

"Do you know why? What it was about?"

"Something you said?" he guessed.

"That's what I'm asking."

"You have to ask?" He baited the retriever to his side with an Oreo. "Look. What the hell you were blathering on about, who knows—but there's no mistake about it. Whatever it was, you're the one who set her off. What it was? I don't have a clue."

"How about an opinion," Cy asked. "Was her death an accident?"

"What else?"

"Murder."

"Perry give me up for it?" he joked.

"Brent!"

"It was a joke, Amy."

"Why would you even joke about something like that?"

"Because this whole damned thing is a one big sick joke," he snapped. "Who the hell cares how it happened?"

"I do. Your sister does. Your father—"

"*Step*father."

Cy put his mug down. "Let me be real sure I understand you. Are you saying it wouldn't matter to you one way or the other if your mother was murdered?"

"That's not it at all."

"Then suppose you tell me what *it* is?"

"*It* was an accident. You get that? You think I wouldn't toast good old Uncle Perry if I could? If the son of a bitch really had killed her? Or the judge or his crazy mother? They're all a bunch of self-righteous maggots as far as I'm concerned, but there wasn't any murderer. No villain, see, means you don't get to ride into town and be the big hero. Sorry. But that's the way I see it."

"Funny," Cy mused aloud. "I thought your mother was still alive when you ran out."

"So?"

"So if you were gone," Cy pressed, "how do you know no one killed her? Maybe you didn't run that far off. Maybe you were hanging around waiting to see what would happen. Maybe you saw your mom run out of the house and fall and then you took off."

"Bullshit. I didn't see anything because I was long gone."

"You can't have it both ways, bud. Either you were there to see an accident, or you weren't there to see the murder."

"Or it was an accident I didn't see."

"Then we agree you don't really know what happened," Cy concluded. "So what I want to know is, who planted you with the conviction that your mother's death was an accident?"

"Stick it," Brent snarled, dragging a hand through his hair. "No one planted a story on me."

The dog had wandered back to rest her head in Amy's lap. She sat stroking Fritzy's silky, graying head, watching Cy dealing with her brother.

Ignoring Brent's denial, he leaned back in his chair. "I'm thinking it had to be Perry. You know. Quid pro quo. He covers your ass, you cover his. Stick to your guns and nobody has to go down."

"Except my ass didn't need covering—" Brent broke off, recognizing the trap too late.

"But Perry's did. Imagine that." But Cy wasn't done yet and he didn't give Brent the chance to put a different spin on what he'd said. "Maybe yours needed covering after all."

"Why, because I ran off when I should have stuck by my mom? Big effing deal."

"Not exactly. You ever heard of felony menacing? How about reckless endangerment?"

"I don't know what you're talking about."

"Amy."

"That's a lie." But he paled. He couldn't prevent the slow, tortured drop of his Adam's apple. "That's a goddamned lie."

"Hey," Cy jibed, spreading his hands. "Why would your own mother accuse you if—"

"Because she was crazy as a loon too."

"Brent," Amy interrupted, signing, "I don't think you meant to hurt me—ever. But—"

"I didn't do anything to you, Amy," he complained

bitterly, turning to Cy. "I played with her for Chrissake. I was the one entertaining the little freak-show brat all the damned time—"

Amy shivered violently.

Brent broke off, staring at her, his eyes wild and savage as a cornered badger. Cy looked at her too, waiting for her to say something, but she couldn't. Her stomach heaved and heaved all the harder again, and it was all she could manage to breathe and keep herself from throwing up.

Cy misunderstood. He turned to Brent, his expression full of contempt. "Maybe you're the one who killed your mother."

"That's another lie—"

"Is it, Brent? She blamed you for what had happened to Amy. You must have been really pissed. You shoved her down. Maybe she hit her head then. Maybe that was what killed her. Is that how it happened?"

"Sure," he sniped. "I did it. I killed her."

"And then Perry hauled her body outside and set up her so-called accident?"

"Yeah, old Perry. He'd be sure to cover my ass all these years."

"You're playing with the spinmeister of all time, Brent," Cy warned. "If you didn't do it, maybe you should give him up for it before he leaves you hanging in the wind."

Brent slammed the heels of both hands into the table's edge so hard that its legs jolted, screeching against the floor. "I think it's time you got the hell out of my house and off this mountain."

Chapter Nine

But it was Brent who tore out of the house.

Frozen in place at the kitchen table, Amy could feel his rage resounding through the floorboards of the old Victorian mansion, and sense the change in the flow of air currents when he jerked open the front door and then slammed it shut behind him. And even once outside, she knew by the percussion of shock waves roiling through the thin mountain air when the engine of his pickup roared to life.

Cy sat waiting for her, his front chair legs off the floor. The stillness returned, outside, if not in her heart. She didn't know where to begin.

"What's wrong, Amy," he signed. "Talk to me. You remembered something. What was it?"

She shook her head. "Not that he killed her."

His eyes narrowed. "What then?"

"It was the freak-show thing, Cy. When he said he was the one entertaining me?"

"Yeah."

She shivered again. "He...it was...I remembered what happened. Or maybe it's just that I finally understood what he had done."

"Go on."

"Julia had sent us outside. I was holding my March

Hare—my stuffed rabbit?'' Cy nodded and she went on. ''I took it with me when she sent us away. Brent snatched March Hare away from me. Jerked him right out of my arms and ran away.

''He kept running and running. I couldn't keep up with him. I was so mad I couldn't even see straight. I was crying. I fell down a couple of times. By the time I caught up with him he was sitting beside the ventilation shaft smoking one of Julia's stash of cigarettes and I couldn't see March Hare anywhere.''

Cy's jaw tightened. She nodded. ''He threw March Hare down the shaft. I think I knew it but I didn't want to believe it. I begged him to tell me where March Hare was. He just sat there laughing and smoking, but then I heard these terrible cries coming from the dark hole.''

Cy swore. ''Amy, you knew Brent was making the cries, didn't you? Didn't you always understand the voices he made for your animals were for pretend?''

Sitting at the kitchen table where she and Brent had so often conspired together, Amy continued, lost in the scene.

''I lay down on the ground so I could see inside the mine shaft. I saw March Hare. He hadn't fallen that far. I thought I could reach him. I had to save him. I'm certain Brent didn't push me, but somehow I reached too far. Brent was screaming at me to stop it, but I couldn't. I got hold of my rabbit and then I was falling. He made a grab for me, I think, but it must have been too late.''

She stared into her mug, gently swirling the last swallowful of her tea. A sense of relief, of finally knowing what had happened settled over her, easing the biting nausea. Brent had been scared. He'd always been afraid—of family ground shifting beneath his feet, of his mother's loyalties dividing, twisting, always threatening to collapse away from him.

''He wasn't so very different from me at all, Cy.''

He understood. He couldn't much sympathize with Brent. He'd as soon beat the living daylights out of Amy's brother as look at him. But he understood her relief. What Brent had done with her March Hare to make Amy disappear as well made a terrible poignant kind of sense to her. It proved she wasn't crazy or dim or suffering childish delusions or warped and dangerous memories.

She wasn't the only one so adversely affected by the disastrous currents swirling between their parents. In his own way, Brent must have shared the same forebodings that had always haunted Amy, crowding her into spying on her grown-ups, even goading her to awaken and creep down the stairs to hear what would happen after her father had rocked her to sleep.

It hit him, then, like the full force of a steer hitting the end of a rope, that Amy had it in her to forgive what her brother had done. What scared the hell out of him was the shock of his own desperate insight that there was nothing he needed so much in this life as the kind of forgiveness Amy dispensed with so much heart, so little rancor.

His own heart thumped. He couldn't look at her, couldn't not look, either. He could feel his pulse high in his arms. He knew then that he was so far gone with love for her that he wasn't going to make it back to a time when he thought he would be better off for cutting himself loose from her.

He didn't know what to do. He didn't even know who he was if he could chuck his creed of honor out the window for the sake of weaseling the forgiveness he needed out of Amy Reeves. The only honorable thing to do was to cut her loose.

He didn't know how.

He started to get up, take his mug to the sink, but then

sank heavily back into his chair when it struck him what a fool he had been. Sensitive to every nuance of his expression, Amy leaned forward anxiously.

"Cy. What is it?"

He wasn't sure he wanted to go with her where the sudden thought had taken him. He met her eyes. "Can you tell me what happened when you woke up that night?"

She shrugged. "I climbed out of bed. I took March Hare. I left my room and walked in the shadows and sat down on the landing where I always sat."

"Why?"

"They were fighting. It scared me. Mommy and Perry. I…" Something out of place, out of time chafed in her mind, but she couldn't quite grasp it.

"Take your time, Amy. They were fighting. Do you mean fighting physically, or arguing?"

"They were arguing, but she was…I don't…I didn't—"

"Did you see them, Amy?"

"No, I couldn't see them from—" She struggled to remember. "I was on the landing where I showed you. I was crying. I had to be quiet, because if I wasn't they would catch me." Her mother would scold, she told Cy, and Fee would scold *her* and Daddy would catch her up and take her back to bed, not mean, never that, but put out with her.

"Except your dad wasn't there that time."

"No. It was Perry who came. Who…who found me spying on them all again." A tiny wrinkle of worry creased her brow. "We've been over all this, Cy. I don't understand—"

"Humor me," he urged. "Did Perry accuse you of spying on them?"

"Yes, he said—" She broke off. Confusion swirled all about her. "Dear God." She looked at him, stricken.

"I could still hear him. I could still hear them fighting, Cy! Otherwise, how could I have known what it sounded like when all Granny Fee's music boxes were playing at once?"

Her hands described a clamoring that tugged at his heart, not so much for the noise, but for the question clamoring at her now.

He'd gotten it all wrong. They both had. The question was never really what it was that had turned her into such a vigilant little creature, but what it was she heard that night that had forced the terrible, unconscious decision to close her ears forever.

THE SNOWFALL HAD LET UP, and in one of those weather switchbacks the Rocky Mountains were famous for, the sun was shining when they left the forbidding ill-kept house where Brent still lived.

Outside, the road was what it had always been, twisting, winding, wending through a forest of towering old evergreen. The snow was piled deep. The sun shone, sparkling cold and bright. But inside Amy, her world, her landscape, her thoughts, little remained of the old order.

She could still hear, long after the ordeal everyone supposed was the cause of her deafness. She'd grown so used to the silence that she'd forgotten she had always known she wasn't really deaf.

She was, but not for any reason she could either grasp or heal.

And she still didn't know where to find the precise moment her terrified, subconscious young mind had shut itself off from hearing even one more thing. Had she been playacting, and forgotten how not to pretend? Withdrawn to safety only to forget the way back?

Huddled across the bench seat from Cy, she braced herself against the jostling of the pickup on the rutted, snowy road like any sane woman, but she was deep into pretending again. Pretending she was only pensive, a tiny bit sad. Because she thought if she didn't, she would go mad, join her Granny Fee in a place meant for people who heard too many voices...or none at all.

She knew how to put on a happy face. She'd learned it at her father's knee when she understood that the grief and guilt inside him over her lost hearing was so staggering that only her smiles would keep him with her.

Cy's sorrow was much the same. She'd seen it in his eyes.

He thought she didn't know how hard he resisted his feelings for her, how he fought to keep himself from investing himself, his heart and his mind and his sexual feelings in her, but he was wrong. She knew.

Falling in love with a hearing woman was one thing. Ordinary flaws only required ordinary lovers. Steeper ones like hers took a quite heroic man to overcome. But while she was convinced with all her heart that Cy McQuaid was such a man, he would find terrible fault with it even seeming heroic—to her or anyone else—that he loved her.

Even if Cy could rise above his reservations, she fought a constant seesaw battle of her own. He attracted her on every level. He told the truth, even when it was difficult. He treated people, from his partner to her uncle to Granny Fee to her, with respect.

He listened.

He paid attention.

He kept an open mind, and he held himself to incredibly high standards. But he was also a man who assumed charge, took control and wouldn't hesitate to pull rank on her...when she needed to stand on her own, be her own woman, make her own choices, take her own risks, and needed those freedoms like she needed the air she breathed.

By asking for his help, she'd opened herself up in ways she hadn't ever, ever done before.

So she put on her pensive, independent smile for him when he looked at her.

"You okay with going on into town?"

She nodded. "Yes."

"Sure?"

"I'll be fine, Cy." She might as well believe it.

The agent who had interviewed Brent had searched the coroner's financial records. The theory had been that Courson might have demanded a payoff on the spot to deliver a finding of accidental death. But nothing in twenty-five years of federal income tax returns or bank statements had even come close to looking like ill-gotten gains.

While on the drive up it had occurred to Cy that it made sense to look through records of real estate exchanges in the county offices as well. In a ski town like Steamboat, resort property and real estate, even twenty-five years ago, were considered better than money in the bank.

Cy downshifted to slow the pickup as it neared the highway. But it was half-past noon by the time they reached town, and likely that the county offices were closed over the lunch hour. They bought a couple of deli sandwiches and got back into the pickup. Cy drove down near where the river cut through town, onto the end of the rodeo grounds, and parked.

He peeled back the wrapper on his sandwich and took a bite, gesturing with a tilt of his head toward the chutes across the arena, blanketed now with snow. "Busted my butt there one year."

"How?"

"Bull riding."

"The bull won?"

"Hell, no." He sulked, pretending to be offended. "I was in second place going into the final round. That's second as in a point off of first, woman."

Amy smirked. "I see. Eight seconds to glory."

"Damn straight."

"Come hell or high water."

"Are you poking fun at me, Amy?"

Her lips curved gently. "No more than you're poking at yourself." Her head tilted. "I guess you don't grow up on a ranch in south Texas and not turn out a cowboy, huh?"

"Not hardly."

"Do you have an accent?"

He looked at her. "That's a weird question. Why do you ask?"

"A lot of the words you use are total throwbacks."

He missed it. "Total what?"

"Throwback." She spelled the word.

"That's what I thought." He glowered and didn't even know it.

"A throwback in a nice sense, McQuaid. Polite. Gentlemanly." She smiled. "So do you? Have an accent?"

He shrugged. "I didn't think so. Not till we moved to Colorado. The western slope. I was thirteen, belligerent as hell. It didn't take me more'n a week to get the drift, though."

"What...drift?"

"You pretty much crawled out from under some rock

if you thought you could transplant yourself to Colorado and strut your redneck Texas drawl.'' He grinned. ''We all took our licks—''

''We all, who?''

''My brothers and me. Cameron's a sheriff over in Chaparral County. Matt went back. He's a Texas Ranger. I can hear Texas in his voice, but I don't think I've got much of any accent left.''

''So what are you now, in your heart? Colorado or Texas?''

He drew a deep breath, squinting against fierce sunlight glinting off the field of snow, passing a glance out the window at the side view mirror. ''My mother is buried in Texas. A part of my heart will always be there. But this is home now.'' He sat silent for a moment. ''Do you know what a Texas accent would sound like?''

''Dimly.'' Amy stared a moment across the pristine field of snow ending at the rodeo stands above the chutes. In April it would be knee-deep in mud with the spring run-off.

She felt truly pensive now. She rarely thought of times when she could hear. Fiona's voice had come to her in dreams and odd waking moments, and sometimes the voices Brent made for March Hare and the others.

She looked at Cy, finding that she couldn't keep hope from her heart. Maybe there wasn't such an impossible chasm between them if she could remember what things sounded like. ''Mostly what I remember,'' she signed, ''is music. Lyrics. I was thinking Texas must sound sort of like the woman who sang, 'Mamas, don't let your babies grow up to be cowboys.' ''

He grinned. ''That'd be close, darlin'. Though my personal favorite Texas country song went something like, 'Kick me, Lord Jesus, through the goalposts of life.' ''

She smiled and shook her head. "I loved cowboys."

"You are making that up."

"No. I swear." She crossed her heart.

"Who?"

"Billy Kidd for one. You might have heard of him. He came from Steamboat and won the downhill in the Olympics when—"

"Oh. I see," he scoffed. "Cowboys on skis. Billy Kidd could knock the hell out of a mountain, but a Stetson doesn't make a cowboy."

"He wasn't the only one—"

"He isn't even one."

"You're being dumb as a post, McQuaid." He opened his mouth, but her look must have shut him up. "It's the character, you know? The loner, the stars in the sky for a roof over your head. The one man who always tips his hat to a lady. It's the macho thing too, the boots and vest and chaps, all that leather. All that sexy cowboy stuff." He was laughing at her now. "Okay, maybe it was only a romantic notion of a cowboy that I loved, but when the rodeo comes to town, every girl in town wants one."

He glanced at the rear- and side-view mirrors, then gave her long look. "D'you ever kiss a cowboy?"

"Before you?" she teased. "Almost." She wrinkled her nose. "He had chew in his mouth and it grossed me out, so…no. You are my first cowboy."

The painful, obvious question popped into her mind, whether she was his first deaf girl. No boy had ever said that to her, but some of the crueler girls had, apparently at a complete loss as to why any guy would take her out aside from the kiss-and-can't-tell novelty of it.

She took another plunge instead because she knew the question would make him angry. "How did you learn to sign?"

He shifted his weight, stretching his stiff leg out over the transmission. "A deaf kid in rehab I got to know. He'd about killed himself in a motorcycle accident. His legs were mangled worse than mine. We both had to learn to walk again. You can learn a lot of signing when you're together twenty-four-seven for months on end."

She nodded. "I went to a boarding school for deaf children, but I was still pretty little. I loved to sign." Then, though, she thought, it must have seemed an adventure because she still thought she was only pretending to be deaf. "What was his name?"

"Seth."

"Did he make it out?"

"Everyone makes it out, Amy. You either make it or you don't. Sooner or later they bounce you."

"No, I mean—"

"Did he walk again? Yeah." He crumpled his sandwich wrapper and stuffed it in the paper sack, checking the mirrors again.

"Is that just a habit of yours?"

He looked at her.

"Checking everything out. Looking in the mirrors."

He frowned. "Yeah, it's habit."

"Is someone following us?"

"I wouldn't rule it out." He drew his leg back under the steering wheel, put in the clutch and turned on the truck. "Just a feeling."

"YOU'LL NEVER GUESS who turned up at the house this morning."

"Are you on a secure line?"

"No," Brent cracked angrily, kicking a box out of his path, the cell phone in one hand and a Bloody Mary in the other. "I went looking for a phone anyone could tap into."

"Calm down. Tell me what happened."

"Amy happened. All these years, you never expected that, did you?"

"If you can't deal with your sister, Brent, maybe you ought to just go blow your head off and get it over with."

Pacing the stock room of the bar and packaged liquor store, Brent swore. Stupid SOB would like that, wouldn't he? Solve all his problems. "It's the G-man hanging out with her I don't trust. The guy's filling her deaf-and-dumb little head with all kinds of crap."

That gave his uncle pause. "McQuaid?"

"That'd be the one. You said—"

"I know what I said," Perry cut him off. "Nothing has changed. The truth is exactly what it always was. Nothing more, nothing less."

"Oh, yeah. I forgot. We've cornered the market on the truth."

"We have." His uncle sighed. "You're going to be better off if you remember that, Brent. I don't have to remind you it's *your* neck in the noose, do I?"

"No, you don't. But you always manage to, don't you?" His chest felt like it was about to explode. Like the night his mother accused him of hurting Amy, his heart pounded till his ears filled with the sound of it, till he thought he'd stroke out.

Why did she have to say that? Why did she have to make him so mad? Couldn't she see all he wanted, all he ever wanted was to have things back the way they were before—

No. Things were well and truly screwed up enough. He couldn't…he couldn't let himself get sucked down into the nightmares, couldn't let it happen. No. He had to keep it together. He'd been doing it all these years, he could do it now.

Screw Amy.

Screw her lover.

They couldn't make him lose it, not if he—

"Brent!" Perry's voice commanded. "Are you there?"

He swallowed. Couldn't believe the stench of fear on himself, the cold sweat soaking his shirt. "I'm here."

"You've got to hang tough, boy," Perry soothed. "The truth is what you've always told. What I've always said it was. There is no evidence to the contrary. None. You're safe. No one can ever say anything else happened because *nothing else did happen.* No one can prove any different. Are you with me?"

He wanted to believe this so badly tears sprang to his eyes. "You don't know what it's like. You don't—"

"It was an accident, son."

No, it wasn't. "I hit her. I meant to hit her. I didn't mean her to—"

"It was an accident," Perry repeated, his voice gentle, firm, commanding. "Say it. Come on, Brent. Say it. It was an accident."

"It was an accident."

"There you go. Say it again. *It was an accident.*"

"It was an accident."

"Again. 'My mother's death was an accident.'"

"My mother's death was an accident." *Now, if he could only believe it*… Believe he hadn't killed her. Believe it. But he'd been saying those words like a mantra for too many years and he knew better. Saying so didn't make it so. He had all the demons in hell in his dreams, taking him dragging him, kicking and screaming *itwasanaccident.*

Chapter Ten

"Another week or two, Brent. That's all you have to get through, and then you'll be home free."

"You never counted on Amy."

"Amy is nothing. She can't hurt you. Listen to me, now. She can't hurt you. There is nothing she can say or do that will take you down, son."

Brent's throat tightened. Most of the time Perry calling him "son" simply galled the piss out of him, but now the word just made him want to curl up and die. He was nobody's son and he had his mom to blame for that too.

Why'd she have to get rid of my dad?

He swallowed on the stinging, bitter bile staining his throat. Resolve curdled inside him. He didn't need this shit, didn't need the judge's brownnosing, nothing, toadying brother telling him what to do, treating him like some dullard half-wit offspring he could hardly tolerate.

What a freaking fool. *Amy knows nothing. Amy can't hurt you.* Like hell.

He folded up the cell phone, disconnecting the bastard who had both held his mother's death over his head and protected him from the consequences all these years. He hurled the phone into a trash compactor filled nearly to the brim with empty bottles and cardboard packaging.

Amy knew.

He couldn't understand a word she signed, but he could see with his own eyes when it had hit her what he'd done to her and how he'd done it. If she remembered that, God only knew what would trigger the next thing and the next thing after that.

No. Amy knew plenty. He'd seen it in her eyes.

SLOUCHED INSIDE his rented car down the street from the Ski Town USA Saloon, Zach had just learned a lot. On the seat beside him was surveillance equipment anyone could lay their hands on with a particle of ingenuity. With it he had picked up Brent Reeves's whiny phone call to his uncle, all but confessing to the murder of Julia Reeves.

What a moron. A cell phone was no more secure than bellowing at each other over tin cans connected by string. Even if Brent Reeves knew better, he didn't care, and not caring who heard that call made him a fool—and a dangerous one. A loose cannon.

Zach plucked the pack of cigarettes out of his shirt pocket, lit up and took a drag. He let the smoke drift out his nostrils, thinking what he was going to do with this story now.

The plot was sure as hell not shaping itself into the blistering exposé of the judge that Phillip Gould expected to see. That angle was, in fact, a big nothing, a pathetic shadow of what it had promised to be.

No one cared. Not Jessup's family, not the DOJ, not the public, not even story-starved TV news mags or the typically salivating producers of unsolved crime shows.

With the results he was getting, he didn't have to wonder why. Another riveting read, Zach thought sourly. A notch above tabloid fodder, not much more. Still, he couldn't quite give it up. He was just perverse enough to believe that in this case, less was promise of more.

There was something here deeper, meatier, nastier than he knew right now, but he intended to find it. Whatever it was.

Crushing out his cigarette, he spotted McQuaid and Reeves's daughter coming out of the county office building into the painfully bright sunshine. He felt his spirits rise a bit, his interest piqued. Why the hell would McQuaid be escorting Amy Reeves around unless she was the cache of real gold in all of this?

No reason Zach could think of. He had to hatch a plan that included weaseling into the good graces of Cy McQuaid. At least negotiate a trade. Quid pro quo.

Brent Reeves's taped confession for an answer to the real puzzler in all this. Despite traipsing all over the country, questioning every lead, angle and player, Zach still didn't know why Senator Gould had his shriveled, creepy little heart set on scuttling Byron Reeves's nomination to the Supreme Court.

He straightened, turned the ignition of the rental car, and smiled grimly to himself. He would have to force McQuaid's hand. A risky proposition with an armed and dangerous *hombre* like McQuaid, and not likely to earn Zach any warm fuzzies. But once he had McQuaid's undivided attention, the straight-arrow lawman would surely see the upside of a little collaboration.

Cy SPOTTED THE GUY tailing them within about fifteen seconds of leaving the County Hall of Records. Ducking low inside a parked dark blue Nissan sedan now, their pursuer had been driving a white utility vehicle with a rental-agency logo on its bumper when he finally passed Cy's truck on the downhill side of Rabbit Ears Pass. Cy might not have made the connection, except that he'd seen the sedan in passing when he pulled up and parked at the end of the rodeo grounds.

He switched sides with Amy so that he was between her and the inept jerk following them. When they reached his truck, he unlocked her door and helped her in. From where the sedan was parked, Amy was safe once inside and he didn't tell her what he was doing till he got in, pulled out onto the street and pulled a U-turn headed toward the middle of town—which the sedan immediately copied.

He turned to her. "Someone is following us."

"Who?"

Keeping an eye on the traffic, he told her hadn't gotten a decent look at the face.

"What are you going to do?" she asked, abbreviating her form.

"Park," he answered, his gaze constantly moving, "and double back on him. I want you to duck down and stay down till you see the whites of my eyes. Clear?"

She nodded.

He told her there was a small handgun in the dash and asked her if she knew how to use it.

"Never held a gun in my life."

That was probably just as well. He didn't expect to let the guy get within shooting distance. He drove until he found a setup he could work with and pulled into the lot. He waved Amy down, got out, shut the door of the cab and crouched low. From the right front corner he watched the sedan pull over on the street next to a fire hydrant.

He wouldn't stay there. Cy figured him to be trying to make up his mind whether to circle around the block or make the left-hand turn that would put him on the street to the side of the lot. Then the guy shrugged his shoulders and turned off his ignition.

Cy pulled his sidearm from his shoulder holster and took advantage of the guy's indecision to move closer, staying low, but a woman shoved out of the dry cleaners, spotted him and started screaming her head off. "He's got a gun! Oh, my God, somebody! He's got a gun."

He swore under his breath, stood, pointed his firearm at the creep in the sedan. "You. Don't move. Do not even breathe." Two bruisers and an old man came running out the door of the package liquor store, the old man carrying a sawed-off shotgun aimed straight at Cy. His sidearm trained on the cretin in the sedan, he shouted at the gun-toting old man. "FBI. Put your weapon on the ground. Nobody's gonna get hurt here. Do it! Now!"

"I don't see any freakin' ID—"

"You are looking at the inside of a cell if you don't back off and get that shotgun on the ground."

It wasn't his threat that made the guy back off, but Amy moving slowly, fearlessly, aiming the empty handgun at the old man, holding up the jacket from his pickup with F.B.I. in nine-inch yellow letters on the back of it.

The two wise guys backed up and opened their arms. The old man stooped low and put his deadly sawed-off relic on the iced-over pavement.

Amy waved the gun in a direction that ordered all three men back where they'd come from. The woman got up and bolted for her car, sobbing hysterically. Amy backed up till one of the parked cars shielded her body from the storefronts, positioning the gun over the roof.

Cy approached the parked sedan and broke out the driver's window with the butt of his gun.

"Get out. Make it slow. You make one stray move and it'll be the last one you ever contemplate."

When Cy saw who it was climbing out, it took everything in him not to double up his fist and rearrange every internal organ Zach Hollingsworth possessed.

And busting Amy for impersonating an agent and putting herself in the middle of it wasn't a far distant second thought.

CY HERDED HOLLINGSWORTH after Amy through the swinging doors of the Ski Town USA Saloon, sent Zach a make-my-day look and turned to the barkeep. "You got a back room?"

"Yeah." The spare, ponytailed bartender dried his hands on fresh white towel. "But it ain't open, pardner."

Cy pulled out his FBI credentials and let them fall open where the barkeep could get a real good look. "It is now."

"Sure, but it's gonna cost—"

"Where is it?"

The barkeep jerked his head toward the far end of the bar.

"Fine. I want a pitcher of beer, three mugs, chips and salsa and an hour." He drew a fifty from a money clip and tossed it on the slick, polished patina of the bar top. "This ought to cover it."

ONCE AMY, CY and Zach Hollingsworth were sitting in a back room and served with a pitcher and chips, she took the initiative. "What were you thinking, Mr. Hollingsworth?" Cy sat with the front chair legs high off the ground, his arms folded over his chest, and repeated her question to Hollingsworth. "Were you trying to get yourself busted?"

"Were you?" he tossed back. "Because I've got to tell you, Amy, from where I sit, Mr. McQuaid here is about as put out with you as he is with me."

Cy didn't even blink, and Amy realized, suddenly, because he wouldn't look at her, that it was true. "We're talking about you now, Hollingsworth, and right now, you're looking at obstruction of justice on one end to stalking and felony menacing on the other."

"Make it Zach," he offered, unfazed. He pulled a pack of cigarettes out of his breast pocket and sent Amy a questioning look. "If you don't mind—"

"She does."

"She," Amy signed, her hands somehow acerbic, "*doesn't*. I am allowed to say that, aren't I?"

Cy's lips tightened. "Say anything damn thing you want, Amy," he signed, "but *not* now." He signed the word for emphasis.

"Let me just get this one thing straight. I'm the one who defused the situation in the parking lot, and I'm in trouble?"

"I asked you to stay put."

"No, you *told* me to stay put. My mistake. I guess you would rather have gotten yourself shot up again."

"Hmm," Zach interrupted, wincing visibly, belatedly thumping the pack of cigarettes back down into his shirt pocket. "Stepped right in it that time, didn't I?" He sat forward, his forearms resting on the table. He had a weathered look, a face that hadn't aged well, and steady, ordinary brown eyes. "Look. I didn't mean to cause that kind of trouble. I have information I think you need. I didn't want to wait for the Feebs to decide I wasn't just angling for information myself. And frankly, Amy...I wanted to talk to you, but I didn't think McQuaid, here—" he looked at Cy "—would let that happen." He paused. "Naturally, I'd appreciate whatever leads...insights you care to share."

"What information?" Cy asked, still smolderingly pissed at Amy, though no more than she was at him.

Hollingsworth picked a small tape recorder out of his jacket pocket and put it on the table. "While you two were in the county building, I was on the street in the car. Your brother, Amy, got on a cell phone—which, as you may or may not know, is pretty simple to listen in on."

"You want to give us a short synopsis?" Cy asked, finally setting the front legs of his chair back on the floor. "What's on it?"

"Brent Reeves dialing up Uncle Perry, reading him the riot act because you and Amy are on the verge of proving Brent killed his mother."

Amy's glance darted between the two men. Skeptical, Cy drained his mug and poured more, angling the mug to minimize the foam. "You've got our attention. Let's hear it."

Keeping eye contact with Amy, Zach's hand closed over the small recorder and he thumbed one of the small buttons. Cy put down his mug, rested his forearms on the table and began to listen intently. Amy had to touch his arm before he remembered she couldn't hear it.

He signed, adept now, easily identifying Brent, then Perry for her as the recording played on, closing his hand when one of them stopped and the other began. At the tape's end, Cy took a deep breath and settled back in his chair, his big hands resting on the table.

"Interesting listening, huh?" Zach ventured, still trying to humor Cy. "Is he cracking up, or what?"

Amy shoved her beer away, ignoring Zach. "He's scared. He knows I remembered what happened when I fell into the mine shaft, and he's worried I'll remember more."

Cy shook his head. "He's worried, but your uncle is right. All Brent has to do is hang tough. It's exactly the same thing you said yesterday. All either one of them has to do is stonewall us long enough and this thing will go away.''

Zach began drumming his fingers on the tabletop. ''This is all pretty interesting in a silent-movie sort of way, but would you guys mind sharing with the signing-impaired?''

Amy had to smile. ''Will you tell him?'' she signed, posing the question to Cy, her smile gone.

''We're off the record, here. So long as you understand that.''

Zach shrugged. ''I'll take what I can get.''

''You know basically what's going on?''

''Not when I started this.'' Zach took a couple of swallows of beer, then wiped his lips with the back of his hand. ''One of our esteemed leaders on the Senate Judiciary Committee tossed me the Jessup bone. As far as I can tell, Senator Gould would like it—like it a lot—if Judge Reeves's nomination tanked. He won't care how it happens—except he obviously wants the judge to go down in public. Then this murder thing opened up. I still want to know why Gould has it in for the judge.''

Amy shook her head. ''I'm not sure I've ever even heard of him. Do you know anything about it, Cy?''

Gnawing on the inside of his lip, Cy frowned and shook his head. ''Your father is extremely well connected, Amy. Gould would look like a jackass to openly oppose him.''

''Well, there's the rub, huh?'' Zach muttered. ''He isn't openly opposing Judge Reeves, but he sure as hell wants his nomination scuttled.'' He shrugged. ''But look. Here's what I know.'' He began ticking off his fingers. ''I know Julia Reeves died under uh…uncertain circumstances. I know who she was, that things weren't swell between her and the judge. I looked up the public record of the autopsy report. I know Courson, the coroner, called it an accident.'' He met Cy's hard look unflinchingly. ''My sources at the

DOJ tell me Courson changed his mind, and put that on paper. And now, thanks to this tape, I'm guessing Brent did the deed and old Uncle Perry has been covering his young ass for the last quarter century.''

''And if you go to press with that,'' Cy warned, ''Perry Reeves will name you and every publisher you peddle this story to in a libel suit you're unlikely to forget.''

''Been there, done that,'' Zach said, shrugging.

''Not with my uncle, you haven't,'' Amy signed, and Cy repeated.

Zach thumped a crumb of tortilla chip onto the floor. ''So are you telling me you don't remember any of this, Amy? Because from where I sit, you look sweet for the key witness to your mother's murder.''

Cy shook his head. ''It doesn't matter. Even if she were an eyewitness, even if she saw who did it and how it went down, there is no court in the country that will allow her testimony. She was five years old when it happened. She'd already been traumatized. Her recall twenty-five years later wouldn't even get into evidence.''

''Yeah, but does Brent know that? That's the question.''

''My uncle does. That's all that really matters,'' Amy signed.

''Are you telling me if you leaned on Brent right now, he wouldn't crack wide open?'' He looked at them both, then straightened and kited another angle. ''Okay. I get it. You two don't believe Brent did the deed at all. What? Is he taking the fall for Perry? Why would he do that? More important, why would Perry Reeves off his brother's wife?''

''That's your story, Hollingsworth,'' Cy conceded. ''But since there's no proof he killed her—or that anyone did, for that matter, it doesn't really matter what his motive was. You go to press with nothing but idle speculation, then Perry Reeves will bury you alive.''

''So.'' Zach shoved his chair back from the table and rose, leaving his recorder on the table. ''If the case is so hopeless, why are you still dogging the thing?''

NIGHTFALL CAME hours before Cy drove through to the back of Amy's father's property, to the small guest house where she lived. He walked her to the door, where her porch light came on automatically.

''Will you come in?'' she signed. ''Let me feed you?''

He leaned up against the stone siding. ''You don't have to do that, Amy.''

''I want to. I'd like you to stay.'' She thought he wanted to stay too, for a while, for reasons other than a brief respite from the road and the relentless pursuit of difficult answers to her past. For easing the tension between them over what she had done in that parking lot.

He took off his hat. ''I eat a hell of a lot.''

''Good. I make one hell of a *boeuf bourguignonne*,'' she spelled. ''French for beef stew. Leftovers, but a lot of it.''

''I'm sold.''

She stood there smiling, so befuddled, suddenly, that she forgot to open the door. He took her keys and opened the door. She shed her coat and hung it up, then took his and hung it next to hers. She couldn't remember when she'd done that. Hung a man's coat by hers and liked the way it looked. The way it smelled. She had never cleaned out a drawer or half a closet for a man, but Cy's coat hanging there pleased her, made her think of more radical things. More intimate adjustments.

When she turned, she turned into him. He had his arm

on the wall, trapping her in such a small way. Her lips parted. Her pulse beat hard beneath her breast.

She placed her hand on his chest.

He cupped her nape. His hand was still cold, and she shivered till he eased her head up with his thumb and kissed her. His lips were cold too, at first, but her shivers had more to do with the thrill. With the sensation of his shadow-dark whiskers stabbing her chin, and the pull of his hand through her hair.

Her lips parted. He took it for an invitation. His tongue touched hers, and the thrill took hold as low as her breasts, as deep, abiding pleasure both pinched and unfurled.

She felt the shape of her name on his lips, and answered with the breath of his name against his tongue. At some deep, mute level, he understood her attempt and a wildness overtook his holding her.

She knew it. Got what it meant to him that she would try saying his name. His hand closed tight in her hair, then he broke off his kiss and backed away, way too soon.

"I wasn't ready to be done with that, Cy."

Shoving his hands into his jeans pockets, which in an instant of startling feminine clarity, she understood for exactly what it was. He cleared his throat. "Me either."

"Is that true?"

"I wouldn't lie to you, Amy."

The thrill moved deeper inside her.

Chapter Eleven

She nodded and moved past him, turning on low lights as she went through her small living room, with the burgundy leather couch and deep, white-on-white embroidered club chairs, through the dining room where she lit half a dozen white, jasmine-scented candles, to her kitchen. She pulled out a fat container of leftover bourguignonne and set it to warming on the lighted gas burner.

Cy had followed her, and sat in one of the chairs at her breakfast nook looking at her arrangement on the wall beside him of small pen-and-ink sketches in a variety of pewter and delicate wrought iron frames.

"Did you do these?"

She nodded. "Doodling, really."

"I'm no expert, Amy, but these are exquisite."

His awe pleased her. "Thank you."

"Was that trophy I saw in the living room the design award Fiona was talking about?"

"Yes."

"What was it for?"

"A zoo, actually. Mine was an aviary design. I'll show you the elevation sketches if you want."

He thought she'd signed "elevator." She laughed, spelling out "elevation."

He grinned. ''Well, that's not the worst mistake I've ever made.''

She poured a couple of crystal goblets of wine, then prepared a small platter of sliced cheese and crackers, adding a few capers, sprigs of fresh parsley and tiny red peppers for color.

He looked as if he couldn't quite stand touching it, making a mess of her arrangement.

''It's only cheese and crackers, Cy,'' she signed, teasing. ''You should see what I can do with a radish.''

''Show me.''

She looked at him, considering, then went to the refrigerator and brought back a large radish. ''Trade,'' she signed. ''Tell me what's the funniest mistake you've made.''

''Okay. You first.''

He got over it, and started on the cheese and crackers.

She began to carve on the radish with a tiny paring knife. In a few moments of deft slices and intricate carving she'd produced a swan between petals of red radish. She held it out to him with a *voilà* gesture. ''Your turn.''

He shook his head, awed again. ''You'll laugh.''

''You promised.''

''Okay. But I don't know—''

''Cy, just spit it out,'' she demanded.

''Okay. It was with Seth. I should have taken a clue when he taught me to say my name. Turned out what he taught me was 'dickhead.'''

She grinned. ''The battle of the deafie and the hearie began.''

''Exactly. So one day—he's sixteen now—he's telling me he's screwed, only I thought he spelled scrod. He hadn't ever even heard of scrod. He asked me if scrod was 'hearie' for *screwed* in the past tense. So I'm explaining screwed is already past tense, and he's following this whole English grammatical thing and he asks, is scrod the verb form in the past perfect tense?

"I threw up my hands. *I* don't even know what the hell past perfect tense is."

Now she was awed. "What an incredibly bright kid!"

Cy nodded. "He knew it too. It got him into trouble all the time. He had some great teachers he could run circles around."

"So what happened?"

"I told him to forget about that. I told him a scrod is a fish that, at the latitude of Boston, is a real delicacy. But the lightbulb comes in Seth's devious little mind and I can see he's going to work on this verb thing and I'm thinking, I'm not gonna get it. I'm gonna look like a real moron. He signs, 'So did you hear the one about the Boston cab-driver?' I fall right into it, and shake my head, like no, I haven't heard that one. So he signs, 'This guy gets in the cab and asks the driver, "You know where I can get scrod in this town?"' The cabbie says, 'Mister, I've been asked that about a hundred million times, but never in the past perfect subjunctive.'"

"Wow!" She smiled. "Did you get it?"

He scowled. "Yeah. Sort of. A couple of beats later." He looked suddenly very pensive. Forlorn. "That's how it went with Seth. He needed someone to get it. Someone to admire him. Someone to tell him to knock off playing his video games in the middle of the night."

Amy nodded. "He didn't know they make noise?"

"Not a clue."

She thought about a boy, a sixteen-year-old deafie, so smart he could invent a joke that worked in ASL and English, so innocent and unwitting he didn't know video could also make sound.

She thought about all her own small embarrassments, the way the only chance she had stood was to see them for precious, comic, funny moments that made the tragic and unhappy ones endurable—especially now. Especially struggling against all odds to learn what it was she once had heard, once known about her mother's death.

She understood with all her heart what a gift Cy and Seth had been to each other. What a gift Cy was to her, right now. "You're a hearie with a deaf-heart, Cy McQuaid."

She got up to serve him her piping hot stew in an antique ceramic tureen. The beef and burgundy wine scent steamed into the air, rich as the moment Cy also got what she meant dubbing him a deaf-heart.

IN HER FATHER'S courtroom late the following day, the attorneys for the government were lined up at a table to one side, like birds on a wire, those for the defendant on the other side, facing them. The afternoon sun slanted steeply from the west.

She knew from the way her father held his shoulders that he had listened as long as he was willing. He would have read the stacks of documents submitted on appeal, not once, but many times.

He would know the case inside and out. Better than the attorneys for either side. In her own experience, when he knew better than you, you usually knew it, so if the attorneys were paying attention, the oral arguments were very nearly done.

She had no doubt that her father had seen her when she slipped inside the courtroom with Cy. Still, he had given no indication. When she was very little, if she had been very quiet until he was done and the courtroom cleared, he would let her come sit in his chair and preside over his pleadings. She would bang the gavel to her heart's delight, but always, always, in her little universe and the courtroom she ran, her daddy's impassioned arguments carried the day.

Of course, the case usually boiled down to who loved her best—her daddy or her March Hare.

Her daddy always won.

He looked bone-weary to her. And older than she remembered him looking less than a month ago when he had come home to Denver for Christmas. He spent a couple of moments poring over his calendar after he'd cut off the last of the oral arguments, then announced when he would render his decision. He rapped his gavel and was gone from the bench and the courtroom before the bevy of attorneys all came to their feet.

Amy got up with Cy and left by the side exit to avoid the crowd, then keyed in the code to open a door, marked Private, off the narrow corridor. Through a second door, they entered her father's chambers. The judge finished hanging up his robe, then turned to embrace her.

She inhaled his warmth, the scent of his aftershave, the powerful, commanding essence she had always associated with him. "Daddy," she signed against his grizzled cheek.

"Amy." She both felt the familiar vibration of her name in his chest, and his hand, spelling her name against her cheek. The ritual was old between them, small comfort in the beginning, more necessary, more cherished every year since she had gone deaf. He pulled back for her to see on his lips what he said. "You should have called. I'd have had my driver pick you up." He turned his gaze on Cy, offered his hand. "We've met, Mr. McQuaid."

Cy extended his hand to shake. "I'm surprised you remember, sir."

"What was the occasion?" Amy asked, more surprised that they had ever met.

Her father hadn't stopped taking Cy's measure. "Some D.C. soiree or other."

"One of Candy Orenthal's, wasn't it?"

"Yes. That's right."

Amy shot her father a warning look. "Don't bother, Daddy. You know exactly."

"A bit off my game, am I?" He shot her a rueful look. "Just an old man's vanity. No strokes today, however." He turned away and sat at his desk. Behind him, dark, mahogany-stained oak bookshelves stretched the length of the room.

Arched, elegant, multipane windows gathered in the last of the daylight. His chambers were furnished with antique brass, a spittoon and coat tree, and several western bronzes. "I assume you've come the distance to talk. Shall we do it here, or would you rather I take you out to dinner?"

"Both?" Amy teased.

"Both it is." He leaned forward to grab up his phone. "Helena, make reservations for dinner for me, will you? Three at nine. More private than less." He hung up without waiting for any response, and turned his attention to Cy. "I understand you sign well enough to keep up with my brilliant daughter."

"Not that well, I'm afraid," Cy answered, glancing at her, "but almost."

"I'm sorry for your loss."

"What loss?" Amy asked.

Cy didn't answer her, only stared hard at her father. "You're well-informed."

"Always. Amy's uncle makes it his personal business."

"Makes what his personal business?" she asked. "What loss, Cy?"

"Amy." He turned to her and signed. "It's a long story. I want to tell you. I will tell you, but this is not the time. Not here. Not now."

She felt blindsided, excluded not to know what they were talking about, and as if she were being patted on the head for asking.

Cy must have seen the flare of resentment, the heat in her face. The tension between them over what she'd done in the parking lot the day before was only barely resolved.

For her father's benefit he said aloud, "Amy, all it means is that your uncle has been vetting me, and passing along what he gets to your father."

"Daddy." To be perfectly clear, she took the time to spell out her question. "Did you ask Perry to do that?"

"No, but I confess having read the material, and throw myself on your mercy."

"It's not funny."

Her father looked down, drew a deep breath, then answered her. "No. It's not. But it is the truth. I give your uncle credit for looking after my interests, but in this case he has overstepped himself. When he learned that you had gone to see Brent—well. He is…troubled that you would pursue this, Amy, after he went to the trouble of explaining what had happened to you. And to the FBI—Mr. McQuaid. Very troubled, I should say."

"He should be troubled, Daddy. Did he provide you with a file on all the investigating agents?"

"No." Leaning back, her father loosened his tie. A look encouraged Cy to do the same if he chose. He drew a deep breath and waited. "But perhaps we should get to the point."

She took a moment to compose her thoughts. Her father

was a brilliant, complicated man and she knew, suddenly, watching him sit there waiting to answer her questions, that the little sidebar with Cy could not have been an accident or an unwitting slip of the tongue.

Her father wanted her to understand what her uncle had already done to thwart her, the power he wielded, the resources he had at his fingertips—enough to invade the privacy of a federal agent and compile a report, all within twenty-four hours of her questioning Brent.

Cy had tried to warn her that she had no idea what she was getting into. By her father's carefully constructed charade, she finally got it.

He had to know what was on her mind, what she had learned. He had never given her any reason to fear that he would cut her off emotionally, or in any other way, but Perry was on the warpath now, and she didn't know what to expect. Had her father intended to warn her that he would not take her side when he threw himself, in jest, on her mercy?

"Am I troubling you, too, Daddy?"

"You were always trouble, Amy." He gave her a bittersweet smile. "It usually made my day."

She smiled too. "Thank you. But I mean—"

He cut her off. "I know what you mean, Amy. I want you to know that there is no question in my mind that what you're doing is necessary as breathing to you, or you wouldn't be doing it. And your continued breathing, by the way, is as important to me as my own."

"Will you tell me what happened that night?"

He frowned. For some reason, he hadn't followed her question. She looked to Cy.

"She asked, sir, if you will tell her what happened the night of your wife's death."

"Ah." He turned to her. "I'm sorry. I assumed that you had come to ask about the Jessup story."

She exchanged glances with Cy, a look meant to confirm their decision to put off telling her father about their encounter with Zach Hollingsworth. "That too, Daddy. But about my mother…"

He began to toy with a pen on his desk. "You already know it, Amy. To my knowledge, everything happened the way your uncle described it to you. I can't account for what went on after I left the house to go find Brent. But I have no reason whatever, nor have I ever had reason to believe that your mother died that night of any cause but a freak fall."

Her throat tightened. "Could you start at the beginning, Daddy? Start with what had already gone so wrong in our family?"

He took a deep breath. "Our marriage was in trouble, Amy. Your mother and I had been at serious odds even before you were born."

"Why? What happened?"

He rose from his chair, crossed his chambers and stood looking out the windows at the city lights. "Up until yesterday, when Hollingsworth's piece broke, I believed it would not serve you to know." Cy repeated in sign for her. "Your uncle told me that he was quite harsh with you. Too harsh, perhaps. But he has always respected my wish to protect you from ever learning the sordid details."

Amy had never seen her father so ill at ease, so uncomfortable in his own skin. He was a man of strong opinions and rare doubts. If she had ever witnessed the slightest degree of uncertainty in him, she couldn't remember the occasion. But now…was he saying, as Perry had claimed, that he would lie to her face to protect her from the harsh realities?

"Would you go so far as to lie to me, Daddy?"

He lowered his head, almost as if praying. "I hoped the questions would never arise. Even so, were it not for what you already know from Hollingsworth's article, I would not be willing to discuss my private life with your mother. Now you are entitled to certain answers—what your uncle has or has not said or done was intended to discourage your ever asking."

She believed Perry's motives in bullying her went far beyond discouraging her questions, but that was another subject.

"Was she leaving you, Dad?"

"I suppose that was her plan, yes."

"How did you know your wife's intentions, sir," Cy asked, "when you were in Denver, and then en route back to Steamboat right up until Amy was rescued?"

"I learned of it in the couple of hours after Amy was pulled out."

"Do you know why?"

"I never learned her reasons. She had threatened before. I assumed it was the accumulated weight of her various complaints. But the simple truth of the matter is, I refused to listen to her."

He looked consideringly at Amy, deciding, she thought, how he would tell her. "Your mother was furious with me for taking you, for shoving her out of the way when the rescue team brought you up. She went on ahead to the house. She'd run a warm bath for you by the time I got back with you, but I wouldn't let her take you from my arms. You were clinging to my neck, Amy. You wouldn't have gone to her anyway—which only infuriated her more. Do you remember?"

Amy shook her head. According to parade of therapists, hearing specialists and physicians she had been to, it would be highly unlikely for her to remember the trauma of her fall or its aftermath.

Even the question of what she had seen or heard that night was dicey from the standpoint of "recovered memory"—which was known now to be far more unreliable than psychologists had believed years ago.

All she could hope was that something she learned now might trigger fragments of recall that would stand up against Perry's stonewalling.

"Did she leave then?"

"No. She insisted that we had to talk, then and there. She said your grandmother should 'get off her scrawny ass' and come take care of you. 'Make herself useful,' she said, 'for once in her pampered existence'—referring to Fee of course. We argued. Briefly. Bitterly. She must have said something to the effect that she was leaving me, but I ignored her and told her again to get out." He broke off, cleared his throat, unfisted his hands. "You'd already been through a hellish experience, Amy. I wasn't about to leave you with anyone else. Not even your grandmother. I told her that *I* was the one who was going to take care of you. That you came first, and that she would have to wait."

"Surely she could understand—" Cy began, but her father shook his head.

"On the contrary. Julia was utterly incapable of putting anyone but herself first."

Cy frowned. "Even under those circumstances?"

"Even so." He shrugged. His shoulders seemed suddenly less substantial to her than the image of him she carried in her mind. "She might have been more reasonable," he went on, "if Amy had been more obviously injured by her fall. Physically damaged in some way." He looked at her. "If you'd had broken bones, gashes or abrasions that needed tending, but—miraculously—you didn't. In her mind, you had *always* come first with me, Amy. This was just one more affront to your mother and she wouldn't stand for it.''

''Why did she hate me so much?''

''It wasn't you, Amy. It was never you—only that you reminded her of someone…someone else. A woman she believed was a—a rival, I suppose. A woman with whom she accused me of being in love.''

''Let me guess.'' Cy grimaced. ''We're talking Pamela Jessup now.''

DELAYED BY THE insane amount of traffic on I-70, Brent didn't clear the westbound Eisenhower Tunnel till nearly four o'clock. He didn't know what time people knocked off work at the fancy-assed architectural firm where Amy worked, but if he didn't get in for another hour, he'd miss making a call he had to make.

He didn't know where Amy was. He had to find out without at the same time setting himself up.

He pulled over long enough to dig out his cell phone and punch in the numbers, then pulled back into traffic.

For once the cell phone behaved. He got a chipper little answer and asked for Amy Reeves. No surprise, she was taking the week off work. What he needed to know was where she would be and when. He figured she had to have someone running interference for her, doing her interpreting.

He schmoozed the Sykes & Bladestone receptionist till he got the name of Amy's personal assistant, then hung up, pushed redial, and this time accessed the maze of the company directory till he could select Jessie Verdell's extension.

He nearly swallowed his tongue when the woman answered. He had to talk to someone, there was no getting around it, but he was shaking now. "Jessie, hi. You don't know me, but I'm Amy's brother, Brent Reeves—up in Steamboat Springs."

"Yes?"

He gripped the phone hard. His hands were sweating. She wasn't exactly extending herself. He had no way of knowing what Amy would have told the woman about him. "I hate to bother you, but…I need to get a hold of my sister and I thought maybe you could help me."

"Amy's out of town, I'm afraid. She went to see your father. I…yes. She left yesterday before noon."

Little bitch… God only knew what she was telling the old man. "Yeah, I knew that much," he said. "I thought I'd surprise her. You know, drive down to Denver and pick her up at the airport."

"It may be a waste of your time. She seems pretty well taken care of with that FBI guy—"

"Cy McQuaid." The more informed he seemed to be, the more likely she was to take him at his word. He improvised, playing on the faceless woman's sympathy. "Ames is pretty upset about all this going on with Dad. We both are. We just sort of need to stick together now. Problem is, in all the uproar, I can't find her flight information."

"All I know is that she won't be in until late tomorrow."

Close enough. "Well, thanks, Jessie. That'll give me plenty of time to check with Dad. I appreciate your help."

"No problem. Tell her we're all thinking about her here."

"I'll do that. From what I hear—" he hadn't heard anything, but so what? "—she's in with a pretty great bunch of people. Oh, wait. One more thing." He knew when, now, but not where, and he couldn't think how to get an address out of the dim bulb without her getting suspicious. He couldn't take the chance of asking directly whether Amy was even working on a house renovation now or not.

About the time he figured out what to do, he realized his silence had grown awkward. "Sorry about that. Never mind. Hey, listen, Jessie. Thanks for your help." He went through the drill again, rang off, then punched redial one more time, then 0 for the Sykes & Bladestone receptionist.

Putting on a rough, construction-worker voice, he said, "Yeah, this is Acme Building Supply. Got a wrong delivery address here. We need the renovation site for Miss Reeves."

"Sixth and Holly, you mean?"

"Yeah." The ease of it made him damned near giddy. "That'd be it."

Chapter Twelve

Let me guess...Pamela Jessup.

Stunned by Cy's intuition, Amy stared at him. Her father looked down, then blew off a deep sigh. "Your performance evaluations, however brilliant, have fallen a bit short of the mark, Mr. McQuaid."

Cy shrugged. "I doubt that, sir."

"Daddy...were you ever planning to tell me?"

"I'm sorry you're only learning of this under these circumstances, Amy. Your mother's family was never a part of your life. It's no secret anywhere, even the public record, for that matter, how I felt about what happened to Pamela, or how I tried to help her—but yes. Pamela Jessup was your mother's cousin—and the one with whom she imagined I was in love."

"But Hollingsworth's story had only to do with your prosecuting—"

"Not exactly," Cy interrupted.

"How did you guess?" she demanded, conveying with her hands her bewilderment.

"Remember, Hollingsworth's article alluded to 'higher stakes.'" Cy looked back to her father, signing his question for her as well. "Will your relationship with Pamela Jessup be next on Hollingsworth's agenda?"

"God only knows," her father answered. "To my knowledge, your mother's family never believed Julia's jealousy or her accusations had any merit. He won't get any encouragement from them on that. On the other side of it, they did believe that I was somehow willing to sacrifice their good name on the altar of the almighty law."

"I don't understand," Amy signed. "What happened that made them think that?"

"Pam was raped, Amy. Raped by the son of old family friends—now," his expression riddled with scorn, "the estimable Phillip Gould, senior—"

"*Senator* Phillip Gould?" Cy asked incredulously.

"Yes." Amy's father took a deep breath. His hand closed in a death grip on his Mont Blanc fountain pen. His knuckles whitened. An old and deep-seated anger smoldered in his eyes. "The son of a bitch raped her and got away with it."

Sickened, exchanging looks with Cy, Amy swallowed hard. This was what Zach Hollingsworth was looking for, Gould's reason for taking dead aim at the possibility of her father's nomination.

"Unfortunately for Pam," he went on, "the family was disinclined to believe her. The Goulds were friends. And higher up the social ladder by more rungs than they wanted to count. In the end, her father, your mother's uncle, threatened to disinherit her if she humiliated them, her sister Candace—whose debutante season would come next—or even the Goulds, by pressing charges. I encouraged Pidge—Pamela—to go to the authorities anyway."

"Where did my mother fit into this?"

"She was several years older than Pam, but their grandfather had cut your mother off financially as well, over some teenage indiscretion. I suppose she hoped her own infractions would seem so insignificant compared to Pam's defiance that she would get back into her grandfather's good graces.

"I told your mother privately," he concluded, "that if the family cut Pam off, I would support her. I thought your mother sympathized. As it turned out, I was mistaken."

"She thought you were in love with Pamela?"

"She was convinced of it."

"But if it wasn't true," Amy signed, "how could she have been so wrong?"

"I was fond of Pam, Amy, I won't deny it. I watched her grow up from the age of thirteen or so. I was aware that Pidge had an adolescent crush on me, but she grew out of it. Your mother didn't see it that way."

Amy had never known her mother's family, never visited the family estate in the California wine country, where their fortune was made generations before she was born. She had never been taken to see them as a child, after her mother had died, and never wanted to as an adult. "Did you manage to persuade Pam to go to the police?"

"I didn't have to convince her. She wanted to press charges. She'd told Gould she was going to go through with pressing charges. It might already have been too late in terms of physical evidence, but she never got the chance. Two days after the rape I dropped her off at a hair salon where she had an appointment. I never saw her again. She was kidnapped coming out of the salon appointment."

Cy shook his head. "Quite the lucky break for Gould, wasn't it?"

Byron grimaced. "Don't think the thought didn't cross my mind. For two cents I'd have given Eisman, the kidnapper, immunity in exchange for fingering Gould in a conspiracy." He shrugged. "In fact, I tried."

"Nothing ever came of it?"

"Eisman refused the bait. We never uncovered a link between them. We did find evidence in Eisman's apartment to suggest that he'd been researching the society pages for kidnap targets. More on Pam than anyone else. There was even a blurb about where the various debutantes got their hair done."

Cy nodded. "Bottom line, he knew enough to have come up with the scheme on his own. Did Gould know you tried to establish a link between him and Eisman?"

"You bet he knew." Her father's nostrils flared minutely. "I wanted him to know. I wanted to make him sweat. After what he'd done to Pam—" he broke off, shaking his head.

Cy looked to Amy. She gave a small nod. "Yesterday in Steamboat we had a run-in with Zach Hollingsworth. Gould was the one egging him on to run with this story in the first place. Hollingsworth figured Gould wants to scuttle your nomination. What he couldn't figure was why."

"And so in my nomination he's found the perfect venue to exact his revenge. A prince of man, isn't he? A bastion of integrity."

A few moments passed. What more was there to say about Gould? Amy drew a deep breath. "What happened then? After the kidnap?"

"A couple of months later, Pam was spotted on the surveillance tapes of a bank robbery in Salt Lake City."

"But she escaped capture?" Amy signed.

Her father gave a tense, abbreviated nod. "Hollingsworth's story is accurate. They all escaped. There was a getaway driver as well. All of them were captured within seventy-two hours. All but Pam. I prosecuted the case for Pam's kidnap as well as the bank heist they pulled off."

Amy shook her head. "What am I missing? Why did they rob a bank?"

"Because the family flatly refused to pay the ransom demand. Eisman and DuLong had their mitts on a rich heiress, but her family stiffed them."

Amy felt her entire body recoil. "How could they refuse to pay? Especially after all she'd been through—"

"There's the rub, you see. They didn't accept that she'd been through anything. Knowing what they had already done to her," her father asked, "why do you imagine they might pay off a ransom demand?"

"She was their *daughter*."

"And they chose to believe she had participated in her own kidnap to get back at them for refusing to believe Gould had raped her. When she was caught on the surveillance footage, they took it to mean she was a willing participant in *that* crime as well." Byron Reeves shook his head. His lips tightened. "It was outrageous."

"To be fair, sir," Cy pointed out, "Jessup was caught on camera toting an automatic weapon."

"She had been held hostage for seven weeks. She was subjected to illegal drugs, beatings, isolation—and that is only what her captors admitted having done to her. Eisman is still in a federal pen in Illinois. Nonetheless," he added, anticipating Cy, "what you say is correct. She was armed and present at the commission of a felony. If Zach Hollingsworth has a point to make, it is not that I was overzealous in the prosecution of Eisman and DuLong because of my family ties to the victim of their kidnap and extortion—"

"But that another prosecutor would have pressed harder to catch Pamela Jessup," Cy concluded.

Her father met Cy's gaze with his own, flinty and unapologetic. "Yes."

"*Did* you exert your influence to get them to call off the dogs?" Cy asked, equally unrelenting. Looking from one to another, Amy thought how alike they were, both of them unbending men of a certain code, posturing at one another like mountain stags locking horns.

"Yes." He refused to soften his answer, justify it or make the case for himself that any prosecutor would likely have granted Pam immunity for her testimony, or at the very least gone lightly in the charges laid against her.

"Are you prepared to answer for that now?"

"Cy, my father is not answerable to you or anyone—"

"He is, Amy," Cy interrupted, signing fiercely. "No man is above the law. Especially one who officially sits in judgment of others."

"He's right." Her father took his suit jacket from the coat tree. "I'll just say this, though I don't intend to make any statement to the press at all. The office of the U.S. attorney was not used to aid and abet the flight of Pamela Jessup from prosecution."

As far as Cy was concerned, the clarity and precision of Judge Reeves's assurance to Amy seemed a little disingenuous.

Riding in the front seat of Byron Reeves's car with the chauffeur, en route to the restaurant, he decided Reeves would know exactly where to draw the line. If Pamela Jessup had been aided in any way in her flight from prosecution, Byron Reeves had done the deed personally, carefully separating his personal and professional lives.

If he had done it, he'd done it for values he must believe superseded the law. Cy had the feeling Byron Reeves would stand up and say so publicly if it came to that.

Grudging admiration curled in his gut, and he squirmed. He felt pulled in two directions. His own code of honor had always been unstinting. Still, as he'd told Cameron, things were never all black or white, and Cy had to wonder what he would have done if he'd been in Reeves's shoes. Would justice have been better served if all the stops had been pulled out to track down Pamela Jessup?

The limo delivered them to the front steps of the restaurant, and a few minutes later they were seated in a small, elegantly appointed alcove. Her father preoccupied with the menu, Amy sat stiffly, smoothing the fanfold pattern of creases from her napkin.

The image that had haunted Cy from the start came back. Amy sitting on the landing of that daunting old staircase trying to hear what danger was coming next, calming, consoling herself by stroking the flocking on the wall beside her.

Consoling herself again, stroking the whiskers on his jaw when he kissed her and must have reeked of his regret to her.

He wanted to give Amy something else to touch besides the linen. His hand for instance.

Instead he stretched his arm across the pristine white tablecloth and spelled her name where she would see him doing it. She needed a shove to get out of her head and put her questions on the table. "Amy."

She watched his hand.

"Ask him," he signed, "what you need to know."

Judge Reeves closed his menu and set it aside. He'd missed nothing. He tolerated the discreet appearance of the waiter at his elbow, ordered, then ordered for Amy at her request, and waited through Cy's request for rare prime rib. Then he took Cy on. "My daughter has never needed anyone's encouragement to speak her mind to me."

"Don't, Daddy," she signed. "Don't make this into a pissing contest between you."

She had shocked her father. She'd intended just that, spelling the word, meaning to stop him cold.

"I have...this isn't easy for me. If it weren't for Cy I wouldn't be here, asking you what happened. Things I have needed to learn for a long time."

He sighed heavily. "My apologies to you both. What else can I tell you?"

"Finish with what happened the night my mother died."

Reeves nodded. "There isn't a great deal more to say." Waiting until the tureen of oxtail soup had been served, he picked up at the point where Pamela Jessup had become relevant and he'd become sidetracked.

He referred back to Julia's tirade. "It was true that you weren't physically harmed beyond a chill and a few cuts and bruises, but I was so angry at her selfishness that I told her again to get out. She finally left and I sat down with you in the rocking chair in your room. I stayed until you had fallen asleep.

"When I finally arrived back downstairs," he concluded, "Brent had taken off, and your mother was over the edge with worry about him."

"Do you know, of your own personal knowledge, that she was worried about Brent?" Cy asked. This was the moment to confirm with her father whether Brent could have been responsible.

He frowned. "Yes—"

"Is there any possibility that your brother intercepted you as you came downstairs and told you Brent had run out? That you didn't actually see Julia at all before you left to go after your stepson?"

"No." The creases about his eyes and on his brow deepened. "I did see her. She was—"

"Still alive, sir?"

"Of course she was still alive! We even argued about

which of us would go after Brent. I prevailed. She wasn't in any shape to be chasing after the boy.'' He paused. ''Are you asking if there is any possibility Julia was dead before Brent left?''

She exchanged looks with Cy. ''He believes she was, Daddy.''

''Brent?'' He shoved his soup bowl away, rested his elbows and laced his long fingers. ''You can't be serious.''

''Yes.'' She was. ''Brent believes he was responsible for mother's death.''

The waiter removed the soup bowls and now served their main courses. ''Why would he think such a thing?''

''That's the point, sir,'' Cy answered. ''Why would he believe it, unless it was true? Or unless someone—your brother for instance—went to a great deal of effort to make Brent believe he had somehow killed his mother?''

''Wait,'' her father demanded. ''One thing at a time. First, did Brent tell you that he had killed his mother?''

''He didn't,'' Cy said. ''What he did do, within a couple of hours of our visit to him, Amy's and mine, was to call your brother long-distance on a cell phone.''

Her father's chest seemed to deflate. ''I presume the conversation was intercepted?''

''Yes.''

''By the FBI?''

''No, sir,'' Cy answered. ''Hollingsworth got it on tape.''

Her father scowled. ''Got what on tape?''

Cy gave him the gist of the conversation, all the times Perry Reeves had tried to calm Brent, reassuring him that there was no evidence to bring him down, urging him over and over again to repeat aloud the assertion that his mother's death was an accident.

''I am aware, sir,'' Cy went on, ''that the tape is proof

of only one thing. Your brother and stepson have had a long-term understanding between the two of them as to what happened the night your wife died. Your brother's version of the events has been consistent from day one with your own. But it's hard to imagine that Brent would be so riddled with guilt if, in fact, when he left the house, your wife was still alive."

"Unless Brent was lying in wait for her somewhere outside. Is that it?" The judge's mind worked quickly, arriving in a few short seconds at the only other possibility.

He described a scenario in which he had missed Brent, going further and further afield looking for his stepson so that when Julia followed, she and Brent had clashed again in an argument that ended with her death. "The logic of it is impeccable— but wrong. Brent wasn't hiding. It had begun to snow right about the time I arrived back at the house with Amy. Brent's footprints were clear. Easy to follow in the snow. He bolted, he went down the front steps, and I followed the trail he left all the way down the mountain. He angled through the forest on a direct course for the highway leading into town."

"Then the question remains," Cy replied, unfazed by the dismantling of a theory neither he nor Amy had ever believed. "Why did Brent panic? Why did he make that call to your brother?"

"I have no idea," Judge Reeves answered. "Do you?"

"We think she must have lost consciousness, Daddy," Amy signed. "Uncle Perry told us that she was having terrible asthma attacks all day long. Maybe she passed out—at least long enough for Brent to run because he thought he'd hurt or killed her when he shoved her down. If Brent is panicked, then it has to be that Uncle Perry has let him go on believing all these years that she died because of whatever he did."

Cy spoke along with her signing, translating for her because although her father could follow her fairly well, he was more deeply upset than he showed.

He made an obvious effort to regain his composure, lifting his heavy silver flatware, cutting carefully into his roasted quail and delicately seasoned new potatoes.

"I take it you still do not believe your mother's death was an accident, then?"

"I don't, Daddy. I don't accept that Uncle Perry was trying to make me back off for my own good. He could have asked. He could have said I should talk to you. He had no reason to bully me, Daddy, but he was. And Brent—"

"I have to say, sweetling, that I am at a loss." He placed his knife on the rim of his plate. "While I agree with you that it would be a heinous, despicable act on Perry's part to have fostered Brent's belief that he was responsible for his mother's death, nothing you have told me disproves the simple conclusion that Julia's death was an accident."

Amy looked steadily at her father. "I am asking you to consider another possibility."

"That your uncle killed your mother." It took no special insight to guess.

She nodded. "Can you do that? Can you imagine it's possible?"

"Anything is possible, Amy," the judge chided gently, "but what would be the point?" He paused. "I don't believe it. I'm frankly astounded that you can even entertain the notion. I don't pretend to appreciate Perry's tactics in discouraging an investigation, but that is a very long way indeed from the commission of a felony murder and cover-up." He began to fiddle again with the silver flatware. "What is it that you want? The assignment of blame?"

"Isn't that what we do? Isn't it everything you stand for—to hold people accountable for their crimes?"

"Yes. So is the doctrine of innocence until guilt is proven. But even if I were to suppose your uncle killed your mother, Amy, if I entertained that possibility, then blame would have to be assigned, and it would fall to me."

"With all due respect, your honor—"

"Spare me the honorific, McQuaid," her father commanded. A rigid expression seized his features. "Let us suppose, for the sake of our discussion, that Perry killed Julia. If so, he has kept it to himself with exquisite care. I would not in a million years have suggested he get rid of her either, but the fact of the matter is that my brother has hardly taken a step in thirty years that wasn't calculated to further my interests."

"Maybe," Cy argued, "but since we don't hold people liable for the murderous action of others, why hold yourself to a higher standard? You weren't even an accessory to the murder unless you knew—"

"Is there some doubt in your mind, Mr. McQuaid," he interrupted jokingly, "that I am somewhat familiar with the threshold for accessory-to-felony murder?"

Cy cracked a grin. "None."

The tension between them broke, but her father sighed deeply and his disbelief was still thick.

"There's more, Daddy."

He sighed deeply. The waiter removed his plate. "What is it?"

Amy deferred to Cy for the sake of her father's ease of understanding. "We have assumed in the Bureau," he said, "that the notarized letter in which Dr. Courson recanted his original finding of accidental death never saw the light of day—not until the extortion attempt began last week. If it had, our forensic accountants figured to follow the money. As you know, there wasn't any obvious pay-off.''

Her father nodded. ''No evidence whatever of a lump sum or an income stream which couldn't be explained.''

''Exactly. But your brother told us that he was in the midst of a complicated real estate transaction on the day Amy fell and your wife died. As real estate was his area of expertise, I thought it might be worthwhile just to give the records a cursory check. Amy and I went to look through old county records, beginning with that day, going forward. Again, there was nothing, no sale of record by Courson or his wife. No—''

''Are you coming to a point?'' her father interrupted wearily.

''Yes.'' Cy's jaw tightened. ''We were referred by the county clerk to corporate sales of time-shares in various properties. Six days after your wife's death, on the date of first release of the coroner's findings, Greg Courson became the owner of a time-share that sold then for fifty thousand dollars down and equal amounts every year after. The records indicate 'For value received by Magenta Corp'—which has holdings at the finest resort locations all over the world.''

''Dad,'' Amy signed, ''Courson didn't have fifty thousand dollars to plunk down anywhere. Not then. Not every year since. And Uncle Perry is listed in the secretary of state's office as one of the directors of the Magenta Corporation.''

''I'm guessing, sir,'' Cy concluded, ''that your brother has been paying all these years for the time-share Courson used.''

''Don't bet your ranch, Mr. McQuaid,'' her father warned. He had listened carefully, but as if it all applied to a case being described to him that involved someone he didn't know. "If Perry orchestrated this deal, you won't find a trace of his participation."

"Are you saying," Amy signed, "that this is not enough—"

"Legally, no," he answered, anticipating her direction. "Is it coincidence that Courson wound up with such a plum, and on the date of his release of findings? Again, no." He paused to take a drink of his wine. "What you are left with, however, is identical to the old joke about the evidence for the existence of a vast right-wing conspiracy in this country." He laughed gently. "The proof is in the utter lack of any proof."

"Daddy, *stop it!*" Amy signed angrily. "This is not some intellectual exercise. This is Uncle Perry paying hush money to the coroner so that—"

Her father held up a hand. "I know what this is, Amy." His chin began to tremble. "I know what this is."

Chapter Thirteen

Cy couldn't sleep. Judge Reeves had insisted he avail himself of one of the guest rooms in his D.C. town house. He lay in his boxers on the floor, his head and shoulders propped up against a chair. Beside him a fire burned in the gas-log fireplace and he sat staring at the flames flickering with only the slight hiss of fuel.

A gas fire was a far sight cleaner than wood, but he missed the scent of burning pine or cedar or oak, and the sounds. The crackling and popping of real wood on fire. As far back as he could remember, he'd loved the feel of the heat of a good hot fire on his face—and the taste of flaming marshmallows melting Hershey bars on a graham cracker.

He laced his hands behind his head. The heat felt good on his damaged leg as well, but his heart was sore and his groin ached, unrelieved from an hour ago when he'd kissed Amy good-night at her door down the corridor from her father's room, and ended up, somehow, with her blouse half-off and her bare breast filling his hand. Not a wise move when the judge had barely retired to his rooms some fifty feet away.

His instinct must still have been fairly blunted. He didn't even see Amy in the doorway to his room till she'd been standing there for quite a while in her long black satin nightgown, watching him.

He lowered his arms. There wasn't much he could or cared to do about his bare chest or boxers bulging. Nothing was going to happen here tonight. "You shouldn't be here, Amy."

Her gaze took in the length of his body. She looked flustered. There was no way she didn't know what condition he was in, but she stood her ground. "Can we talk?" she signed.

"No." Maybe she could. He couldn't.

She closed the door and locked it behind her. "I know about Seth."

His heart squeezed tight. She must've taken herself off to her daddy's file cabinet and pulled out the report her uncle provided her father on him. He thought if anything would have eased the constant ache in his groin it'd be that, but he was wrong. That she knew, that she was here when she knew the worst there was to know about him made his need still more urgent, made him harder and hungrier for wanting the kind of woman who would persist in the face of it.

He wanted to ask if her uncle's report had happened to mention he'd gone without a hint of an arousal for close to four years now, but he still couldn't talk. Locked in the pit of his mouth, his tongue wouldn't work.

"He was trying to kill himself on his motorcycle, wasn't he? Before you even met him."

"And that's relevant because…?"

"He had more disappointments in his life than your guardianship falling through."

"Yeah." Abandoned at three when it became obvious he wasn't going to be a talking baby, in and out of foster homes for the deaf for another twelve years, the kid was screwed from the get-go. "That broken promise was just the straw that broke the camel's back."

"It wasn't your fault, Cy."

"Whose fault was it, Amy? You read between the lines. You tell me who else was accountable."

"Does someone have to be accountable? Isn't it just possible he hurt too much? My God, Cy! Why don't you ask yourself instead who did more for Seth. Who—"

"I made him believe he could count on me, Amy. It sure as hell wasn't his idea."

"Who do you think you are, McQuaid? God? Did you think if only you loved Seth enough he wouldn't try it again?"

"Yeah," he signed fiercely. "Me and my God complex, that's what we thought."

"Could you have loved him any more?"

Jesus, Lord, what did she want from him? His eyes burned. "Get out, Amy."

She shook her head. "No. I want an answer. I *deserve* an answer."

"Then figure it out for yourself," he snarled, getting to his feet, his tongue, though not his sex, loosened by anger. "Obviously, I could have loved the kid more."

She came toward him. "And you know that because if you had loved him more he wouldn't have had to go kill himself."

"Yeah. That's how I know." He swallowed. His throat jammed, thick with emotion. "You want to twist the knife a little deeper?"

"Sure," she signed, toe-to-toe with him, her hands all but crying aloud. "Let me twist the knife a little more. What about this, Cy? What if Seth was a hearing boy? Could you have loved him that little bit more then?"

"No." His gut wrenched, a god-awful sound came out

of him. It wasn't true. He'd thought it was, but when she put it like that—

"Is that what you're telling me?" Tears filled her eyes. "You didn't love Seth enough because he couldn't hear you say it?"

"No. Goddamn it, Amy, no! I loved him—"

"As much as if he were your own child?"

He shook his head. He gritted his teeth, he couldn't help it. "More."

"Then at least have the balls to admit that there wasn't enough love in the world to keep that child going, Cy, because if you don't, it's the same as saying he wasn't in more pain than he could stand. For a little while, you made a difference in his world, but you couldn't make his world over or right again."

He dragged a hand over his head. He thought he would explode, break down, cry. He swallowed. Shoved the words past his lips. "Amy, why are you doing this?"

"Because I'm afraid." A small sob escaped her. "Because I'm in love with you. Because if you don't love me," her fingers stumbled, "I need to know it now. And if you do, I need to know that too so I have a fighting chance."

He stood there cramped in his arousal and the pain of wanting her, loving her, needing there to be a chance. He couldn't move, but only run the heel of his thumb against his swollen flesh and the scar tissue stretched too tight so nearby, to ease the excruciating throb.

A moment of fiercely indelicate awareness hung between them like the scent of scorched air. He closed his hand tight and endured, then opened it and said the words in her language. *I love you, Amy. I love you.*

He reached for her hips to draw her closer. She rested her forearms on his and sank to the floor with him, to their knees. His strong, powerful, callused hands pulled her bottom tight against him. She cried out with no understanding at all what her cry meant to him, only a fathomless instinct for moving brilliantly against him, shifting her hips, arching, offering, intoxicating, splaying her hands where his haunches gave way to the backs of his legs, the very tips of her fingers teasing the root and most tender, distended parts of him.

He thought he would die then and there.

She brought her lips to his breast and let her lips dawdle, back and again, light as the stroke of a butterfly kiss over the thick, curling black hair that covered his chest. She touched her long-silenced tongue to his nipple. He groaned deep inside, and folding his arms about her, he cradled her head to his chest. For long, exquisite moments, by the tenderness and care and delay of his own pleasure, he held her like that and she knew this language was the language of their common ground and he had told her God's own truth.

Cy McQuaid was in love with her.

He withdrew to cup her sweet face in his hands, to say again that he loved her, to kiss her madly. He dragged his thumb along her cheek to her jaw to the hollow at her throat to the top of her breast to a nipple as taut and tender as he had found his own flesh.

She lifted her gown and he lowered his boxers. She saw his ravaged, shiny flesh then, where a terrorist's bullets had sent him into his years of pain-racked and uncertain wilderness, Seth's years, the ones that had schooled Cy in the fine art of understanding her language. Her touch, there, alone, made the years a more bearable thing. The homage of her lips drove the shadows from his soul and he was not lost in his wilderness anymore, but found.

HE NEVER SLEPT past five, but across the time zones in
D.C. that meant seven. By the time Cy had showered his
deeply satisfied body, shaved his happier face, dressed and
gone downstairs, the judge sat alone in the breakfast alcove. Already done with his grapefruit, eggs and toast, he
sat with his cup of coffee, scanning the morning newspa-
pers.

He looked up, met Cy's gaze and set his papers aside.
"Mr. McQuaid."

"Sir."

"Please. Sit down." He rang a small bell to summon
his housekeeper who appeared at the door as if she had
been waiting behind it. "Mrs. Childers, Mr. McQuaid,"
he said, his eyes never leaving Cy.

"Ma'am. I'm pleased to meet you," he acknowledged
the introduction. He took one of the other two settings at
which a grapefruit had already been placed. The slight,
middle-aged woman nodded, smiled, rolled her eyes out
of the judge's view and ducked behind her door.

"She thinks I don't know she rolls her eyes," the judge
said. "It's Childers's way of putting my guests at ease in
my august presence."

Cy grinned. "It works."

His look suggested perhaps Cy shouldn't be so quickly
put at ease. His heart thumped hard in his chest, but it was
her father who looked away first. Cy cut into a section of
his fruit.

"One of your colleagues rang up twenty minutes ago."

"Who was it?"

"Ted Wilms. One of the Bureau's crime-lab directors.
Seems there was no response from you to his repeated
pages last evening around midnight. Ten o'clock, your
time, or so he thought."

Cy swallowed the chunk of grapefruit whole. He'd been with Amy then.

"I thought I heard my daughter stirring outside her room about that time. I thought I might share a few private moments with her. Perhaps fix her a mug of warm milk to help her sleep."

He paused.

Cy put down his spoon.

His heart pounded. It was in Reeves's power to make him wish he'd never been born. His whole life, certainly his career, hung in the balance. Twisting in the wind from a thread no more substantial than a spider's silk, but he would not insult Amy or her father's intelligence with denials, or apologies he didn't mean.

"What? You've nothing to say in your own defense?"

"I'm not on trial, sir. And what happens between Amy and me is not in your jurisdiction."

"In my house—"

"Or anywhere else."

The judge scowled deeply. "Will you not even give lip service to thinking you're falling in love with her?"

"That wouldn't be necessary. I do love her."

The judge fell back against his chair. Sunlight slanting in the east-facing windows glinted off the brass fixtures of his suspenders. "It's not often I find myself at a loss for words, McQuaid. I'm obliged, as her father, to say that if you hurt Amy, you'll have me to deal with, but the truth is, my daughter is far more likely to be the heartbreaker than the heartbroken."

Cy nodded. He'd never suffered illusions about the emotional gauntlet Amy represented.

The doorbell rang as Mrs. Childers served his eggs and toast. She scurried off to answer the summons.

"That'll be Wilms, I expect."

Cy frowned. "We had an appointment later—"

"We did," Wilms said from the door. "Ted Wilms. Good to meet you, McQuaid." He shook hands with Cy, then Reeves, then took a seat where there was no service setting. "Trouble is, I've been called to a Florida crime scene, and I wanted to talk to you myself. Please. Eat. I'll keep it short and sweet."

Amy came into the room, dressed in her usual black, today a long slender woolen skirt, a deep V-neck sweater, dress boots.

Cy rose, followed by her father and Wilms.

"This is my daughter, Amy. Amy, Ted Wilms of the FBI labs."

"Very pleased to meet you," she signed, no need of interpreting her warmth.

They all sat once again, and Wilms started in directly. "Here it is. We were able to perform some spectral analyses on the autopsy slides from Dr. Courson's files. I won't go into all the science involved. Suffice it to say that we have certain experience now that we didn't have twenty-five years ago. Experience," he clarified, "with the effects of oxygen deprivation in deep sea diving, space exploration and the like. When we ran computer simulations to achieve the effects generated by the analyses on the slides, it became a virtual certainty that Julia Reeves lost consciousness as a result of oxygen starvation *prior* to the blow to her head. She was severely asthmatic. If she exceeded the limits of her ability to breathe, or her medication to keep her air passages open?" Wilms shrugged. "Blackout followed by death."

Wilms looked pleased, or rather, as if they should all have been very heartened by proof that a crime had not in fact been committed. It meant Byron Reeves was on an unimpeded course to his place on the bench of the Supreme Court.

But of the three of them, only Amy's father looked in the slightest relieved. Cy said nothing. Eventually the judge asked, "Does this new evidence put your suspicions to rest, Amy?"

She straightened. There was a brittleness around her eyes and lips Cy couldn't read. "It must, mustn't it, Daddy?"

CY PULLED RANK and got himself and Amy first-class seats on United out of Dulles to Denver International Airport earlier than their confirmed flight. He felt caught between a rock and a truly hard spot.

It wasn't that he had any blind faith that the Bureau labs were infallible. Even Wilms had admitted when Cy walked him out to his car that the meaning of the evidence still depended on the spin.

Seen one way, Julia Reeves had gone out after Byron and her son, finally succumbed to the thin mountain air, fainted and cracked her head in a fatal blow against a rock.

Seen another way, all one had to do was keep her asthma inhaler away from her till she lost consciousness. With no attempt to revive her, no adrenaline, no steroids, no CPR, her oxygen-deprived brain would not function.

However refined and ultra-high-tech the methods of analysis used, the tissue slides couldn't reveal intent to kill, and if Perry Reeves had done it, as Amy believed, he was still going to get away with it.

Justice was sometimes blind, and in Cy's experience, if you didn't roll with the losses, they'd crush you, body and soul.

But as their flight continued, he could see that Amy's feelings only grew more raw, more aggravated. He was the only one who believed in her, and he was fading fast, or at least accepting the inevitable. He knew by now that she needed time to work things through. They spoke hardly at all until the meals had been served and the service removed afterward.

She accepted a second glass of wine instead of coffee, and turned to him. "Do you want to know what Takamura believes?"

"If Hank Takamura has an opinion on this, I'd like to know what it is."

She nodded. Takamura's reputation for insight was no secret from the world. "It was the morning you came. I told him about what Fiona had said to me, what she believes. When I tried to brush off knowing anything about what was going on," she went on, signing, "he asked me this question." She proceeded slowly, because with Takamura's question, the difficulty lay in following him exactly. "He said, 'When a child hears what no child should hear, and when she then knows what she knows but she is told she knows nothing of the sort, what do you suppose becomes of her?'"

Cy could only stare at her as the meaning of Takamura's question sank in. When the truth was turned on its head, what choice would Amy have had but to buy into the lies and accept the insistence of her grown-ups that black was white, up was down, in was out... That everyone loved her dearly, that her brother didn't mean to push her down some nightmarish hole in the ground... That mommy had an accident, fell down and died, and no one who loved Amy had anything to do with it.

But if she wasn't quite strong enough at five to hold out against the lies, maybe her only option was to refuse to hear them ever again.

That Amy had heard her grandmother Fiona's music

boxes had been a powerful tip-off, but Takamura's take on the meaning of Amy's ordeals blew Cy away.

He sucked down the last half of his own Merlot. "Amy, was he suggesting that things were so dangerous for you that it was easier to go literally deaf than to hear anymore?"

"*Not* easier," she signed. "This," signifying a terrifying silence by her hands clapped tight over her ears, "is not easier. Only safer. Takamura believes I will never split one arrow with the second until I overcome this...not knowing. Now, at least, I have an idea of what it is I don't want to know."

Cy couldn't conceive of Amy choosing, even subconsciously, to be deaf rather than hear what she heard in that house, but he had no idea what it was like to be five and so mercilessly threatened. Takamura believed she had chosen it, if his question meant anything, but the possibility stretched Cy's personal credulity.

Like splitting one arrow with another.

But what he saw clearly was that Amy was being asked yet again to accept a lie in place of the truth. To believe that the evidence proved no harm, no foul. Her father was a man who accepted or rejected evidence on its fundamental merits, and he was already predisposed to disbelieve his brother could have committed so heinous an act as murder on his behalf.

Therefore, Amy must be wrong.

If Takamura was right, she had defended against the lies at the unimaginable expense of her hearing. Again, the evidence proved there was no physical basis for her to have gone so utterly, stone-cold deaf, but the truth still hinged on what Amy knew as a five-year-old child.

THEY DEPLANED into the B terminal at DIA at 6:45 p.m. A heavyset woman well into her thirties walked right up to Amy, and the two of them embraced.

Amy introduced her to Cy as Jessie Verdell, her assistant and translator at Sykes & Bladestone, and her friend. "Jess," she signed, "is something wrong?"

Jessie nodded. "Your renovation was vandalized sometime last night. Nothing too serious, but the police called the office and left a message. The back door had been forced open and a lot of obnoxious graffiti was spray-painted on the walls."

Cy grimaced. "Did they catch whoever did it?"

"No. The neighbors spotted the back screen door hanging open this morning. Anyway, I had one of our runners take your car over a couple of hours ago. I thought if your brother wasn't here to pick you up and Mr. McQuaid didn't mind, I'd drive you into town and—"

"Her brother," Cy interrupted. "Why would he pick her up?"

Jessie looked uncertain. "Didn't he reach you at your father's place?"

"No." Amy sent Cy an irritable look about letting her ask her own questions. "I don't understand."

Jessie described Brent's call to their office the day before. "I had the impression he wanted to talk to you—that he'd be here to meet you, but then this thing came up with your renovation and I thought you'd want to know right away. The police want to talk to you ASAP also. They're meeting us at the house at eight o'clock, and the new locks should already be installed. A triple bolt, I told them."

"That's great, Jess. Thanks for handling it." They'd reached the underground train station back to the main terminal and stood waiting for the next train. "Cy, I think I will ride to the site with Jess, if you don't mind."

He shook his head. "I don't think it's a good idea."

Amy squared off. "Cy, the police are going to be there. Did you get that?"

"*Amy,* the place was vandalized within hours of your brother making some lame-assed excuse for determining your whereabouts. I don't think it's a good idea. I think you should come home with me tonight." Embarrassed by their clearly personal confrontation, Jessie began looking everywhere but at the two of them. The train came. They crowded on. "I'll call the cops and square it for tomorrow."

"I don't need you to 'square it.'" She looked at him. "Whatever Brent was thinking, he obviously changed his mind. I need to take care of my business. I've been doing that for a long time now. And I'd like a little time with Jessie." He could see she was trying to compromise with him. "Cy, please. This is what I do. It has nothing to do with anything else. What if I drive up to your place after? Would that be okay?"

The train stopped at the A terminal and then the main one. He wasn't going to argue with her. He couldn't stop her risking her reckless little neck, but if she was going, he was going, even if he had to sneak around behind her back to do it.

"Yeah. It'll have to be, won't it?"

She gave him a brilliant smile. She thought she'd gotten her way. She trusted him.

He trusted no one, and he wasn't going to back off to save himself her anger.

"I'll just draw you a map."

"AMY, ARE YOU SURE you should stay here alone?" Jess began to worry after the police took one last look around the house and drove off. "I don't mind staying. I really don't."

"I'll only be here a couple of hours," she signed. "I promised Cy I would come. I can't be too long, or he'll call out the National Guard."

"I know, but I'd—"

"Jess," she signed, standing in the deep-freeze temperatures with her friend, depending on the light of the street lamp for each of them to see the other's hands. "Vandals strike when no one is around. I'm not staying, I'm just going to take care of the windows. The police have been through the house twice, the place is lit up like a Christmas tree and the new lock has a triple bolt. I'll be fine."

"All the same, call me when you get home?"

"I don't need a keeper, Jessie."

Jess frowned. "What is that supposed to mean?"

"Nothing. Sorry. Just tired of being looked after twenty-four-seven."

"Mr. McQuaid?" Jess's breath made tiny clouds in the bitter cold.

Amy nodded.

"Part of his job, don't you think?"

"Self-appointed keeper of the deaf girl?"

"Don't," Jess snapped. "Don't even start with me. He's got a right to be worried. It wouldn't matter if you were deaf or not."

"Wouldn't it, Jess?"

"No. He's in love with you. Don't tell me you don't know that."

Amy swallowed hard. Her face, her breasts flushed with heat. She had every reason to know Cy was crazy in love with her. But somehow she'd thought a man who loved her, no matter how reluctantly, would also know her well enough to understand the thing she needed as much as his love was his respect.

To be treated as if she were a competent woman.

An equal, damn it. Not a willful child in a deaf woman's body, in need of constant supervision.

Brent hadn't shown up, his excuse was lame and he had surely been lying about any intention to meet her flight in the first place, but to make the necessary leap in logic that all of that meant he intended her any harm just didn't fly.

"If you ask me, Amy, you're scared and looking for any excuse. From my point of view, Cy McQuaid is treating you as if you were priceless to him. If you don't knock it off, he won't have any choice but to walk away from you—and it won't be his fault."

Jessie jerked open her car door and sank into the driver's seat, looking at Amy as if she had been personally insulted.

"Jess, don't go away mad," she signed, pleading, her fingers stiff with cold, her eyes watering. "I am scared."

She started the engine. "Let me tell you something, Amy. I'd give anything to be scared like that."

She swallowed. Life was so hard. Jess deserved to be scared like that. A little thrill, a little danger, hope and a good man causing it all. "Thanks for arranging all this. And I will call you."

Jess smiled, then rolled up her window and backed out of the drive.

Amy turned and dashed across the crunchy layer of snow for the front door. The space heater probably had the living area up to fifty-five degrees, but compared to the outside it felt like a sauna.

And looked like hell. Spray-painted graffiti now defaced nearly every wall in the living area, but what concerned her were the clerestory windows. They looked as if they'd been damaged with a pea-shooter or slingshot, and in the extreme cold, which was expected to snap in the morning, the windows would fall apart, dropping glass, and in the worst case, letting melted snow seep down onto the ceiling.

If the water got far enough, the expensive antique molding she'd just put up would be ruined.

She had to seal off those windows, and she wanted to be done with it before Cy got antsy.

She half-rolled, half-dragged her scaffolding to the center of the room, then heaved the four-foot roll of heavy construction-grade plastic up one level, then the next. She put on her tool belt and climbed up onto the scaffolding.

When she was done she'd go home, throw a few things together and drive up to Cy's place. Maybe on the way she'd think of a way to fend off her fear that Cy wouldn't ever quite believe that she needed to take care of herself. Or that she could.

DAMN NEAR NINE-THIRTY. And thirty below with the wind chill. Huddled in the space between the outside door of the root cellar and the half door leading into the cramped basement, Brent still felt every freaking degree.

For a minute he'd worried Amy was going to leave when the cops left. But she must have only walked the dim bulb Verdell woman out to her car, because she'd come back inside.

Alone.

His luck was holding.

The cops had been all through the place, even rattled his cage door from the inside, then decided it hadn't been opened in fifty years. He imagined she felt safe now. Pissed, no doubt, at the vandalism, but safe.

She was wrong.

He felt around his coat pocket for what he needed and began prying open the root cellar door, not giving a crap when it groaned. Amy wasn't going to hear it.

The eeriness of it began to get to him. The place was dead silent. No TV blaring, no voices, no radio, no CDs, nothing but the scrape of things being dragged across the floor.

He thought he knew exactly what she was doing.

He avoided thinking, in the bigger picture, what the hell it was *he* was doing. She was his kid sister. He never meant for her to get hurt, but if it wasn't for her his mom would have left Byron Reeves. She would have packed up their stuff and taken Brent and gone back to California, and then none of this would have ever happened.

He'd wished a million times he hadn't hurt his mom, hadn't killed her, hadn't gotten so angry he couldn't see straight because she was dead now, and Amy was like a dog with a bone she wasn't going to give up.

He didn't think they'd ever get him for murder one, but even if they got him on involuntary, the suck-ups would make sure the kid who killed Judge Reeves's wife spent the maximum time in the slammer, even if he was her son.

But Amy wasn't going to leave it alone and he didn't have a choice.

Crouching in the dark, freezing cold basement he imagined he could hear the hiss of gas fueling the space heater on the main floor. In any case, cold as it was, he knew she would long since have turned it on. All that was left for him to do was to dissolve the seal and loosen the fitting on the furnace.

The gas would rise up through the house at a pretty good clip. She might even smell the nasty sulfur scent the gas company added to natural gas to warn of exactly such a leak. But by the time it penetrated her clever little brain that the gas she was smelling wasn't the gas powering the space heater, he would be safely removed. The concentration of gas would reach an incendiary level. The pilot flame on the safe, innocuous space heater would ignite and the place would blow, lighting up the blistering-cold night sky. And it would all be the fault of the brand-new furnace installers.

Chapter Fourteen

By nine-thirty Cy began to think he'd overreacted to a nonexistent threat. He'd parked on the street at the side of the house and observed every movement for the last ninety minutes. The cops went in, the cops went out, the house was obviously secured to their satisfaction. Then Jess left without Amy, which settled it. He wasn't leaving, he didn't care how lamebrained it felt. At this point, he could just show up. She wouldn't ever know he'd been watching over her the whole time.

He gave her till ten, then got out of his truck and made his way across the street when a movement in the dark alley behind the old Victorian house caught his eye. He jerked open his down coat, drew his sidearm from the shoulder holster and flattened himself against the eight-foot fence to the side of the house across the alley.

Tentative footsteps at first, then a more jaunty pace coming toward him, then whistling. Goddamned whistling. He knew the chances this was an innocent stroll down the alley by a citizen were about nil. Which meant this was anything but innocent. He cocked his gun and held it out, his arm straight out from the shoulder and tight to the fence.

When Brent Reeves moved into his line of sight, it was

all Cy could do to prevent himself cracking the guy's head open with the butt of his gun. Instead, very deliberately, he disarmed and replaced the safety on the gun and then moved in behind Amy's brother and jammed the piece into the base of his skull.

"Anybody ever tell you it isn't nice to stalk your little sister," he snarled. "Now move it. Nice and easy across the street."

Brent stuck his hands in the air like he was bored. "You're outta your skull, McQuaid. I was just checking to see she was—"

He never got the word out, or if he did Cy didn't hear it for the explosion that ripped through the house and the hail of debris. The sound deafened him, the impact threw him onto the ground on top of Reeves. He roared in his own uncontained anger, and in a split second he had cracked his gun over Brent's head and lit out at a dead run for what had been the front of the house.

In some surrealistic slow motion, he saw the metal scaffolding Amy had been standing on, flying upside down, then crashing into the sudden flames. He screamed for her without thinking she wouldn't hear him. The air had to be hundreds of degrees and he began to choke through his screams when he saw Amy, shielded by the open trunk of her car, standing in the only place she could possibly have survived the horrific force of the outward blast.

A heavy beam had landed on the roof of her car, crushing it and several smaller pieces skidded into and burned in the V made by the open trunk.

In shock so deep she couldn't look away from the flames, she didn't even see him till he lifted her off her feet and carried her to his truck through a gaggle of neighbors and the screams of fire-engine sirens.

HE TOOK HER HOME with him. The danger to her was over. Brent had been apprehended and hauled off to jail within an hour of the explosion and wouldn't see bail. But though Amy came willingly with him and let him hold her for what remained of the night, Cy was scared.

He didn't want her gratitude. He didn't want to play hero to her vastly unwilling damsel in distress. He didn't even want to say he'd told her so, although he had.

Somehow, all that weaseled into her feelings anyway. It had to do with his being there at all when the explosion tore into her certainty and proved her wrong about her ability to survive on her own terms. No survival instinct, not even the vaguest sense of discomfort had sent her out of the house, only the need of a pair of shears when her knife blade broke.

So Cy was right and she was wrong, but instead of leading her to trust his instincts, it only made her doubt her own, and he was turning into the cause of her doubting herself.

They sat at his kitchen table over coffee. He made the case for himself that these were extreme circumstances, that she might never again be in the kind of danger he'd foreseen and she hadn't. That in ordinary times, the rest of their lives, she wouldn't feel smothered and manipulated and her instincts discounted.

But he knew she was right when she pointed out that it was the extreme circumstances that laid them both bare, that put into stark relief the truth of their feelings about each other when they couldn't be gussied up with flowery words.

He hated it. Goddamn hated it. But the world was filled with marriage vows made and then broken, because people wouldn't look at things between them that sorely needed looking at first.

She dressed warmly and went with him soon after the sun rose to take care of his critters. Outside the barn he broke up the two-inch-thick layer of ice on the water trough. Inside, she curled up on a bale of hay with the mouser, a pearly-gray little cat he called Smoky. He shoveled dung out the stable door and onto a flatbed in a few deft strokes, then doled out oats and such to Charlie and the others.

Amy banged a foot on the rough wooden floor to get his attention. "Your horses are beautiful, Cy. What are their names?"

"This clown," he said, jerking fondly on the gray mane, "is Knight to King's X. I call him Charlie. The little sorrel mare is Molly. That's Sassy, Lightning and Dandy." He came around the backside of his stallion, his hand trailing over Charlie's rump. He couldn't believe Smoke was sitting still for her. Or, he supposed, he could. He would.

Her eyes filled suddenly with tears. "This is all over but the shouting, isn't it? He's gotten away with it, and I'll never know what I heard or...what I said."

His heart slammed hard against the wall of his chest. He had to do something, say something. "I have a friend, Amy. She does work with cancer kids. Hypnosis." He didn't think there was a snowball's chance in hell that it'd work. He saw she wasn't pinning any fresh new hopes on what amounted to one last-ditch effort, but she agreed.

"Nothing much left to lose," she signed, "is there?"

He nodded. "I have a meeting that ought to be over by five. I'll call Marcee and see if we can meet at her place after supper."

"Where does she live?"

"I don't know. I'll have to look it up. But I'll come get you."

"I'll drive myself, Cy."

"Fine." It wasn't, but it would have to do. "I'm done here."

She looked at him. Her chin angled higher. "I was hoping you'd show me the loft."

He couldn't mistake, by her body language, what she meant to be shown in the loft. His mouth went dry as dust. "That happens in the summertime, Amy. It's freaking cold out here."

"But…" She shoved Smoke out of her lap and began unbuttoning her coat, then her sweater, beneath which she was bare. "I want it."

He thought what she wanted was not to have to think too much about what would happen after they left the barn. It was all too clear to them both that they'd reached a stalemate, a place between them where things weren't quite right, and there might never be another time.

He turned around, aroused just looking at her bare breasts, her nipples puckering tight in the cold, grabbed a pitchfork and climbed the ladder to the loft.

She watched him break up a couple of bales of hay and spread them around. He jammed the pitchfork into a third bale, away from the bed he'd made for her, then began to open his clothes.

His sheepskin coat. His shirt. His button-down fly.

She stood.

He wanted to warn her not even to take that first step up if she thought this amounted to a farewell, but he couldn't even shape the words.

MARCEE BLEIGH looked skeptical.

"Cy, Amy. I understand what you're after, and why. It may have been something you said, some inadvertent repetition of something you heard, that set your mother off—but I have don't have the foggiest idea—"

"C'mon, Marcee. You do this all the time. Use a little imagination. Give it a shot. If it doesn't work, we haven't lost anything. If it does..." Cy shrugged. "We might get lucky."

Her sharp, homely features softened. "Do you mean *you* might get lucky, Cy?"

He didn't mistake her comment for crudity, but he didn't know how to answer her either.

Amy looked stricken, and signed, "Are you thinking if I could only hear what I heard that night that my hearing will suddenly come back? *Is* that what you're thinking?"

Marcee looked back and forth between them. The air seemed thick with tension. "To be fair, Amy, I don't think Cy brought you here with that agenda in mind. Or that—" she broke off, looking down at her hands a moment. When she looked back up, she gave a pained, somehow bitter-sweet smile and spoke only to Amy. "You're a very lucky woman, do you know that? Because this big lug loves you. I would have snapped him up in a heartbeat. And for what-ever it's worth, I don't believe he won't still love you when your hearing doesn't miraculously return."

"Marcee—"

She looked up at him. "It's all right, Cy. I raised the question of your motives. I thought Amy was entitled to know what I think of you." She said to Amy, "I didn't mean to put you on the spot, either, about Cy. I guess I just want to make doubly sure you even want to try hyp-nosis. You're talking about a pretty awful time to try and tap into. I'm not convinced you understand the power of your subconscious mind to defend against your messing with your psychological defenses. Your...well, I'll just say it. Your deafness."

Meeting the warm brown eyes of Cy's friend, Amy signed. Cy translated. "That's the one thing I do understand in all of this, Marcee. I could still hear when my mother died. I know that. But if I can't somehow get at whatever it was I heard that day, it's not only hearing that I've lost.''

Amy gritted her teeth. She couldn't even look at Cy. Because she loved him, loved who he was as a man, what he had been willing to do for Seth, how he was struggling to make it work with her, she could give this a try. If she didn't, even if Cy was harboring some futile hope of her ever hearing again, she didn't deserve him—and feeling that way would ruin whatever chances they had.

"It's like I've lost the soul of me, Marcee," she finished. "I don't mean to be overly dramatic, but the rest of my life feels…somehow…at stake.''

"Then let's do it.'' Marcee sat forward in her chair, directly facing Amy. "Cy, I want you to sit as far out of Amy's visual range as you can and still be able to interpret her for me. Yeah. Over there. Amy, now, if you just focus on my face, do you see Cy?''

She shook her head. "Barely.''

"Enough," Marcee asked, "to distract you?''

Again she shook her head no, but her nerve was slipping. Marcee had Cy lower the lights, then kept up a running commentary, encouraging Amy to look only at her, only at her lips, to focus and relax and let herself go. Reassuring her that nothing would happen that she couldn't go along with. That Cy was there for her. That she was moment by moment more deeply focused on Marcee's lips, only her lips, all the tiny grooves, the shape, the shapes they made, the meaning she imparted.

Amy began to relax. To remember times when she had done this herself as a little girl, like touching her fingers to the pattern of flocking on the wall, watching her daddy's lips just reading to her from her storybooks, just reading to her till after a while what he said and what shape his lips and mouth and tongue took began to make sense to her. Began to be faithful symbols for the words of stories she had already known by heart.

"Okay, Amy," Marcee's lips said, "When I say the word 'now' I want you to close your eyes for one minute. Don't worry about how long that is. Don't count, just trust your mind to know. When I say 'now,' just close your eyes and at the end of one minute, open your eyes, and then you'll be back in your house, in the house in Steamboat where you were a little girl, early in the day before you fell down the mine shaft. Do it 'now.'"

Amy's eyes closed. Marcee looked at Cy. Both of them checked the second hands of their watches. He gave her a thumbs-up. She tested the whole thing by speaking aloud to him, to see if Amy was not yet there and could still sense a separate conversation even with her eyes closed.

"I'm flying by the seat of my pants, here, Cy."

"Pretty fancy pants, Marce."

She shot him a half-lewd gesture and sat monitoring the time. At precisely sixty seconds, Amy's eyes opened, trained on Marcee's lips.

"Amy, you're doing fine. Brilliantly for such a little girl. Now I want you to imagine that you are so smart that you know how to read my lips and say anything back to me in sign language. Can you do that? Spell 'yes' for me if you can."

Her fingers raced through y-e-s. Cy was holding his breath. He figured Marcee was checking out whether the trance Amy had achieved was going to survive the discrepancy of hearing and not hearing and signing before she ever went deaf.

"That's great, Amy. When you see me turn and talk to

Cy, you won't be worried. It will be okay. You'll be fine. You are fine. Can you tell me how old you are?''

F-i-v-e. "I'm five. How old are you?''

"I'm thirty-five.''

"My daddy,'' Amy signed, entranced, Cy repeating aloud for Marcee, "is older than you.''

"What about your mommy and your brother?''

"Mommy's thirty-two. Brent is almost thirteen. Granny Fee is older than God.''

"I bet she is!'' Cy told Marcee, because they'd not thought to mention the fact earlier, that Fiona Reeves was a diagnosed schizophrenic. She followed up on it. "How is Granny Fee today?''

"Mommy says she's in a twist.''

Marcee laughed. "Is that right?''

"No...well, really, Mommy's in a twist too.''

"Why is that, Amy?''

"She...she—'' Amy seemed to freeze.

Marcee looked at Cy.

"It's all right. Nothing is going to happen. You're able to wake up if you want to, Amy. Is this the day that you went outside with your big brother and fell down the mine shaft?''

Amy gulped. A tear formed in one eye. "Y-e-s.''

"You don't have to do this, Amy. You don't have to do anything, or go anywhere you don't want to. But maybe you could be a really big girl and go back to before Mommy was in a twist. Can you do that? Go back a little ways?''

She shivered violently. Y-e-s.

"Good. Good for you. You're warm and safe, Amy. What are you doing now?''

"Playing with HooDoo and Pilly. March Hare and Pigeon too.''

"Is your brother Brent there?"

"No, it's just me and my—"

Cy swore softly, unable to decipher her meaning.

Marcee just went with it. "You and what? Could you spell that for me, Amy?"

M-e-n-a-g-e-r-i-e. She signed again. "My imaginary friends. That's what Brent calls all my 'maginary friends.' "

"He's pretty smart, too, isn't he? But he's not there right now?"

N-o. "Just me and them."

"So who is Pigeon?"

"I don't know." Amy looked thoughtful, curious maybe, but not confused. "She just came. She's shy. She won't come inside. All the others are scaring her."

"Will she come in and play, do you think?"

"I keep asking her, but she's shy."

Marcee turned to Cy. Amy sat peacefully waiting. "I can't believe this is working, Cy. Do you know where she's going with this?"

He shook his head. "I don't know."

"Should I go on with it, or move her ahead?"

He shook his head. What was happening was the other side of what he would have accepted as real. "Just take her through it, Marcee, till her mother comes into the picture, at least."

Marcee turned back to Amy. "Is Pigeon a 'fraidy cat?"

Cy watched as Amy's spine curled down, limber as a child, her chin resting on her fist like a child considering what to do with an imaginary friend that wouldn't come in to play with the others.

N-o. "She's going to be o-kay. She's done with it. I keep asking her but she won't come inside and play."

"Maybe Pigeon will stay nearby and—"

Amy suddenly blanched, then flushed. "Uh-ohhhhh."

Cy's heart about crashed out of his chest. Amy had verbalized her dismay. Said it aloud. *Uh-ohhh.*

"Shit, Cy! Did you hear that? What the—"

"Go with it Marcee. Uh-ohhh. Just go with it, quick!"

"It's okay, Amy. You can wake up any time. What is uh-ohhhh?"

Amy's expression grew fiercely angry. Again she spoke aloud. "What-did-you-say? What-was-that-you-said, you-little-bitch! What-was-it?"

As if she were playing, speaking for each of her animals, taking each role, Amy shifted back to her littler self, but every word was coming out of her mouth, as perfectly pronounced as if she had never been mute.

"Nothing, Mommy. *Don't-you lie-to-me-who-were-you-talking-to?*... M-m-my M-march Hare. I was just playing—" Her eyes flew wide open, still focused in her trance, but her face stretched tight in fear and the cords in her neck stuck out. "No, Mommy, I won't play it anymore—"

Marcee broke in with her cue word. "*Now,* Amy. *Now* you can relax, it's all over."

She began to shiver uncontrollably. His insides roiling, Cy got up to go to her. Marcee warned him off. "Give her a minute, Cy. Leave her be. She needs to come the way back by herself."

"No way—"

"Cy, if you touch her, I'll tear your heart out with my bare hands! Now *back off.*"

He shot her a look and whirled around, walking away, pacing the room behind Amy, his hands fisted and crammed into his pockets. "Then for God's sake help her, Marcee."

But Marcee just sat there, waiting, for what he didn't know. It was all he could do to stand back, but he could see Amy had stopped shaking so hard. She clamped a hand over her mouth to prevent her own cries, then signed to Marcee. "I don't know what any of that means! What did I say? What was it that I said to her?"

Marcee looked to Cy. "We don't know, Amy. We don't know what set her off. I need you to take some deep breaths now—"

"You mean—" her hands flailed helplessly. "You mean," she signed, "all this meant nothing?"

He couldn't take it anymore. Couldn't stand her wild disappointment. He strode to the sofa and crouched low in front of her. Tears stained her cheeks. He wanted to hit something, lash out somewhere, God knew where. "It's okay, Amy. We'll figure it out. I promise you. We'll figure it out."

But he could see she had no idea she had spoken aloud. And he had no idea how he was going to keep his promise. He moved out of her way when she stood, but he thought she'd turn to him. Instead she looked uncertainly around her, at him, at Marcee and then asked for a cool washcloth to wash her face.

He ought to be used to her turning away from him by now, doing something else, any damned thing except let him have any part of being there for her. Holding her, for Chrissake. Was it too damned protective of him just to want to hold her?

He guessed it was. He paced the confines of Marcee's comfortable, plain-potatoes living room like a caged animal. When his pager began to vibrate on his belt, he started.

The number was a 970 exchange he didn't recognize. He snatched up the portable phone sitting on Marcee's rolltop, logged in the string of numbers to access his calling card account, then the number on the pager. The voice at the other end stopped his pacing cold.

He listened for a couple of minutes, asked what questions he thought Susan could handle, then told her he'd be in Cedar Bluffs as soon as he could get there.

"Cy?"

He turned around. Marcee was the one who had spoken, but Amy was the one he told. "My dad's had a stroke."

She came straight into his arms. Now, he thought bitterly, when it appeared to her that he was in need, it was okay, when comforting wasn't okay when she needed it. She was so hard, so prickly, so fiercely independent she couldn't even see she was giving him what she wouldn't take for herself. He wanted to turn away from her, wanted to make the point, but he was scared this was going to be the last time he would hold her.

He buried his face in her hair and clung to her for all he was worth for all of thirty seconds, then pushed her back gently as he could, which wasn't very gently at all, and picked up his hat.

"I'm leaving now, too," she signed, sensing more was going on with him than worry over his dad's stroke, grabbing up her coat. "I'll walk out with you." She turned and took Marcee's hands, wordlessly thanking her for what she'd tried to do.

Marcee stopped Cy at the door. "Tell Susan for me, they're both in my prayers, Cy."

He gave her a brief hug, then walked out. Amy didn't catch up with him till he had his truck door open.

"Cy?"

He flung his hat onto the bench seat. "What, Amy?"

"What's wrong?"

"We're what's wrong, I guess." He shrugged. His heart

felt leaden. His jaw cocked sideways. "You tell me. We aren't going to get past this, are we?"

"Not if you won't tell me—"

"Cut it out, Amy." He swore. "You turn away from me when you've just gone through something like that—" he flung his arm back toward Marcee's bungalow "—and I'm supposed to take it and still think you could give a simple damn whether I'm there or not?"

"Cy, it wasn't like that—"

"No?" He took hold of her arm. "Do you get what would happen if you weren't deaf? If we were what...Jesus, I don't know...*ordinary people?* If you weren't scared half to death that I'll think you're a weakling or defective or inadequate or God knows what if one time, *just once* you let me be the strong one?"

She swallowed convulsively, hurt and angry, misunderstood—another shortcoming he wasn't ever likely to defeat. "I'm not ordinary, Cy. I *am* deaf. I can't hear you. I'm not defenseless, but I'm afraid when you look at me, that's what you see, no matter what pair of rose-colored glasses you put on.

"When you tell me to stay put no matter what danger you're in...or you have to make sure I'm not in walking into an ambush or when you want to take care of every little thing. I can't live like that. If I could suddenly hear you, Cy, I couldn't live like that." Tears skidded down her soft, alabaster cheeks. "I didn't mean to turn away from you. I didn't mean anything by it. I love you till I ache with wanting to be right for you, but I don't know how else to be besides the grown-up version of a little girl who had to pull up her own socks and go on."

"Amy." He pulled her into his arms and cradled her tight, till he couldn't tell anymore if it was his own heart flailing that he felt, or hers. He still didn't know when he found himself still standing in the middle of the godforsaken street watching her taillights fade away like autumn bonfires in the night.

Chapter Fifteen

He had to go take care of his horses and stock, but by seven o'clock in the morning, Cy walked into the Chaparral County Community hospital in Cedar Bluffs. Between the three of them, he and his brothers had been stitched up, X-rayed, patched together, bandaged and encased in plaster casts so often as teenagers that the emergency room nurses knew them by name, birth order and usual reason for the ER admission.

His father, though, had never been a patient here, and would rather have found himself pushing up daisies than occupying one of the sixty beds. If he'd had any say in the matter, they would have had to knock Jake McQuaid cold to keep him here.

Walking the short, brightly lit hall on the second floor, Cy found his father's room. Susan greeted him at the door, her prettiness ravaged by worry and a sleepless night. She waved him inside, then moved silently into his arms. He held her tight for several long moments, and watched his dad stretched out, sleeping peacefully though there were tubes hanging out of him and monitors everywhere.

It hit him that he'd never seen his father sleeping. Not once. Not even dozing through some television program.

It wasn't right, Jake being so out of it, laid out on the slab of a hospital gurney.

Susan pulled back and shoved a hand through her graying blond hair. "They tell me he's going to make it. They just don't know about any lingering brain damage."

Cy nodded. "I spoke to the doctor. He told me they used some new drugs to dissolve the clot?"

"Yes. Some kind of blood thinner. They have to be concerned for the next couple of days that the medication doesn't make him bleed, I guess."

"How doped up is he?"

"He hasn't woken up yet. But I guess that's what they want. He's responsive to pain, so they're not worried about him being in a coma." She touched his lapel. "Can you stay a while?"

"Sure. Why don't you go on home for a bit and get some rest?"

"I don't want to leave, Cy. I couldn't sleep anyway. But I wouldn't mind going downstairs to get a hot chocolate or something. As long as you're here with your dad."

"I'll stay, Susan. And I'll have them come get you if he wakes up."

He sat in the chair next to Jake where Susan had stationed herself, probably holding his liver-spotted hand, when a memory flashed in his head of his dad kneeling on the kitchen floor, washing Susan's long, narrow feet with a terry cloth towel worn down to the nub.

A pang of envy so strong he forgot to breathe went through Cy. He and Cam and Matt thought of Jake as about as tough as a man came, but what kind of dyed-in-the-wool tough guy washed his woman's feet?

Yeah, it was jealousy, pure and simple. He lost his train of thought when his pager vibrated at his waist. He took the pager off his belt, checked the number and reached for the phone. The switchboard in Denver connected him to Brimmer's office. Mike's secretary told him the President was about to preempt nationwide programming with a statement on the Reeves nomination.

He hung up and used the bedside control to switch on the TV mounted near the ceiling opposite the bed. Susan reappeared with a mug filled with hot chocolate just as the presidential seal gave way to the news anchorman prefacing the President's remarks.

He started to get up out of her chair, but she said she'd rather stand, so to sit still. "What's going on?"

"Something to do with Byron Reeves. My office just paged to let me know."

The video feed switched to the President preparing to speak from the podium where most major White House press conferences were held.

Leaning against the door frame, Susan sipped at her chocolate. "Do you know what he's going to say?"

Cy started to shake his head, but the camera angle widened and he knew then. "He's about to name Byron Reeves to the Supreme Court. Reeves is the one standing closest to the President. The other one is the judge's brother. Perry Reeves."

"Your investigation must be over then?" she asked. Cy didn't know how to answer Susan's question, but he was spared when the prepared speech began.

"In recent days, as we have all come to know, there have been various attempts made to blacken the name and block the appointment of the Honorable Judge Byron Reeves to the Supreme Court. Despite the passage of so many years, Judge Reeves's successful prosecution of the Jessup kidnapping and Salt Lake City bank robbery has been cited as an example of poor judgment unbecoming a nominee to the bench of the Supreme Court, in its most

favorable light, and a case of felony conspiracy with the kidnap victim herself in a less friendly interpretation of the facts.

"These charges have been found unfounded, unreasoning, and insupportable at every level of the Department of Justice. Case—" The President looked around the room, seeming to connect and command all pairs of eyes, *"closed."*

"Is that true, Cy? It's over?" Susan asked.

Surprised that she might have followed the case at all, he didn't know how to answer that question, either. Certainly it wasn't over where Zach Hollingsworth was concerned. "The President saying so doesn't mean the media will lay off, Sus."

"Oh. Well. You'll want to hear the rest." She looked back up at the television while the President gave an abridged description of the extortion threat and murder allegations against Amy's father.

"We now know," he stated unequivocally, *"by forensic testing unavailable a generation ago, that Julia Reeves did in fact die of oxygen starvation. Her son, whom Judge Reeves adopted at an early age, has now confessed to keeping from his mother the simple remedy of an asthma inhaler that would have saved her life. He is being charged as we speak with manslaughter.*

"Two nights ago, this deeply troubled young man made an attempt on the life of his half sister, Judge Reeves's daughter, Amy, as well—"

"Oh, my God—that was Amy? The explosion in Denver?"

Cy nodded. Susan must have seen something in him he'd rather she hadn't. Her eyes lingered on him rather than returning to the set.

"—out of some terribly misguided fear," the speech

went on, *"that she could and would expose him as the murderer of their mother. Amy had already suffered at his hands. At the age of five, and on the day of her mother's demise the night of February 15, twenty-four years ago, Amy lost her hearing in an accident her brother caused."*

Cy swore softly. The President's spiel had Perry Reeves's spin written all over it. "Son of a bitch didn't miss a trick—Susan, what's wrong?"

She had gone stark white.

"I—what…the date."

The President was laying on the kudos now, formally placing Byron Reeves's name into nomination for the Supreme Court, but Cy wasn't paying much attention. He got up and took the mug from Susan and helped her into the chair.

He sank to his haunches in front of her. "Sus. What is it?"

"I don't…something about the date stuck in my mind. I think…I heard somewhere his birthday is February thirteenth. The day before Valentine's Day. Didn't they say his wife died…Amy Reeves lost her hearing the…the, um…the fifteenth?"

He didn't get it, didn't see what Susan was getting at or why she was obsessing about the date. "It was the anchor, Sus, in the introduction. Remember? Before the President came on, the anchorman was giving the judge's vital statistics. 'Born February 13, educated'—blah blah blah. Is that what you mean?"

Her head moved awkwardly, half agreeing, half not. "It must be." Her hands fluttered near her face. If she'd been another woman he was questioning on a case, a woman he didn't know, he'd have thought she was feeling threatened. Trapped. "I just can't imagine how awful it must have been for them all. For his little girl. For Amy. She's deaf. You didn't tell me.''

She'd gotten none of her color back. She touched his face and stunned him again. ''You're in love with her.''

Slam dunk. All that, he thought, because Susan had seen he was heart-staggered over Amy, even before she heard the part about Amy's being deaf.

Nothing got by Susan. Nothing much ever had. He shouldn't have been surprised she'd made the connection in time to Reeves's birthday, either. It was her twenty-first birthday, the luckiest day of her life, the way she told it, when she woke up to find Jake and his sons watching over her.

With Susan, ever since, all their birthdays had been week-long events when everything good was supposed to happen, and nothing bad. One of the reasons, at least, that the barbecue she was planning for Jake's seventieth was so important to her.

''Cy?''

He looked up at her, and realized he wasn't going to get off this hook with her, recognizing maybe he didn't want to be off the hook. That he needed to tell her.

He gulped. How often was a man obliged to tell the woman who had raised him that he was in love?

Or that he'd screwed it up royally.

''Yeah. I'm in love with her.'' He took a deep breath and stood because his leg couldn't take the deep bend anymore.

She took his hand and looked up at him. ''Tell me what's wrong.''

He squeezed her hand. ''I screwed up, Sus. I don't think it's going to happen.''

''Is it that she's deaf that...'' she trailed off, unwilling to put in words a thing so shallow.

He could see she was going to be sorely disappointed in him if Amy's being deaf was his problem. Susan was the only person he knew who hadn't thought he was completely addle-brained for going after guardianship of Seth. "You don't know what it's like, Sus. I love Amy, but apparently it's not enough." His jaw up and locked. He had to pry the words out of himself. "I didn't think it was enough for me, but it turns out to be the other way around. It's not enough for her."

Susan let go of his hand and stood up, going around Cy to get closer to Jake. Cy moved to the other side of the bed. She stroked his dad's head, running her hand gently over his thinning, gunmetal-gray hair.

"Did you know I came close to leaving your father once?"

He shook his head. He hadn't known.

"Your dad and I weren't seeing things the same way." Her eyes roamed over Jake's rugged face. "He wanted to take care of me. Fix things for me. Set everything right when I couldn't even tell him what was wrong."

"He did take care of you." He felt surly and didn't care. Disingenuous, because his beef with Jake was always about what he had and hadn't done for Susan, but he didn't care about that either. "What the hell else was he supposed to do?"

"Just love me." She looked at him. Looked trapped again. In some fundamental way, he wasn't getting it, wasn't seeing what she was trying to tell him. He didn't get what was bringing that half desperate, half resigned look to her eyes. "Don't let her get away, Cy, because you think love isn't enough."

HE STAYED TILL Jake woke around two o'clock. Cy took it as a measure of how out of it his father still was that he failed to pick up on the lingering tension between him and Susan.

Since that wasn't anything that would escape his father if he were a well man, Cy thought he'd better stay till the doctors had a chance to confirm that Jake was out of the woods.

Susan shooed him away.

She said what mattered was that his father knew Cy had come, when what she meant was a whole other thing in the vein of, if Cy was going to have a chance with Amy, he'd better do what his father had done when Susan was prepared to walk away—which was to get off his high horse and make an amend or two.

He got into his pickup at three o'clock, figuring to be in back in Denver by seven if the weather held. His mood couldn't have been worse. He didn't know what amends to make. Amy had made it pretty clear she didn't need or want him to take care of her, order her around, tell her what to do or forbid her to do for him what he would do for her.

She'd asked for his help, but he'd crossed some line he didn't even recognize. If Susan was right, it was his hard-headed lawman cow-punching take-charge savior complex getting in the way, but he was damned if he could see it, and damned if he couldn't.

A heartache the size of all Chaparral County filled his chest. "Sorry" wasn't going to cut it, even if he could dredge it up.

Nothing with Amy was simple, nothing easy. Loving her was like reaching for the primrose at the heart of a thorny bush. And still, loving, being loved by the judge's beautiful hard-core-independent daughter was all he wanted.

He filled his gas tank at the convenience store by the

entrance to I-70, bought himself a couple of prepackaged roast beef sandwiches and headed east toward the mountain passes between Cedar Bluffs and Denver.

He thought about her listening to her uncle's spin on the events of her life as told the nation by the President. One more blow to the truth? One more insult, one more chorus of *Amy must be wrong*.

He was haunted by the sound of her voice in those few moments when she had been taken back to the hours before she went deaf.

He flipped on the radio and forced himself to concentrate on the drive, but the simple physical memory of sound, of a voice out of Amy's mouth, brought his thoughts full circle back to Susan, and he didn't know why, and not knowing made him wary.

He went over every reason he could think of. His mind came around to the superficial resemblance between them that even Cam didn't see, then to the stricken, ghastly shade of pale Susan turned when she learned Amy was deaf...even before that, when she heard the date of Julia Reeves's death and matched it up in her mind to Byron Reeves's date of birth.

He didn't get it. It struck him that her reaction was on par with out-and-out guilt, as if she were in some way responsible for—

His blood began to roar in his ears, his mind to stagger. He jerked the wheel hard right to pull off the highway before he caused a terrible accident. He sat there staring at the walls of the Glenwood Canyon, his hands made into fists over the steering wheel, telling himself it wasn't possible.

But as his granddad always said, wishin' a thing didn't make it so. He got out into the dog-ass cold of arctic winds whipping through the canyon, slammed the door shut behind him and dialed his father's hospital room.

A BURST OF APPLAUSE went up in the lovely old room that served as a living area for the residents and staff in Granny Fee's wing. Amy had taped the President announcing her father's nomination. Everyone at Chamberlain House knew and loved him. Everyone here had an emotional stake in Fee's son reaching the Supreme Court.

No one knew how deeply upset he was. Even Amy didn't entirely understand his reservations. They'd sat, thousands of miles separated, writing back and forth over the Internet this morning after the announcement was made.

She knew he felt as if the nomination were the fruit of ill-gotten gains, and that before it came to a vote in the Senate, he might yet withdraw, even retire. She didn't understand why. Nothing her uncle had done, even in her father's name, changed Byron Reeves's suitability for the nomination. She felt as if there were things he wasn't telling her, reasons maybe too private or personal, to offer her. But if there were, he gave no hint of what they might be.

Was he ill? No, nothing like that.

Amidst the congratulations of her friends, Fiona seemed more dazed than pleased. Her head moved in tiny, birdlike gestures, searching for Amy, so befuddled that when Amy knelt right in front of her, it took Fee long seconds to make the connection between the face before her and her granddaughter.

She got unsteadily to her feet. Amy walked with her down the long gracious hallway back to her room. She sat in her rocking chair and seemed for a moment to doze off. Amy sat watching her, longing to sit at her grandmother's feet and rest her head in Fee's lap, to be able to pour out her heart and be heard by a woman who loved her.

With the failure of her last-ditch effort, all her hope of any possibility of ever learning what lay locked away in her mind had died. In her uncle's game of winner take all, she had lost. For the President to have made any statement at all regarding the death of her mother, he had to have bought into her uncle's deft lies.

They could have left it alone, reiterated that her death was accidental. Instead, Perry must have taken Ted Wilms's crime lab results and cried foul. Confronted with the proof, Brent had confessed. End of tragic tale, end of any chance of nasty exposure.

But Perry was also Fee's son, and even if Amy could tell her grandmother what he'd done, how ruthless he was in the pursuit of his ambitions for her father, she wouldn't have had the heart.

But about Cy...it would have been so precious to have Fee mentally there to tell, to share. To have the benefit of a wise old granny's advice.

"Sweetling?"

Amy drew near and knelt before Fee. "What?" She mimed scribbling, asking should she get out paper and a pen. Fee shook her head. She seemed less lucid, more confused than ever now, and only waved in the direction of her music boxes. Amy rose and selected one at random, the smallest, a miniature pipe organ that, according to the label, played Pachelbel's Canon in D.

But Fee shook her head, unhappy with Amy's choice. Her hand stretched higher, pointing. "The Strauss, sweetling," she cried, though Amy had only Fee's distressed expression to rely upon.

She knew the one. The antique box, at least eight inches deep, was carved from white ebony, and the Strauss waltz was the one tune she could dimly recall. She turned away and picked up the pad of paper and pen, and wrote, *G. Fee, the Strauss has been broken for years. You remember, don't you?*

Fee's head began to tremble as if she were palsied. She took the pen from Amy and bent over the pad. Her spidery writing took several long moments. *Open the Strauss, sweetling.*

HE REACHED SUSAN on the first ring. "Sus—"

"Cy? Is that you? Are you—"

He lowered the phone. The pain inside him was fear-some, worse than when his leg was nearly blown away.

"—what's wrong? Cy!"

He cleared his throat and spat. "Sus. Take it easy. I was just thinking...couldn't think what it was you used to—"

"Used to what?" came her voice. "Cy, are you drunk? Hurt? What? I can barely hear you."

His days of calling home drunk were long since over. But hurt? Yeah. "I'm on the highway. Glenwood." God help him, he had to know. He jerked his hat down tighter on his head to keep the wind from tearing it off. "I was just trying to think what it was you told me once. What your nickname was when you were a kid?"

"My nickname? Pidge, you mean?"

Pidge. As in, *I encouraged Pidge to go to the authorities anyway.*

As in, *March Hare and Pigeon too.* Amy's new imaginary friend. The one she'd asked again and again to come in, with only her mother to hear, to grow enraged. Heartsick, his gut heaving, Cy finally got it. Somehow he managed to hang up with Susan, but his head wouldn't stop spinning the disc, the image of Byron Reeves on the phone with Susan.

She must have called him on his birthday, and set in motion the disastrous events that led to Julia Reeves catching Amy innocently repeating the words she must have overheard her father using. A nickname, *Pidge,* and words Julia would not have mistaken for idle chatter.

Susan.

Dear God. It was Susan who had been kidnapped. Susan who had endured her captors long enough to be caught up in the Salt Lake City heist. Susan who had escaped the federal dragnet, run to Texas, come to be the only real mother he and Cam and certainly Matty ever really knew.

Susan was Pamela Jessup. The girl whom Phillip Gould had brutally raped.

DEEP INSIDE the white ebony music box, Amy found her mother's inhaler, jammed somehow between the antique mechanism and the side of the box. For one brief horrifying moment, she imagined it had been Fiona playing keep-away with Julia's life, but no.

Between that errant thought and her next, between what was true and what was the truth, between hearing and then, not hearing, Amy knew what the last damning, hideous sounds she would ever hear had been.

Her uncle's taunts.

Her mother's futile, gasping, dying pleas.

Fiona's music boxes cranked up, every one, to drown out the sounds of her son Perry letting Julia's life slip away.

Afterward, when Perry must have carried the lifeless body outside and dropped her hard enough that a blow to her head could be mistaken for the cause of her death, Fee had stashed the light green plastic holder with its canister of steroids in the only place she knew to hide it.

But Granny had begun to sing to herself, now, and Amy knew she would never learn whether Granny Fee had concealed the inhaler to protect her son, or to preserve the evidence of a murder.

Chapter Sixteen

Amy drove like a bat out of hell down the table mesa roads, through the switchbacks, up the canyon, around the winding curves that led home.

She let herself into the guest house, half expecting to find her uncle there, making himself at home in her space, sipping sherry in the dark, ready with some utterly reasonable, gloating proposition for letting bygones be bygones between them. He would believe she had no other choice.

He would be wrong. He was the one with the audacity, the sheer arrogant effrontery, the brass, to have taken Wilms's evidence and with it, called her mother's death a murder. His spin *de grâce*. With it, he had nailed himself, for it wouldn't be Brent's fingerprints on the inhaler, but Perry's.

He just didn't know it yet.

She tossed her keys and bag into an easy chair, then turned down the hallway to the bedroom she had converted to a study of her own. She flipped on her computer and summoned up her E-mail program on the nineteen-inch screen her computer-assisted-design software demanded. Her fingers flew over the keys, addressing the urgent electronic missive to Cy. She hadn't the heart or the patience to sit still, typing in the details, how, when and where she had discovered the inhaler, only that she had found it.

She changed from her black silk skirt and blouse to warm-ups and a tank top, then threw on a winter parka and walked in the dark, frigid night up the path to Takamura's converted barn. He was not at home, and would not be for several days, but she had her own keys, and a desperate need to ground herself.

Cy would find her soon enough, but if he didn't, she still had to do something with the rawness inside her, the glare of emotion, the rage.

Granny Fee had sacrificed what remained of her sanity in the wake of Julia's murder. Amy had sacrificed her hearing. She had been playacting, deciding at some level in her childish, accomplished mind that if she couldn't hear, then she couldn't have heard the terrible thing, and if she couldn't have heard it, it must not have happened the way they said it had.

But the price exacted from her now was the one to break her heart and goad her to rage. Her deafness had made her into the woman Cy McQuaid loved—just not enough.

She turned on only one of the bank of lights and closed the door of Takamura's converted barn behind her. She would see, now, if having come to the heart of her deepest fears, she could split one arrow with another.

She shed her coat and took the leather case from a rack along the south wall and drew out her bow, strung it and then fixed a target to the batt of straw. She selected her arrows, a dozen to warm up with, and two more, the ones that in her hands felt as precisely balanced as it was possible for arrows to be.

She began to breathe, to become as one with her bow, and each arrow in turn. She assumed her distance from the target batt and shut out all other concerns, but her sorrow refused to fade and her anger clung to her like her own skin.

Then, she thought, her anger must be meant to stay, to accompany her as armor to the heart of her fears. She put on her leather arm guard and dispatched six of the twelve arrows inside a few minutes.

In the second set, drawing her ninth arrow, she became aware of the slightest draft, of an intruder slipping inside with her, the air going still again, and her mind went to Cy. She focused deep inside herself, drew her awareness to her arrow only, to the quality of tension of her drawn bowstring, to the release of her fingers, the arcing flight of the arrow, the dead-on bull's-eye strike, the lowering of her own arms, the unrelenting focus of her eyes on her target.

But as she nocked the tenth practice arrow, her heart began to pound and an uneasiness crept into her mind. She sensed rather than saw or heard the intruder mounting the stairs to the loft. The eleventh still flew straight and true, lodging as if welded to the batch of ten before it...but by then she knew that, whoever it was, it wasn't Cy.

By the draw of her twelfth and last practice arrow, she knew her uncle had come to deal with her.

She knew by the dance of a tiny red laser light over her left breast, over her heart, that he had her in the sights of a deadly weapon.

An unearthly calm filled her. He could drop her where she stood, but she knew he wouldn't do that. Wouldn't risk spilling her blood here in Takamura's pristine practice hall. Wouldn't even risk threatening her with slugs perilously close because they would lodge in the floor where they could later be found.

He would have it in mind to force her to run, because

she would be crazy not to. He could pick her off with the ease of shooting a hapless fish in a barrel.

But he could have chosen no worse venue for himself than the place where Takamura had long since trained fearlessness into every cell and fiber of her being.

She let her arrow fly, then lowered her bow and looked up, above and to the right of her target batt where the laser beam originated from the loft. Where Perry stood with his weapon, unsmiling.

Saddened.

Dismayed. "She was going to destroy your father, Amy. I had no choice, you see. No more choice than I had in monitoring your E-mail." He began to walk about the perimeter of the loft. Forced to follow his progress, to turn in place, to keep her eyes trained on him, she read his lips and waited for an opening, a flaw in his attention to the detail of his aim.

"She would not have let it go," he went on. "Little Julia knew what she knew, so paranoid she rivaled your grandmother. She always had her suspicions, always mistrusted what your father told her. Always believed cousin Pamela was going to steal Byron away from her."

He gave a bitter, mocking laugh; Amy knew only the barking motion of his head, the sneering shape of his lips. "The irony was always that she was right! Your mother was right!"

Amy began to shake her head no. No, It wasn't possible. But her uncle went on, carried away with himself, telling his tale as if even now he could not begin to fathom the foolhardiness, the sheer folly of his brother's behavior.

"Imagine your father, Amy, the respected, upstanding federal prosecutor, the man of bedrock values, brought to his knees over the plight of a poor little rich girl crying rape!

"Imagine him risking his career, his reputation, his family, everything he had worked for, everything I had done to assure his path, *imagine him meeting her!* Imagine him taking her call in the Salt Lake City hotel room, paid for by the government, the very next night after she escaped! Picture him meeting her in some hole-in-the-wall dive, sitting down with her, giving her money, trusting the slippery, lying, felonious little bitch to turn herself in." He shook his head. The wonder of it still held him in thrall. "For the sake of that selfish, conniving little piece of tail your father was willing to risk it all. Imagine it!"

But all Amy could imagine was the depth of her father's compassion, the courage of his convictions, that he was willing to risk all that he was and all that he had for the sake of a girl who had been so faithlessly abused and abandoned.

He had admitted to her what he felt for Pamela, and she believed him. To do what he had done, what he had not admitted to her, he had to have believed with all his being that no one and no principle or letter of the law would be served by making the victim into the scapegoat—not only of her family, the scummy bastard who had raped her and the men who had kidnapped her, but of the judicial system as well.

To her mind, unlike her uncle's, those qualities made her father a hero. What was justice without mercy?

But she understood, now, her father's deep reluctance to sit another hour on the bench, much less the highest in the land.

Perry's aim never wavered despite his stroll about the perimeter of the loft. The spot of laser light on her tank top never varied more than an inch.

"Can you see it, Amy?" He shook his head. "Can you even begin to imagine your mother's fury, when out of

your mouth, five years later, came the spoils of your in-
cessant spying?''

Her composure began to crumble. Her fingers tightened
about her bow.

"Yes, Amy!" he taunted. "It was you who betrayed
your father's secret. 'Pigeon,' you said. 'Won't you please
come in,' you asked. 'You will be safe. Everything will
be okay,' you said."

She felt herself slipping, no longer knew what to expect,
no longer trusted that he wouldn't gently, regretfully
squeeze the trigger and kill her for the weight of all her
innocent transgressions. All he had to do was dump her
into one of a half-dozen local ravines, and if her body was
ever discovered, it would appear she had been hiking, and
had fallen victim to a careless hunter's rifle.

"It was you," he accused, "your constant prattling,
your fault, Amy, that your mother learned your father was
still in contact with Pamela Jessup. Your fault, Amy," he
charged, pointing at her, thundering, *"and your bloody
fault I was the one present to deal with your mother's
wrath."*

Unimaginable pain roared like a derailed train through
her head. Face-to-face at last with the truth of her innocent
complicity, her mind gave up its pretense, its power to
keep her from hearing ever again. To keep her deaf.

Each word struck her vulnerable eardrums like the explosive blasts of cannon-fire, touched off one after another
after another. She sank her knees, tried to cover her ears
to blunt the terrifying discord of hearing again, but her
bow brought her left hand up short and somehow penetrated her consciousness till she did what she had been
trained to do, to create about herself an aura of absolute
concentration, and then more, to do what she must to protect herself.

She had the instant, only one, when her uncle froze with the staggering realization that she could hear again, to act. In a blindingly fast, deliberate succession of movements, she took her thirteenth arrow, nocked it and drew back and sent it hurtling into the heart of the circle of lights. She heard her bowstring vibrate as if magnified a thousand times, her arrow slicing the air, her own battle cry and then the shattering of glass, the sparks and popping of the lights shorting out, plunging Takamura's converted barn into blackness.

But her own heart beating deafened her mind. Her own lungs drawing breath made her head throb unbearably. She drew her last arrow from the quiver through the staggering pain of hearing again. And then the door to Takamura's barn flew open.

A rectangle of dim starlight framed Cy. Her uncle's howl of outrage reverberated till her mind shut down and then she saw the red beam of the laser trained on Cy's throat where in the same split second her name was torn from him.

The instant expanded in time for her. All rational thought halted, every intention save his survival fled her mind. She gauged the direction and distance of the laser beam, turned, pulled and shot the arrow that rent the air and found its mark and buried itself deep in the flesh of her uncle's shoulder. His flawless aim jerked wide of its mark. He fell heavily to the deck, and crashed through the railing, and his rifle clattered uselessly to the floor below.

But his screaming cries of pain and vile epithets finally broke her, shattered the barrier of her focus and Amy fell into Cy's arms covering her ears, crying desperately, "Make it stop, Cy. Please God, make it stop."

THREE DAYS LATER, with Cy standing to Amy's right and her father to her left, they buried Perry Reeves in the cemetery in Steamboat Springs. It was a Tuesday, the last in January and the first time Amy had seen her father since her hearing had returned.

Her uncle had suffered a massive heart attack; Amy's arrow had stopped his firing on Cy, but come nowhere near even a major vessel. It was his rage that had killed Perry Reeves.

Cy had taken her to the only place he knew where silence could be depended on, to his ranch in the high country meadows where her fragile ears could go unguarded.

When he spoke, he signed.

When comfort was what she needed, he held her so closely all she heard was the beating of his heart.

And when she began to crave the sound of his voice, he read aloud to her.

In reverse then, she began to associate the sound of words with the shapes his lips made, but somewhere deep inside her mind were the memories of spoken words, and when she let her mind get around the fact that she knew them by heart and how to make them, that she had in some way always heard the words inside her mind, she reproduced them as faithfully as she had in Marcee Bleigh's living room.

Still, she had hardly slept. She could blame the furnace coming on, or the wind coming up, or the bed creaking when she moved. But in her heart, what she blamed was the tension, the awkwardness lingering between her and Cy. There was this unbearable uncertainty with each other, a hopelessness for where they had been, for the impasse they had come to before she even imagined she would hear again.

If he couldn't love her enough before, or tried too hard

to take care of her, not accepting her strength and self-sufficiency, how would he be now?

Amy held up through the police interviews, through dropping the charges against her brother. Brent had spent a lifetime paying the wages of his uncle's sins. Enough, it was finally agreed at her urging, was enough.

And still the sense of impossibility wrangled in her heart. She was no longer deaf, and no matter how Cy had eased the beginnings of her transition to hearing again, he didn't know how to deal with her now. He walked around her as if on eggshells. Against all odds, he had fallen in love with her, but he no longer knew who she was. She hardly knew herself. What she knew was that he was struggling with some private demons she knew nothing of, and when she couldn't stand his silence any longer, she followed him outside his ranch house to the barn where they had made love in the frozen loft to have it out with him.

He was busying himself currying the hide of his beloved stallion Knight to King's X—Charlie.

"I want to know, Cy," she signed, "what is hurting your heart."

"If you want to talk to me, Amy," he answered harshly, refusing to make his lips accessible to her sight, "then talk."

She battled back her tears and crammed her hands deep in the pockets of the coat of his she was wearing. Every halting sound that came out of her mouth offended her ears, but she drew a deep breath, repeating aloud what it was she wanted to know. "What…is…hurting…your heart?"

His currying stroke lengthened, slowed. His jaw cocked sideways. It took him several long moments to arrive at what he wanted to say.

"When I was a kid," he said at last, "twelve going on

thirteen, my brothers and I were out cruisin' around town. The old man was the county sheriff. Mostly we'd leave school and go get Matty from the woman who watched him afternoons. The three of us would walk over to the jailhouse. Straight out of Mayberry, minus Aunt Bee. Dad'd take us over to the Yellow Rose Café for supper, then we'd have to wait around another little while till he was ready to close up.

"One night we were hanging around later than usual. The old man had to deliver a summons, so it was long after Matty should've been home in bed when we stumbled over this girl. She was just lying there, crumpled up and beaten half to death, in a back alley beside a motel across the street from the bus stop.

"Cam lit out looking for Dad. Matty and I stayed with the girl. I could tell she was alive, not much more. Dad had us haul a mattress out of one of the unoccupied jail cells. We lifted her onto it, then slid her and the mattress into the back of the old pickup and took her home with us." He picked Charlie's silvery-gray hair out of the currying comb, hung it up on a nail behind him and chose a soft brush.

"She wound up staying on," he continued, his voice soft as the daylight filtering into the barn, deep as the shadows where the little gray cat Smoke sat licking her paw. "Got to be we were a family. Matty thought Susan hung the moon and stars. His mother ran out on us when he was knee-high to a grasshopper. The old man took a shine to Susan, too. She was pretty, and fun. She made him into a different man." His voice thinned. "She had the biggest heart in all of Texas, but we never knew who she was or where she'd come from or why somebody'd beat the living daylights of her and leave her for dead."

Amy formed the words in her mind, and then spoke them aloud. "Did you ever find out?"

He shook his head, then looked over Charlie's back at her. "Not one clue. Not in all these years. It never seemed to matter. She was with us. That was the only thing that counted. But when I was driving back from Cedar Bluffs, about the time you found the inhaler in Fiona's music box, it came to me. The only thing I remember Susan ever letting slip about her past was that when she was a little girl, her family called her Pidge."

As THEY DROVE to Perry Reeves's funeral in Steamboat Springs, Amy argued coincidence. Haltingly, as much from emotion as the foreignness of shaping words aloud, she brought up Hollingsworth's article, reaffirming that Pamela Jessup had died within a few short years of her escape. Surely if she had survived, if the evidence of Pamela's death was bogus, Zach Hollingsworth would have uncovered the truth.

But, Cy thought, Amy hadn't seen the panic-stricken look on Susan's face. He knew now that it had all come together for her in his dad's hospital room, Susan had finally realized what her call to Byron Reeves on his fortieth birthday had cost his family. He told Amy all that and then gave the disclaimer he didn't believe.

"I'm only guessing, Amy. Putting the pieces together. But I'm not wrong." He didn't expect some miraculous other explanation out of Byron Reeves, or Susan, either. But the whole thing ran up against his lawman mentality, against a code of conduct, a code of honor and justice he'd learned at his daddy's knee, a code where mercy came in last if it came in at all.

A code he had been raised to embrace and uphold. He

had to wonder if his father knew, or if Susan had kept her secret even from Jake.

So now he was faced with the same dilemma Byron Reeves had stared into twenty-five years before.

The same, he thought, watching the miles go by, except that this one shoved an immovable wedge between him and Amy, in a relationship so fragile he had pretty much lost all hope anyway.

She would not leave it alone. "You have to let it go, Cy."

"It's not that simple, Amy."

"It's *just* that simple. Pamela Jessup is dead. Susan is someone else now. If you expose her, you mock everything she has been to you."

"But she's living a lie that has cost us all—"

"And you know better," she cried, her words halting and distant from each other, "better even than my father what she went through. Where is the harm in letting it go? Letting her be…at least letting her make this decision?"

Now that she could hear, it was almost as if she could hear his thoughts. Susan had suffered enough. And every time he thought of what she'd been through, from the rape right up to the moment he'd come across her battered and bruised and broken and unconscious, he wanted to throw up.

But then all he had to do was look at the results of Susan's flight from justice. It wasn't only that her deceptions, however unwittingly, had soured the regard of Cy and his brothers for their own father.

Cy's dad must have made his own peace with her secrets, however much or little he knew of Susan's past. He'd be the first, had been first countless times, to warn his sons off judging what went on between him and Susan.

And Cy knew Amy's father had acted out of his enormous compassion for Susan—Pamela's plight. But Byron Reeves had broken the law and lied to his wife, and the consequences to his family, to Amy, to Cy and Amy together all these years later, hadn't stopped raining down yet.

Maybe Amy could hear now, but that could never make up for having learned the hard way that of everyone she loved, and everyone who loved her, the only one she could trust or believe in was herself.

Still she argued compassion.

"If you do this, Cy...if you have to be right and someone wrong...if you won't let me believe you are more than your badge or your honor...more than your precious code, then what is there to believe in?"

He didn't know. His throat felt thick with tears, his jaw set rigid against crying. He just didn't know how to make it right or how to transcend himself and his judgment of right and wrong to be the man she could believe in.

On the way to the cemetery, in a limousine with her father, Byron told Amy he had already withdrawn his name from consideration by the Senate Judiciary Committee for the Supreme Court. He had gone this far protecting Pamela Jessup's right to the life she had carved out of nothing but pain and loss for herself. The only way he knew to get Zach Hollingsworth off her case was to remove himself from the limelight.

He believed the "missing heiress" angle would pall for Hollingsworth after the front-page appeal of a link to him and to his nomination was eliminated.

Seated in the limo beside her father and across from Cy, Amy looked at Cy, as if waiting to see if he would begin to destroy the life her father had sacrificed so much to preserve. Pamela Jessup's life.

Susan's life.

After the words were said and done at her uncle's grave-side, Amy took the flowers she had picked one by one for their simplicity from the florist in town and laid them at the base of a memorial marker to her mother.

Amy touched the marble face of her mother's marker, her wrist doing a small, elegant turn, her third and fourth fingers curled under. Signing *I love you,* in the language she knew best, to her negligent mother, the only mother she knew.

And in that moment, the shaft of Amy's arrow, which Cy knew was already lodged in his heart, was split by another, cracking it wide open, leaving room for compassion and justice...and the triumph of love.

When she turned her face to his, what she saw must have betrayed his heart, because she stood up slowly, her eyes never leaving his, and walked into his open arms.

Epilogue

Seventeen hundred miles away, unhappy and snowed in at O'Hare International, Zach Hollingsworth made his TV debut with the hot news of the death of Perry Reeves, and the tip he'd received that Judge Reeves intended to bow out of the nomination to the highest court in the land.

He'd supposed, one day, he'd have to give in to the talking-heads syndrome that had become the journalistic venue of the millennium. He didn't like it. He was a print man from start to finish. But he was a survivor as well, so he coiffed himself and put on a tie and delivered, like the professional he was.

What he delivered made his gut sour. In his mind, Perry Reeves's death had put yet another spin on a story more stubbornly guarded than any in recent memory. It suggested to his lean and hungry soul that Julia had been meant to die that night nearly a quarter-century ago, and her preadolescent son doing the deed just didn't make sense.

And if she had been meant to die, there was a reason. One heavy-duty reason. Zach wasn't letting this puppy go just because Byron Reeves had given it all up.

The cunning Senator Gould was one happy man. Zach was not.

When the network anchors let him go, he ducked out of the blinding camera lights and tossed aside the mike. He had the neon gauntlet of O'Hare's concourse tunnel to run. He intended to be on the first plane out, to anywhere between Denver and Salt Lake City.

He was all but free of the camera-heads when one of the interns caught up with him on the down escalator with a cell phone in hand.

"Some woman," the kid said. "Says she has to speak with you now."

He took the cell phone. His instincts began to hum. "Hollingsworth."

"Mr. Hollingsworth, my name is Susan. Years ago, it was Pamela. If you're interested…if you will come here, I want to tell you my story."

HARLEQUIN®

I N T R I G U E®

COMING NEXT MONTH

#501 A COWBOY'S HONOR by Laura Gordon
The Cowboy Code

Cameron McQuaid was both a cowboy and a lawman, and lived his
life by a code of honor. Yet, when Frani Landon comes to town to
catch a killer, Cameron finds his honor—and his heart—on the line.

#502 FAMILIAR VALENTINE by Caroline Burnes
Fear Familiar

A velvet Valentine's night, a threatening attacker—and suddenly,
Celeste Levert found herself swept to safety in Dan Morgan's strong
arms. He promised to keep her safe and secure, but couldn't offer his
heart—until a black cat played Cupid....

#503 LAWMAN LOVER by Saranne Dawson

Michael Quinn's tenacity made him an extraordinary cop. It also
made him an exceptional lover. And Amanda Sturdevant remembered
everything, every caress and kiss, of her one night with him, but
nothing of a long-ago night of terror that had left a woman dead and
Amanda barely with her life—and amnesia....

#504 JACKSON'S WOMAN by Judi Lind
Her Protector

Everyone called her Verity McBride, but only Vera knew no one
would believe the truth about her identity. But now with a murder
charge hanging over her head, she turned to Jericho Jackson for help
and found a love for all time—even though he thought she was
someone else....

Look us up on-line at: http://www.romance.net